HOTEL
CALIFORNIA

HOTEL CALIFORNIA

AN ANTHOLOGY OF NEW MYSTERY SHORT STORIES BY

HEATHER GRAHAM • ANDREW CHILD • JOHN GILSTRAP
REED FARREL COLEMAN • DON BRUNS • AMANDA FLOWER
JENNIFER GRAESER DORNBUSH • RICK BLEIWEISS

EDITED BY **DON BRUNS**

**BLACK
STONE**
PUBLISHING

Published in 2022 by Blackstone Publishing
Cover design and book design by Blackstone Publishing

Printed in the United States of America

First edition: 2022
ISBN 978-1-6650-2396-2
Fiction / Mystery & Detective / Collections & Anthologies

Version 1

CIP data for this book is available
from the Library of Congress

Blackstone Publishing
31 Mistletoe Rd.
Ashland, OR 97520

www.BlackstonePublishing.com

TABLE OF CONTENTS

NEW KID IN TOWN — ANDREW CHILD 1

LIFE IN THE FAST LANE — DON BRUNS 33

WASTED TIME — JOHN GILSTRAP 59

VICTIM OF LOVE — REED FARREL COLEMAN 85

PRETTY MAIDS ALL IN A ROW — HEATHER GRAHAM 113

TRY AND LOVE AGAIN — AMANDA FLOWER 141

THE LAST RESORT — RICK BLEIWEISS 167

HOTEL CALIFORNIA — JENNIFER GRAESER DORNBUSH 201

ABOUT THE AUTHORS 233

NEW KID
IN TOWN

ANDREW CHILD

Reacher expected a truck, but he wound up in a car. He expected to be kept waiting in the hot Texas sun, but he got a ride almost at once. He expected trouble when he saw a skinny guy in a suit stick his nose into someone else's business, and on that score at least, he wasn't wrong.

The rest area parking lot was maybe half full, but, human behavior being what it is, the vehicles weren't evenly distributed. There were clumps of cars and trucks all bunched up together in some places, and other sections with three or four empty spaces in a row. The skinny guy had been about to climb into a silver sedan on the right-hand side of one of these gaps, thirty yards from where Reacher was standing. Another guy was heading for a dull blue pickup on the left-hand side. He would be in his late twenties, Reacher guessed. Early thirties at the most. He wasn't especially tall, only around five ten, but he was broad. His sleeveless T-shirt was stretched tight across his chest. His arms were thick. They were covered with a bright, swirling mass of tattoos. So were his calves, which bulged out below his knee-length shorts. He wore black boots, unlaced and gaping open. His head was shaved. And he was hurrying after a girl.

She looked around ten years old, with blond hair in braids and a yellow sundress and sandals. She stretched for the door handle, then pulled her arm back and darted toward the rear of the truck.

The tattooed guy grabbed her by the hair and pulled her back.

"Dad!" The girl's voice was shrill. "Let go."

The skinny guy paused, one foot inside his car. He shifted his weight. Set his foot back on the asphalt. Turned to face the other man and the child. "Hey," he said. "Stop that, you asshole. Let her go."

Reacher clamped the lid back down on his carry-out coffee cup and started to move. If it had been any other kind of dispute—a squabble over dinged paintwork, a contest for the most convenient parking spot—he might have left them to it. But this involved a kid. And as things stood, the way he saw them, there was no prospect of a happy ending.

There were twenty-five yards between Reacher and the three people.

The tattooed guy kept hold of the girl's hair for another couple of seconds. He was acting on his own timetable. He wanted that to be clear. Then he put his hand flat on her chest, slammed her against the side of the truck, and held her there for a few moments as if the pressure would fix her in place.

Fifteen yards between them.

The skinny guy took a step, stiff and tentative. The tattooed guy took a bigger step, confident and aggressive. They locked eyes. Neither of them spoke.

Five yards.

The skinny guy edged back. The tattooed guy moved forward. He raised his fist. Cocked his arm. They were seconds away from *game over*. Moments away. Then Reacher stepped between them.

"In the car," Reacher said to the skinny guy.

The guy didn't react for a moment. He was too shocked. The giant, messy figure in front of him seemed to have appeared out of nowhere. Six foot five. Two hundred and fifty pounds. Chest like a refrigerator. Arms like most people's legs. He could have been a villain in a horror movie. Or the thing you run from in a nightmare. Then the guy's senses kicked in and he scrambled backward and did what he'd been told.

Reacher turned to the girl. "In the truck."

She climbed up onto the step, pulled open the door, jumped inside, and disappeared from sight.

"Your kid?" Reacher said to the tattooed guy.

The guy didn't answer. He glared back. But he did lower his fist. Which was smart, under the circumstances.

"Want to keep her?"

The guy strode forward. "You're not taking—"

Reacher shoved him back, one handed. "Do you want to keep her?"

The guy raised his arm again and took a wild swing. He was aiming for the side of Reacher's head. Reacher leaned back and watched the guy's fist sail harmlessly past.

"Behave yourself." Reacher checked the lid on his coffee cup. "Don't make me kick your ass in front of the kid. So. You want to keep her?"

"Damn right."

"Because if you don't, no problem. We can call Child Protective Services right now. They'll take her off your hands, no questions asked."

"No one's taking my kid. Not you. Not the government."

"Maybe. Maybe not. Depends if you hurt her again."

The guy didn't respond.

Reacher said, "Well?"

"I didn't hurt her. You don't understand. Kids, they act out. You have to—"

"Show me your wallet."

"What?"

"Your wallet."

"You want money, you're SOL." The guy took a billfold from his back pocket and held it up. It was made of imitation snakeskin, frayed and stained and sorry looking.

Reacher took it and flipped it open, then turned it around to show he'd seen the guy's driver's license. "Here's something you didn't know. I used to be a military cop. One of the guys from my unit is a Texas Ranger now. I'm going to give him a call. Have him put a flag on your address. Any domestic disturbances, any visits to the emergency room, he'll hear about them. Your kid stubs her toe too often and—"

"What? He'll arrest me? Bullshit."

"No." Reacher shook his head. "He'll call me. Then you'll wish he'd arrested you."

Mason Greenwood sat in his house, in front of his computer, one hundred and fifty miles away, safely out of the heat and the dust. He was working. Although, he was almost embarrassed to call it that when he thought of the way business used to be done. He was earning a living, then. Providing a service. Meeting a demand. There was no arguing with that. And no one could call him lazy. He put in more hours than he had to. Way more. But then he'd always been a hands-on kind of guy. He could buy his stock from elsewhere, but he preferred to produce it himself. He enjoyed it. And he could automate the transactions as well as the security. There are bots that can handle pretty much everything these days. Maybe he'd use them, at some future point. Not yet, though. Not while he was still expanding. Looking for new markets. Like the client he was getting ready to pitch. From Japan. They were sticklers for etiquette, those guys. He'd read all about them. Done his research. They needed to be handled carefully. And he didn't want to risk a lucrative revenue stream for the sake of a few more hours at the keyboard.

Greenwood figured he'd get the deal squared away then head into town, such as it was, and celebrate. He liked the place. In many ways, the two years he'd been there had been the best of his life. Certainly the safest. But it wasn't exactly a heaving metropolis. There wasn't much in the way of fresh blood. Usually. When someone new arrived, it was an event to be savored. Especially if she was young. Pretty. And happy to stick around for a while. As had happened two weeks ago. Greenwood had enjoyed the chase. But now he figured it was time to close another kind of deal.

The old V8 spluttered into life. The truck shivered as the tattooed guy dropped it into Drive. Its rear tires squealed as he hit the gas. Reacher watched until it disappeared onto the highway, then started toward the section where the trucks were parked.

"Hey." The skinny guy rolled down his window. "I want to thank you."

"No need." Reacher kept on walking.

The guy fired up his engine and reversed out after him. "Let me at least drive you to your car. Is it far?"

"I don't have a car."

"Your truck, then."

"Don't have a truck."

"Then where are you going?"

Reacher shrugged. "Wherever the first driver who offers me a ride is going."

"You're looking to hitch a ride?"

"That's what I said."

"And you really don't mind where?"

"Somewhere west of here, preferably."

"Why west?"

"Because I just came from the east."

"Oh. Okay. Well, I'm heading west. South first, then west. Want to ride with me for a while?"

Reacher stopped and looked at the guy's car. He figured it was German. Not new. Ten years old, at least, based on the style and the degree of fade shown by the three expired parking permits stuck on the inside of the windshield. Maybe fifteen years. But a good brand. And it seemed in good shape. Clean. Well maintained. Which meant there was a good chance it would be reliable. A critical factor in that part of Texas. There could be hundreds of miles between one town and the next. Not the kind of place you want to break down. Not unless you want to be dinner for the vultures. "How much gas have you got?"

"Full tank."

"Range?"

The guy pressed a button at the end of one of the stalks that stuck out from the steering column. "Three hundred and fifty-eight miles. If you trust the computer."

Reacher nodded, walked around the front of the car, and climbed into the passenger seat.

The guy shifted into Drive but kept his foot on the brake. "Where's your stuff?"

"What stuff?"

"I don't know. Clothes. Luggage. Suitcases, or whatever."

"I'm wearing my clothes. My stuff's in my pocket. I don't need any luggage."

"The clothes you're wearing—they're all you have?"

"How many clothes can a person wear at one time?"

"What happens when they get dirty? What do you wear when they're in the wash?"

"I don't wash them. I buy new ones."

"Isn't that a bit wasteful?"

"No."

"Oh. Okay. Each to their own, I guess." The guy stretched across and held out his hand. "Charles. Charles Bell. People call me Chuck."

"Reacher."

Bell shifted his foot to the gas pedal and set off slowly toward the exit.

"So," Reacher said, once they were on the highway, "where are we headed?"

"Small town. Near the border. La Tortuga."

"Why there?"

"Long story."

Reacher didn't reply.

"Some . . . thing I'm looking for might be there."

"What kind of thing?"

Bell turned away and looked out of his side window for a long moment. "A place. An opportunity. My background's in power generation. Renewables, most recently. Solar's my specialty. I work for a nonprofit now. Small outfit. Just me, actually. I'm looking to put a coalition together. You know all the talk about a border wall? I want to build one. But out of solar panels. Half the power for the United States, half for Mexico. Something to unite us. Not divide us. And help the planet at the same time."

Reacher said nothing.

Bell said, "You think I'm crazy."

"I was thinking about your idea. This town, it's the place you want to build your wall?"

"I don't know. I've been searching for the right place for a while. A long time. This might be it. Or it might not." Bell loosened his tie. "We'll soon see."

"I wish you luck."

"Thanks." Bell wiped perspiration from his forehead, despite the air being cranked down low. "How about you, Reacher? What do you do for a living?"

"Nothing. I'm retired."

"From what?"

"The army."

"Oh." Bell was quiet for a moment. "I hear that a lot of ex-military guys go into law enforcement. Or join private contracting firms. Things like that."

"Some do. Not me."

"So if you don't work, what do you do?"

Reacher shrugged. "I keep busy."

Mason Greenwood hit the key to end the virtual chat, then double-checked that the secure connection had really been terminated. Some might have called that kind of behavior paranoid. He called it prudent. And he wasn't in jail, or worse, which to his way of thinking was proof he was right to act that way.

He stood up, stretched the knots out of his shoulders, and made his way to the kitchen. It was also at the back of the house. All the rooms he used were. The front part of the building was just for show. Anyone driving by would think nothing had changed since he bought the place, if they thought anything about it at all. It still looked ramshackle. Almost derelict. Or *rustic*, as the sleezy real estate guy he'd dealt with out of Fort Stockton had called it. Keeping it that way had been his biggest challenge. He needed to avoid drawing attention. Not altogether, of course. The kind of attention he attracted personally was fine. The kind in the town. In the bar. The kind that came from being the first person in a decade to land there with money. And no federal warrants. The kind from the local losers, who were looking for ways to get paid. And from the ladies, who were looking for . . . other things. He thought.

It was just his home Greenwood needed to keep discreet. In particular, the part where he worked. His studio. His computers. His pair of satellite dishes to guarantee uninterrupted internet access. And his backup generator to keep everything working when the local supply struggled to keep up. The answer had been to tent the place. Then to hire two construction crews. One made up of old lazy guys who hung around out front, sitting in the sun, drinking beer, wheeling the odd barrow around and occasionally sawing random pieces of wood. And another of top-line professionals brought in from over the border and paid extra to keep out of sight. Their job was to build essentially a whole new house—compact, efficient, and tailored to his exact needs—hidden inside the existing structure.

Greenwood opened the fridge and pulled out a bottle of champagne. Dom Pérignon, 2008. He couldn't honestly tell the difference between vintages. He couldn't tell the difference between champagne and sparkling wine from the grocery store, but he did have a degree of brand awareness. He knew which labels were supposed to be the best, and that's what he felt he deserved. Particularly at that moment. The call had been a success. A triumph, in fact. His preparation had paid off. His due diligence. The guy he'd uncovered was a human gold mine. He represented a group of other like-minded individuals. People with very particular tastes. The kind of tastes he was uniquely positioned to cater for. And on top of their tastes was their appetite. They sounded insatiable. They were going to set him up for life. He popped the cork, grabbed a glass, and headed back to his office. He needed to trawl through his archives. His filing system didn't quite mesh with the way his new best customer defined his group's requirements and he didn't want to miss anything. Not with the kind of volume they were talking about. He reckoned he should have enough material stored away for two months. Ten weeks, if he was lucky. He needed to make sure. Then, start work on a new production schedule. Procuring the raw material might be a challenge.

The specification was very narrow. He checked his watch. There was plenty of time before he needed to leave for the bar. And if he was a little late, so what? It wasn't like he had any competition.

Bell stayed on I-10 for twenty miles, then coasted around a cloverleaf onto a state highway for seventy miles, then switched to a county road. Each one was narrower than the one before. Each one was quieter. Clearly there was no border crossing at the town they were heading for, Reacher thought, official or unofficial. The roads were too small, and the traffic was too light. He turned to ask Bell for more details but paused. It might have been the angle of the sun, or the tint of the windows, but he thought Bell appeared different. His skin seemed a couple of shades paler than when they'd left the rest area. It looked clammy, and his eyes seemed to be bulging a little.

"Chuck?" Reacher said. "You okay?"

"Of course." Bell took his left hand off the wheel and shook it like he'd just washed it and couldn't find a towel. "Why?"

"How much farther are we going?"

Bell checked the odometer. "Fifty miles. Sixty, maybe."

"What kind of place is it?"

Bell shook his left arm again. "Not entirely sure. Never been before. Just seen it on Google Earth."

"Is there a doctor's office there? Or an emergency room?"

"Why? Are you sick?"

"No. But I think you are."

Bell slumped a little in his seat. "I'm fine. Just tired."

"Want to stop? Take a break?"

"No." Bell wiped his forehead. "Got to keep going."

"Why? What's the rush? Is there some kind of race to build this solar wall?"

Bell managed a weak smile. "No. It's just . . . when I set my mind on something . . ."

"I understand. I feel the same way. But a little tactical flexibility can be a good thing."

"I guess." Bell took a couple of deep breaths. "Maybe a rest would be nice. But I don't want to stop. Not for long. So how about we pull over. I get in the back. Stretch out, maybe take a nap. You drive the rest of the way."

It was possible, Reacher thought. He did know how to drive. Although he didn't like it much. It wasn't a technical issue. Operating a vehicle was straightforward enough. He'd been trained in the army. He'd done it many times since then and never had any collisions. Not accidental ones, anyway. It was more a question of temperament. He was better suited for explosive bursts of action or long spells of inactivity. Not the kind of measured concentration needed to successfully navigate traffic and pedestrians. But just then, there wasn't any traffic. There weren't any pedestrians. And there did seem to be a real risk of Bell collapsing at the wheel.

Mason Greenwood was three-quarters of the way through his bottle of bubbly. With each glass, he'd cranked his music up a little louder, which wasn't a problem. No one would be able to hear it. His house was the second-farthest building from the center of town. He'd have preferred the farthest, all things being equal. He'd almost bought the farthest. But there were two things wrong with it. First, the layout. It was basically a big wooden shed. It had been built for storage back in the days when the town straddled a trade route which came up from Mexico and then split, east and west. So there were no living quarters. Greenwood would have had to build two new structures. A fake section, to fool any passersby, and a concealed section, for him to live and work in. Which wouldn't have been the end of the world. He would have considered it, if it weren't for the second issue. The real deal-breaker. A complete lack of water.

With each glass he'd also come closer to the conclusion that he had far fewer of the kind of files he would need for his new Japanese customer. At the rate he was finding them, maybe only enough for a month. Six weeks at the outside. Which might be a problem. It left him far less time to ramp up production. He would have to jump on the procurement issue right away. He hadn't dealt with that specific subset for some time. He'd have to develop new contacts. He couldn't suddenly get back in touch with his old ones. That would be too suspicious. It was more than ten years since he'd done that kind of business, he realized. Where had the time gone? He had no idea. But the length of the interval did explain why he was having less luck with the computer search than he'd expected. Some of his inventory from those days would be on paper. Which could offer a reprieve. If he could find the right pages, he could scan them. Make digital copies. It would be time-consuming but possible. And he could start at once. Get a few batches done. See what the quality was like. Confirm whether he'd found a lifeline, or not. He checked his watch. He was definitely going to be late to the bar. But so what? It wasn't like he had any competition.

Bell passed out on the back seat before the car got moving again. Reacher switched on the radio, tuned it to a blues channel to cover Bell's raspy snoring, and settled in for the balance of the journey. There were fifty-four miles remaining. Reacher covered them in forty-nine minutes. He had no problem with traffic. He only saw three other cars the whole time, all heading in the opposite direction, plus one Coca-Cola delivery truck.

The town of La Tortuga was spread out over a low, shallow hill. First, they passed a scattering of small, low houses, mostly painted peach or yellow, with wide verandas and flat terra-cotta roofs. Then they came to the commercial section, higher up, spread along both sides of a single street. There were a few shops. A tiny post office. A diner. And in the center on the north side, a hotel. The only building with a second floor. Reacher parked by the entrance and turned to rouse Bell.

Inside, they found a stern-looking woman sitting behind a reception counter. The top was made of richly polished mahogany. There was a bud vase holding a single yellow rose and a copper bowl containing three folded copies of a local map. The walls and ceiling were white, the floor was tiled, and above their heads a fan moved lethargically, barely stirring the air. Bell asked for two rooms and handed the woman a credit card. She produced a cellphone, connected a small square device, and pulled the card through a slot on its edge. In his pocket, Bell's phone made a quiet *ting*. The woman returned Bell's card and followed it with a pair of keys on oversized brass fobs, numbered *one* and *two*.

"Rooms are at the top of the stairs," she said. "Dinner's in the bar, five until eight. Bar closes at ten. Breakfast's six until eight. Questions?"

Reacher and Bell shook their heads and made their way to the foot of the stairs. Bell was breathing heavily by the time he'd hauled his suitcase and backpack to the top, and the sheen of sweat had returned to his forehead. He handed a key to Reacher, checked the number on the one he'd kept, and used it to open the door to his left.

"I'm still feeling tired," Bell said. "Think I'll lie down for a while. In fact, I'm going to call it a day. See you in the morning?"

Reacher said, "Sure."

After checking his room, which he found satisfactory—a bed, a chair, a closet, and to his surprise, a little bathroom enclosed in an oval-shaped plastic unit wedged in the corner—Reacher headed back downstairs. He stepped outside, thinking some fresh air would be welcome after the time he'd spent in Bell's car. To the west, he could see the jagged outline of the peaks of the Great Bend National Park. They looked close enough to touch, but Reacher figured they must be at least fifty miles away. The town's single street continued to the east, seeming to lead nowhere in particular. To the south was Mexico, separated by a metal fence. It looked like a line of twenty-foot knife blades, glinting maliciously in the fading sunlight. If Bell wanted his solar project to literally span the border, he was going to have to look elsewhere. Reacher felt suddenly sorry for the guy. His enthusiasm for being outside waned. Plus, it was still oppressively hot. He decided to scratch his walk, go back inside, and see what kind of food the place had to offer.

The bar took up the full depth of the hotel. It had a window facing to the front. Another to the back. And it was about a quarter of the building's width. Which made it bigger than Reacher was expecting. And there were more people than he was expecting. Fourteen, including the guy who was serving the drinks. There was a group of four men, maybe in their forties, thin and wiry and tanned, who probably worked outside, all drinking beer from tall, frosted glasses. There were four couples, ranging in age from late twenties to early seventies, Reacher guessed. And a young woman, sitting on her own. A very young woman. She had shoulder-length blond hair. Bright-blue eyes. No makeup. She was wearing a white sundress with a pink-and-red flower pattern embroidered into it. She didn't look a day over sixteen. And she was halfway through a margarita, with another empty glass at her side.

Reacher took a seat at a small round table with his back against the wall where he could see both windows and the door. An old habit. One that had served him well. The bartender approached, and he ordered two cheeseburgers and a coffee. He watched the other guests while he waited for his food, and the whole time he could feel the woman watching him. She kept it up while he ate his burgers, and when he finished and pushed his plate aside, she took a last sip of her drink and came over to his table.

"Mind if I join you?"

Reacher didn't answer right away.

"I know what you're thinking," the woman said. "This is a setup. Where are the cameras? Where are the cops? But you can relax. I might not look it, but I'm thirty-two years old. It's a family thing. You should see my mother. She's sixty, and she still gets carded. So. Can I sit?"

"I guess," Reacher said.

"I haven't seen you here before." The woman turned and gestured for the bartender to bring her another drink. "What's your story?"

"What makes you think I have a story?"

"Everyone has a story."

"They do? Then what's yours?"

The woman smiled. "Touché. But mine's boring. I'm running away from a bad situation. This is as far as I've got. Kind of run out of steam, I suppose."

"How long have you been here?"

The woman shrugged. "A couple of weeks."

"How long are you staying?"

She shrugged again. "A couple more? Who knows? How about you?"

"I just arrived. I'll be gone in the morning."

"Really? Huh."

The bartender dropped off a fresh margarita for the woman and topped up Reacher's coffee.

"I'm Heidi, by the way."

"Reacher."

"Well, Mr. Here Today, Gone Tomorrow, Reacher. What are you running from?"

"Nothing."

"Then what are you running to?"

"Nothing."

"Really? Neither? You sure?"

"Absolutely."

"How so?"

"Running's not a thing I like to do."

"Interesting." Heidi picked up her drink. She took a long sip and kept her eyes on Reacher's the whole time. "So what kind of things do you like to do?"

Reacher smiled. "Lots of things."

"Example?"

"Some things are easier to show than tell."

"That's very true. Maybe—"

A guy had just come through the door. He was about five foot eight, stocky, with buzz-cut hair and a pinched, pockmarked face. Possibly early forties. Wearing a white dress shirt untucked over loose gray jeans. He was gesturing urgently for Heidi to join him.

"Excuse me." A frown crossed her face. "One minute. Let me get rid of this jackass."

Heidi crossed to face the guy. There was lots of gesturing. Lots of scowling. Eventually, the guy grabbed Heidi's arm. She pulled free and hurried back to the table. She sat down. He followed. He stood about six feet away from her and crossed his arms. Reacher waited a moment to give him a chance to find some manners. The guy stayed where he was. Reacher stood up. The guy backed off, all the way to the far wall, but he didn't leave the room. And he didn't stop glaring at Heidi.

"Ignore him," Heidi said. She took another long swig of her drink. "Now, where were we?"

"He's a little hard to ignore," Reacher said. "Who is he?"

"Some idiot. He hangs around with this other guy. An asshole named Greenwood. He's older. Kind of sleazy. Hits on me every time he sees me. Gets mad if I talk to anyone else. I thought Greenwood might be here tonight. I was glad when he didn't show up. But this one? He's harmless."

"He's annoying. He should leave. For his own safety."

"No." Heidi sucked down the rest of her drink then got to her feet. "We should leave. Carry on our conversation somewhere else. Somewhere more private."

Heidi was gone when Reacher woke the next morning. There was just a tiny depression in the pillow next to his and a slight hint of her perfume lingering on the sheets. Reacher stayed in bed for another five minutes, then got up and showered. He got dressed, folded his toothbrush, put it in his pocket, and went to knock on Bell's door.

Bell cracked the door, then opened it all the way when he saw it was Reacher.

"Feeling better?" Reacher stepped inside.

"I think so." Bell straightened his crumpled blue pajamas and ran his fingers through his hair.

"Then it's time to say goodbye." Reacher held out his hand. "Good luck with your wall."

"You're leaving? No. You can't. I need your help."

"With what? I'm not a solar coalition type of guy."

Bell shuffled back and sat on the edge of the bed. "Neither am I, to tell you the truth. I used to be. I did work in the power industry. I did specialize in solar. But then . . . stuff happened. I lost that job. I'm a private investigator, now. I'm here looking for someone. A missing girl. I'm not feeling well and the kind of people—"

"You're not a PI, Chuck," Reacher said.

"How do you know?"

"Your car. It's too upmarket. It's German. It has Connecticut plates. And it has parking permits inside the windshield and half of a dealer's decal on the edge of the trunk lid. A PI would have a domestic car. Or a Honda or Toyota. He'd have local plates, even if they were fake. He'd have nothing that would make it easy for someone to identify the car if they saw it twice. And he'd certainly have nothing that suggested where he lives. Or lived."

Bell slumped forward and buried his head in his hands. "So you won't help."

"I didn't say that. But if you want my help, you better start with the truth."

Bell looked up. "Only the PI part wasn't true. I am here because of a missing girl. I am looking for someone. I swear."

"What girl?"

"My daughter."

"When did you last see her?"

Bell blinked twice. "Fifteen years ago."

"That's a long time, Chuck." Reacher tried to soften his voice. "Are you sure . . ."

"She's still alive? Fair question. But, yes. I'm sure. Here's what happened. My wife left me. Fifteen years ago. She ran away, actually. With our daughter. I never stopped looking for her. It's why I lost my job, in the end. I only caught up with her six months ago. And by then my daughter had gone her own way. My wife—my ex—was alone."

"What's your daughter's name?"

"Holly."

"Holly's age? Description?"

Bell grabbed his wallet from the nightstand and pulled out some papers. One must have been a picture of Holly when she was little. Bell shuffled another piece to the front, unfolded it, and held it out for Reacher to see. It showed someone who looked like a late teenager. With blond, shoulder-length hair. And bright-blue eyes.

Well now, Reacher thought. *This could get interesting.* The picture looked kind of like Heidi. The woman from last night. Although, there was something strange about the image. It had an odd quality to it. Almost synthetic.

"It's a computer simulation," Bell said. "I didn't have any recent pictures of her. Her mom didn't have any up-to-date ones either, so we had to use this special software. You feed in the pictures you do have, tell it how much time has passed, add any details about accidents or tattoos or piercings or whatever that you know about, and it calculates the person's probable appearance now."

Reacher looked at Bell. Wondered how old he was. Whether he could have a daughter who was thirty-two. Probably not, Reacher thought. But if it was true that Heidi's family looked freakily young . . .

"Eighteen," Bell said. "You asked Holly's age."

Reacher suppressed a smile of relief. "Okay. Good. So, how do you know she's around here?"

"She communicates with her mom via a computer chatroom. I found out her screen name. Then I paid someone I know to hack into the system and trace the IP address of the computer she was using. Most recently, it was here. And before you ask, yes, that was very expensive. And yes, that was very illegal. But we're talking about finding my daughter. I don't care about what's legal."

"No judgment." Reacher held up his hand. "But I do have one question. Something that could be a problem."

Bell looked suddenly worried. "Oh. What?"

"Suppose we find her. What do you want me to do? If she doesn't want to come with you, I'm not going to help you kidnap her."

"Kidnap her? God, no. I'd never do a thing like that. I'm going into this with my eyes open. I know how long it's been. How much water's under the bridge. I'm going to take it slow. Step one, make sure she's okay. Step two, make sure she knows I want to be back in her life. And make sure she knows how to contact me, if she wants that too. And I'm going to be patient. I'm not going to force anything."

"Okay. That sounds good. But not too challenging. Physically, anyway. Which brings us back to where we started. Why do you need my help?"

"Two things. First, finding her. And second . . ." Bell paused for a moment. "Second, honestly, for moral support. I need a friend by my side. I didn't think I would, but I do. You saw me yesterday. The state I was in. The closer we got, the worse I felt. I thought my heart was going to give out."

"I'll stand by you. But finding her? You know where she is. You said your guy hacked her address."

"What? No. Not her address. The IP address of her computer. The chatroom service she uses has all kinds of encryption built-in. To disguise the location of the users. The best my guy could do was narrow it down to this town. Not to an individual house."

"So we're close. This town's pretty small. We should start by show-ing her picture around. Someone's bound to have seen her."

"Yes. Let me change. Actually, I better hop in the shower real quick. I was sweating like a pig last night."

"All right. I'll go grab some coffee. See you downstairs in ten."

Mason Greenwood forced himself to breathe. *It's all right,* he told himself. *Everything's going to be okay. You just have to run. To disappear. You always knew this day would come. It's what you prepared for. The catalyst is different, that's all. No biggie. No need to panic. Just follow the plan . . .*

But which plan? He had two levels. *One,* for if he had a little time. If he picked up a software warning, for example, tripped by the FBI's bots trying to break into his system. Or if he got a coded message from one of the agents whose kids' college funds he was boosting. He'd be able to take more stuff. Personal items that he had in everyday use, or his old paper archives. Things he could load into the RV before tripping the degausser—the device which blasts out a magnetic pulse strong enough to irrevocably wipe all the hard drives in the house—and setting the timer on the incendiaries. *One* was preferable, for sure. But there was also *Two.* The real emergency level. If his perimeter alarm was triggered, say. Or he spotted the feds sneaking through his yard on his motion-sensing, infrared CCTV system. Then he'd have to drop everything and run to the RV. Which was a thing of beauty, he always thought. He'd designed its special features himself. The lead-shielded backup hard drives, so the bulk of his work would never be lost. The high-volume freshwater tank—automatically flushed and refilled every morning—and the additional solar panels for the AC, so he could stay off-grid for longer, even in Texas in the height of summer. The auxiliary gas tanks, which were always completely topped off. The remote switches for the degausser and the incendiaries. The self-detaching umbilicals for keeping the batteries charged. And then the feature he was most proud of, which wasn't actually part of the RV at all. The thing that made the RV unstoppable. The special panel in the garage wall. It looked normal. Felt normal. But it was actually just a thin skin. The RV could burst through with no danger of damage at all. And no need to wait for a door to crawl open. RVs are tall. His was fourteen feet, counting the equipment on the roof. A door would take several seconds to get clear. The difference between escape and capture. He knew because a guy had gotten close once before. Some kind of deranged relative, when he lived in Maine. That time, the door had jammed and he had to bust through a section of frame and drywall. Which did his car no favors at all. He had to ditch it two streets away.

So, level one, or two? Not two, he decided. The situation was serious, but it wasn't desperately urgent. The police were going to find out. There was no way to avoid that. But not until someone alerted them. That could take a while. Then they'd have to make their way out to La Tortuga. There was no police station within fifty miles. That was one of the things that had originally attracted him to the place. He probably had the rest of the day, minimum. Which pointed to level one. Greenwood took another minute to work on his breathing. Then he went to his office. His paper archives were still spread out all over the floor from the night before when he'd been searching for the files he wanted for the Japanese. He'd definitely need them. He started to gather them together, then paused. A new thought had entered his brain. A different way of looking at his situation. The plans he'd made were designed to protect him from threats arising from his professional life. But his current problem had nothing to do with his work. It was entirely personal. There was no connection to his business persona. No trail going back for decades, intrinsically bound up with troves of incriminating evidence. It was a one-off. A blip. Something completely out of character. Something anyone could have done. He wasn't the new kid anymore. The unknown quantity. The person at the forefront of everyone's minds. The one everyone wondered about. But someone else was. Someone who'd been seen in the hotel bar last night. The person who had, actually, started the chain of events that led to the tragedy. The person who should be held responsible. Who would be held responsible?

If Greenwood approached things in the right way.

Reacher was halfway through his second cup of coffee when a guy approached his table in the bar.

"Excuse me, Mr. Reacher?"

The guy was about six feet even, with a big round head, broad shoulders, burly arms, but a narrow waist and incredibly skinny legs. His hair was slicked back and tied up in a ponytail. His shirt was covered in palm trees and parrots like the kind Reacher had seen people wearing in Hawaii. His pants were some kind of pale-colored chinos, and on his feet he had dusty little beige espadrilles.

Reacher took another sip of coffee. "Yes. That's me."

"Come quickly. Please. It's your friend. Mr. Shell."

"Mr. Bell?"

"Yes. Sorry. Bell. He needs your help."

"Why? What's he done?"

"He's not well. He's collapsed. He's asking for you."

"Where is he?"

"Out back. Behind the hotel."

"He wasn't loading the truck on his own, was he?" Reacher drained his cup. "I told him not to. He promised he wouldn't."

"He was, sir, yes. He begged me not to tell you. He knew you'd be mad at him. But please. Come quick. It's bad. I think he needs to go to the hospital."

Reacher stood up. "Which way?"

"Down the corridor. Left before the stairs."

Reacher's standard operating procedure was to never allow anyone suspicious to get behind him, but that day he made an exception. For two reasons. He figured the guy wouldn't make a move until they were outside, where he'd likely have reinforcements. And he wanted to be first to the exit door. He moved fast, to look like he'd bought into the urgency of the situation and to make sure the top-heavy guy had to hurry to keep up. To build momentum. So that when Reacher opened the door and politely stood aside, the guy was past him and outside before he realized the mistake he'd made. Then all Reacher had to do was let go of the door. Let it close. Stand to the side away from the hinge. And wait.

Reacher pictured the scene. The top-heavy guy would slow down. Stop. Look around. Realize he'd come out alone. Glance at his buddies for confirmation, if anyone was backing his play. Conclude that Reacher would be running the opposite way, back along the corridor inside the hotel. He'd rush back to correct the error. Barge open the door. And race through. At which point his participation in the day's events would be brought to an end.

It took twenty seconds for the door to swing open. Reacher was ready. He was watching for it. He knew the exact height of his target. The exact trajectory it would follow. Which led to a perfectly executed blow. Reacher's fist connected with the guy's temple with maximum force. It was lights-out, instantly. And, as an added bonus, the other side of the guy's head cracked against the outside face of the door on his way to the ground. Reacher scooped up the inert body and held it in front of him as he stepped outside, just in case anyone had ideas about gunplay. No one did. There was only one other person there. The guy from the bar, the previous night. The one who'd harassed Heidi. He was standing next to an ancient pickup. A Chevy, with orange and white paint dulled by years of sun and sand.

"Heidi told me you were an idiot," Reacher said. "Is that true?"

The guy didn't respond.

"See what happened to your friend?" Reacher dumped the body on the ground. "That's what's going to happen to you. It has to. It's a rule. It happens to anyone who tries to attack me."

The guy shuffled back a little, but he didn't speak.

"There's only one way to avoid it," Reacher said. "Answer a couple of questions. Are you smart enough to do that?"

The guy's hand started to creep toward the back of his waistband.

"Stop," Reacher said. "Keep your hand still. Tell me who sent you. And where you were supposed to take me. Tell the truth, and I'll let you walk away."

The guy didn't answer. His hand continued to move.

"Last chance."

The guy's hand sped up. Reacher raised his knee and drove the ball of his foot into the guy's abdomen. He flew back and folded at the waist. His face hit the ground. His body slammed down after it. Reacher stepped closer and kicked him again. In the head, this time. Just to be sure.

There was a pistol tucked into the back of the guy's jeans. A Beretta M9. Reacher took it, along with a spare magazine. He checked the guy's pockets. He found a wallet. It held $100 in notes. Reacher took the cash, too. Spoils of war. You lose, you give up your treasure. An ancient tradition. The only other item was a phone. A modern one with a big screen and no buttons. Reacher added it to his haul. He figured he'd investigate it at his leisure when the bodies were secure and he was in a less exposed position.

The top-heavy guy's pockets yielded a similar crop. A gun. A spare mag. Cash. And two phones, this time. One modern. One old-fashioned. The kind that flips open, with a real keyboard and a much smaller display. A second phone was an anomaly. It made Reacher suspicious. He pressed one of the keys. The screen lit up. It said, *Enter PIN* in black letters against a pale-blue background. Reacher tried 1111. The phone vibrated. The screen momentarily went blank, then *Enter PIN* reappeared. Reacher tried 1234. A digital clock appeared, along with a symbol. An envelope. Indicating that a text message was waiting. Reacher used the menu to open it and the screen filled with characters:

Thanks for last nite! Magic! Breakfast at
old warehouse? I have something for you!
Heidi xxx

Reacher read it twice. This was why Heidi had left so early? She'd snuck off to hook up with this guy? Seriously? Then a whole different explanation sprang into his mind. One he liked even less.

The map Reacher took from the hotel's reception showed a place called the Old Warehouse. It was the last site marked on the eastern side of town. When Reacher stopped the captured pickup a hundred yards short, he figured it was more like a dilapidated shed. It looked dirty. Rickety. On the verge of collapse. But his aesthetic and structural complaints were the least of his worries. He'd been drawn into a tactical nightmare. There was only a single road, in and out. He should have scouted an alternative escape route. He should have been approaching from the opposite side. He should have been there hours earlier. In a less distinctive vehicle. And without two hostages hastily secured in the load bed. He should have walked away. He wanted to walk away. But—Heidi. Someone had sent that text. If it was Heidi herself, and it was intended for the top-heavy guy, then no harm, no foul. Under the circumstances, Reacher would be delighted if that was the explanation. Because if someone else had sent it, that meant Heidi was being held captive. Or worse.

Reacher jammed the spare magazines between the squab of the passenger seat and its backrest. He tucked one Beretta under his right thigh. Wound down his window. Took the other Beretta in his left hand. Shifted back into Drive. Shook his head. And continued toward the warehouse. He made it all the way to the structure unopposed. He drove in through a gap in the wooden siding. No one shot at him, so he kept going until he was as deep in the shadows as he could get.

Reacher stepped back out through the gap in the wall and cursed another weakness in his situation. His complete lack of intel. He had no idea how the plan was supposed to unfold. All he could do was put himself in the shoes of whoever he imagined was behind it. Try to anticipate what they wanted to achieve and how they would go about it. And act accordingly. He sat down and leaned gingerly against the wooden planks in the spot where he'd be most visible from the road. Put his hands behind his back. Brought his chin down onto his chest. And waited.

Ten minutes ticked by. The temperature rose another three or four degrees. Reacher felt the sweat prickling his scalp and soaking his shirt. Then he heard a vehicle. It drew closer. Slowed down. Its wheels swapped pavement for gravel. It kept coming. And coming. Straight toward him. For a crazy moment, Reacher thought he was going to get run over. Then it crunched to a stop. The motor died. A door opened. Reacher held his breath. Feet hit the ground. They took a step. Another. Another. And stopped. About level with knees, Reacher thought. He still didn't breathe. He couldn't. Not without his chest moving. He held on for another thirty seconds. Then snapped his head up and whipped both arms around to the front, a Beretta firmly in each hand.

The guy who'd approached leaped back, panicked at first, but he quickly regained control and kept moving, smoothly, until he was thirty yards away. A reasonable position, since he had a hunting rifle in his hands and was pointing it straight at Reacher's chest.

"Drop the guns," the guy said. "It's over. You'd never hit me from there."

"Want to bet?" Reacher got to his feet and darted behind the guy's car. It was a Toyota Prius. Dark blue, with a pale dusting of sand. There was a body in the passenger seat. It was Heidi's. She had no visible injuries, but Reacher knew she was dead. She had the unnatural stillness that only comes when every electrical impulse has shut down and the last vestige of life has passed. Reacher ducked down and shifted to place the car's engine block, such as it was, between him and the guy with the rifle. He cocked the hammer on one of his guns, slid the other into his waistband, then relaxed his arms and rested his hands on his knees.

"What's your name?" Reacher said.

"What the hell?" the guy said. "You're not going to live to tell anyone. It's Greenwood. Mason Greenwood."

"Why did you kill the woman?"

"I didn't." Greenwood smirked. "You did. I was out hunting and I heard a commotion over here, so I came to investigate. Saw you strangling the girl. Then you threw her down. So I shot you, hoping to save her. But I was too late. She must have banged her head on a rock. Shame, really."

"Meaning you strangled her. You threw her down. She hit her head on something else. Somewhere else. And you're trying to pin it on me."

"I didn't throw her down. I let her go. Then she slipped. Hit her head. It was an accident, really. And I'm not *trying* to pin the whole thing on you. I'm succeeding."

"It won't work, Greenwood. Trust me. I used to investigate homicides. Your plan is full of holes. The police will know the body was moved. Your hands are way smaller than mine, so the bruises on her neck won't add up. And you won't be able to find a rock that matches the crack in her skull."

"You know what, Reacher? If we were in a city, some of that might matter. It might matter in a town. Even a small one. But out here? After the sun and the critters have worked on her body for a day or two? Forget it. And there's something else. Whoever drags his ass all the way out here will be at the top of his boss's shit list when I call it in. They're not going to be looking for clues. They'll be looking for a closed case. One that means the next crappy job gets dumped on someone else. And who are you? The new kid in town. The perfect one to take the blame. No one knows you. No one will vouch for you. No one will miss you."

"You have a very depressing worldview, Greenwood. But maybe you're right. Maybe the safest way forward is for me to call it in. And to identify you as the perpetrator at the same time."

"For you to call it in? You think you can call with a rifle bullet in your brain?"

"How's that bullet going to get into my brain, Greenwood? How good a shot do you think you are? Because if you miss high, I've got a clear shot with two guns while you reload. And if you miss low, you hit your car. Most likely immobilizing it. Which is going to complicate your story, some. You heard a disturbance. Shot up your own car. Then shot me? I don't think that'll fly."

"I won't miss. And if I do, I can reload as many times as I want. You'll never hit me from there. Not if you had ten handguns."

"You sure? Let's find out. Take a shot. See what happens."

Greenwood raised the rifle. Took a breath. Started to squeeze the trigger. Then, a box fixed to his belt started to bleep and buzz. The rifle discharged. The bullet hit the side of the warehouse, twenty feet above the ground.

Reacher stood up straight. Feet apart. Shoulders square. Arms out in front. He aimed. Pulled the trigger. And watched Greenwood buckle and fall. He approached the body. Kicked the rifle away. Raised the pistol again, ready for the customary two insurance shots to the head. Old habits die hard. But he didn't pull the trigger. He was thinking about Greenwood's theory. About lazy cops looking for easily closed cases. There might be something in that. In which case he could give them two. And maybe give Heidi's death a little meaning too. It would take a little staging, but maybe he could make it look like she'd defended herself. Escaped from Greenwood's chokehold. Ran a little. Turned. Shot him so he couldn't come after her again. Then slipped and hit her head. It might work. And if it didn't, no one would be any worse off.

Reacher emptied Greenwood's pockets, then went to work on positioning the bodies. It was unpleasant work. Hot. Smelly. Awkward. He didn't enjoy it. But he was pleased with the result. When he was done, he moved into the shade at the side of the warehouse and checked Greenwood's things. There were only two. His phone and the box from his belt that had bleeped and distracted him. Reacher started with that one. It looked a bit like an old-fashioned radio pager, only it was thinner and it had a bigger screen. Part of the screen had a printed, permanent display. It was a list. *Zone One* to *Zone Six*. And the boxes next to zones five and six were checked. It was for a security alarm, Reacher figured. He couldn't think of another kind of system that used zones in that way. Presumably for Greenwood's house. Someone must have broken into it at the exact same time Greenwood was trying to frame Reacher. Which could have been a coincidence, of course. A lucky break for some local hoodlum, chancing their arm. But Reacher wasn't a big believer in coincidences.

The best Reacher could figure it, Greenwood had lured Heidi some-place and killed her there. Presumably out of jealousy. Maybe her death was premeditated. Maybe things got out of control and she slipped, as Greenwood claimed. But either way, he would have kept her body on ice until his stooges delivered Reacher to the warehouse for the frame-up. With the extra cellphone in his pocket, complete with its incriminat-ing message.

Maybe that place was Greenwood's house. A logical place for a rendezvous. Familiar. Not suspicious. And which had just been broken into. Which could have been a coincidence.

Neither stooge had called or texted Greenwood to say they'd arrived, since they were both unconscious. Yet Greenwood arrived at the old warehouse within ten minutes. Which meant his house, if that was where he'd killed Heidi, was likely within visual range. Reacher moved away from the building and looked back toward the town. One struc-ture jumped out at him. The next one in line. Another old place, a quarter of a mile away.

Reacher parked the orange-and-white pickup at the front of the building. It was wide and low, with a deep porch with anchors for a swing chair, made of gnarled old wood, topped with shingles that were warped and bleached by the sun. He stepped onto the porch and peered through the dusty windows. The place looked deserted. He made his way around the side. The wall was plain and featureless. He turned the next corner and almost walked into a car. A silver sedan. German. Connecticut plates. Ten or fifteen years old. Belonging to Chuck Bell. But no longer in good shape. Because it had been driven into the rear wall of the garage. Through the rear wall, in fact. It had smashed into an RV that was parked inside, then it had been pulled back out. The driver's door was standing open, but there was no sign of a driver.

Reacher ducked down and went through the hole in the wall. He skirted around the RV and used a door that led to a kitchen. A super modern space, nothing like the outside of the place at all. It was all stainless steel and granite, and there were all kinds of appliances Reacher didn't even recognize. The only thing he was familiar with was an empty champagne bottle sitting on one of the countertops. He ignored it and moved on to the next room. An office. There were three wide desks, covered with computer monitors. A row of file cabinets along the opposite wall. Heaps of folders on the floor. Along with a person: Bell. He was slumped against the pedestal of the center desk. His face was contorted. His skin was gray. His hair was damp and plastered to his scalp. He was breathing, but fast and shallow. He saw Reacher and managed to lift one hand just enough to beckon him over. He seemed like he wanted to talk, so Reacher leaned in close.

"Sorry." Bell's voice was a rasping whisper. "Lied. Again."

"It's okay," Reacher said. "Don't try to talk."

"Didn't hack chatroom. Hacked this guy. He . . ."

"Take it easy." Reacher put his hand on Bell's shoulder. "I'll get you to the hospital."

"No." Bell paused, gasping for air. "Too late. Promise. Burn it. Burn it." Then his head slumped to the side and the last of the light left his eyes.

Reacher sat on the floor next to Bell and felt for a pulse in his neck, just to be sure. There wasn't one. Reacher stayed for another minute. He felt like rushing away would be disrespectful, somehow. Then he noticed Bell's other hand was crushing a piece of paper to his chest. Reacher pried it free, and immediately wished he hadn't. The paper was letter-sized. It was printed on the other side. A color photograph of two people. A man and a little girl. Both were naked. Both, Reacher recognized. The man was Greenwood. Maybe fifteen years younger. Reacher needed to be sure about the girl. He slid his hand inside Bell's jacket and pulled out his wallet. He opened it and took out a photograph. The one he'd glimpsed at the hotel. Bell's daughter, when she was three.

Bell's ex-wife hadn't taken her. Greenwood had.

Reacher stood. He wished with all his being that he hadn't already killed Greenwood. Because he wanted to do it again. And again. And again. He wondered if that was why Bell had come. For vengeance? And then something Greenwood had said at the warehouse came back to him. *You're the new kid. No one knows you.* He'd meant Reacher, but he was wrong. Reacher and Bell had arrived together. Only Reacher was driving at the time. Bell was in the back seat. Technically he'd entered the town a moment later. So Bell was the new kid. *The perfect one to take the blame.*

Blame? Reacher thought. Or credit?

Reacher hoisted Bell's body up and over his shoulder. He had some arson to attend to. A couple of trussed-up stooges to deal with. But first, there was a shooting he had to restage.

LIFE IN THE FAST LANE

DON BRUNS

Last month, he'd killed Steve Lansing, a Chicago mobster who was responsible for probably thirty murders in and around the Windy City. Gallagher was paid well for the assassination. The planning, the execution took him two days. In and out. Thirty-thousand dollars. Not a bad payday.

Now, Ginger Gallagher had been hired to kill Uncle Willy. Willy the Wonder.

Uncle Willy Anderson, a.k.a. Willy the Wonder, drove a souped-up 1975 Chevy Camaro and lived in Prescott, Georgia. Not a street-legal Camaro, but a hopped-up version with the sixteen and three on the floor. He'd stripped the interior, all except for the driver's seat, and the car was a lean, mean, raging racing machine, meant to scream at the Prescott Raceway, a red-clay, dusty dirt track that packed locals in on steamy Friday and Saturday nights.

Gallagher didn't initially know why he was supposed to kill Willy, didn't really care. Rule number ten in the hit book was "don't ask why." He was in Prescott to do the job, and the job, in this case, paid twenty-five thousand dollars. Good money for a couple of days in the redneck South of Georgia. Although it was now going into days longer than a *couple*. Logistics were challenging, and time and place didn't sync. He'd figure it out.

On a hot, humid summer night when the track was rockin', the clouds of red dust and sawdust could be seen a mile away, and the throaty roar of the minis, bombers, and hobby cars rattled barns in the next county. There wasn't much to do for entertainment in Prescott, except drink, screw, and go to the raceway. And so, half the people who lived there did just that. Maybe more than half . . .the ones who drank and screwed. But the Prescott Raceway did well, the track surrounded by cheap, shaky, wooden stands where the populace bought cheap, shaky beer, and drunkenly swayed in their seats, raising their red plastic cups as the cars thundered by.

Male drinkers crowded long trough urinals in the two men's restrooms, and lines of thirty women waited impatiently for the four stalls in the women's. And, of course, under those unsteady stands, other things went on as well. Oftentimes, the third component: screwing.

And there was the handful of Prescott celebs, Uncle Willy being the leader of the pack. The forty-five-year-old Willy, who must have had one hundred hats at any time in his collection. He wore cowboy hats, baseball caps, fedoras, bowlers, trilbies, Panamas—he never wore the same hat twice. Besides being the local favorite, Willy had the gimmicks. Throwing miniature foil-wrapped milk chocolate race cars to the kids before each race and tossing one of his colorful hats into the crowd after every win, the driver milked his superstar status for all it was worth. And, as Ginger found out, it was worth quite a lot.

Ruhey's Livestock, Pillster's Feed and Grain, Duling Real Estate, Morgan and Morgan Attorney's at Law, and dozens of other companies plastered their names on the famous Chevy. So many stickers, it was hard to distinguish them. When you added up the revenue, plus the purses that he won, Willy wasn't doing that bad. For Prescott, Georgia, anyway. It was all in your perspective.

From the bleacher seat, third row west side, Gallagher took a long pull on his Kennesaw, Georgia, Drivin' 'n' Cryin' beer, straight from the can, and watched Willy's cherry-red lacquered Camaro as it careened around the far curve, leading everyone else by two lengths. The throaty muffler roar was deafening. That man could drive. The car and the driver were in a class by themselves, that was obvious.

Gallagher was impressed. He wasn't good at speed, at reckless driving. Even if he'd been a passenger in that car, he would have been sick to his stomach, ready to hurl at any turn. He admired the man. The man he'd been hired to kill. But now it was time to decide when and how. Two days had turned into four. It was time to kill him and be done with it.

The glamorous demise would be to have Willy's car explode, coming around the turn. The victim would burn in a fiery crash, a final tribute to his daring and determination. But that was far too difficult to orchestrate. He'd have to find access to the car, build the explosive, figure out when to detonate it. Too much work, too long a time, and he was putting other people in danger. Besides, he just wanted to get in and get out. Like the Steve Miller song said, "Take the money and run."

When he started in the business, orchestrating a hit had been, at first, exciting. Then, interesting. Then, a pain in the ass. Now, the act of orchestrating had lost its romance. It was just a way to kill people. Kill them so it seemed like an accident. Just do it, and get the hell out of Dodge. So, Uncle Willy would be dealt with outside of the track. Maybe in his home, maybe on a quiet road as he was driving home, maybe in a bar, restaurant, or while he was involved in another one of Prescott's celebrated activities. Let's see—there was drinking, screwing, and the racetrack.

People talked, and the stories went around that Willy was a womanizer. And apparently, some of his escapades were with married women. So that might be the perfect way to off him. Catch the man doing something with someone's old lady, kill him, and at the same time, claim a moral victory. Gallagher wondered if maybe that was who had hired Paladin, his employer. Maybe a jealous husband who wanted the philandering race car driver out of the picture.

He breathed in the sharp odors of the track. Sawdust, raw fuel, exhaust, stale beer, and piss, and Gallagher realized he really wanted to get out of this town as soon as possible. The next assignment would have to be in a larger, more sophisticated city. Vegas, New York, back to Chicago. While small-town hits might pay well, it was much easier for someone to find you, identify you, question you, and arrest you. Strangers stood out like a sore thumb.

New York? You walked down the street, bumped into your vic, shoved a knife between his ribs, and kept on walking. No one saw a thing. A small town, everyone knew everyone. Even now, Gallagher could feel eyes staring . . . hear voices saying, "Who is *that* guy? I haven't seen him around before." People didn't "visit" Prescott. You lived here, or there was no reason to be here. None at all.

His Glock was back at the Thunderbird Motel. He didn't need it tonight. Weapon of choice was the .308 Winchester, the rifle he'd used in Sniper School at Fort Benning, Georgia. The rifle that he'd used in over thirty kills overseas. Too bad. A guy carrying a rifle in a small Southern town? It was a dead, dead giveaway. There was nowhere he could travel as a civilian in the United States that the .308 Winchester was acceptable. Too bad. One hell of a weapon.

Willy stepped out of the car, took a deep bow, accepted the wilted red roses some young local beauty queen wearing a sash presented. Then, with a flourish, pulled the purple beret off of his head and with his right hand sailed it into the stands. There was applause and a rush for the headgear. A cute teenage blond with ripped jeans and a tight yellow tank top snagged the cap. She squealed and held it high.

And all Ginger could think about, in another world, was what a target Willy would make. Take him out right there. End of story. He'd lie on the roof of one of the low-rise buildings a short distance away, his Winchester rifle cradled in his arms, pressed up against his shoulder. One shot. The hole appearing in Uncle Willy's forehead as the man toppled forward, facedown on the track. His blood coloring the sawdust and dirt a dark red. Another Willy salute, a little game he played with the fans?

But there was a little more to this hit. He was supposed to make it look like an accident, so a simple sniper kill wouldn't work. Gallagher reflected on his work overseas. You targeted the enemy. You engineered the situation, the location, then you shot them. As simple as that. Most of the time. Now, there was a lot more money and a lot more responsibility.

***

The process was always the same. He'd buy a burner phone, call the same number, and simply say, "This is Tracker. I'm available." Within twenty-four hours, Paladin would call back. Paladin, who had made that first very mysterious phone call after Gallagher left the military. Gallagher was never sure how Paladin had found him, but he was glad he did. Forever indebted. He'd answered the cellphone, almost six months after he'd retired. He was working at a hardware store in the exciting town of Wilmette, Illinois, selling a toilet to an eighty-year-old lady, and wondering if this was going to be his forever postmilitary career. Wilmette, Tree City, where one claim to fame was a Guinness World Record domino competition. Good Lord, deliver him. Selling toilets to octogenarians. Domino champions. The phone rang.

"Mr. Gallagher, this is Paladin. You don't know me, but based on your background as a trained army sniper, I can offer you a minimum of five hundred thousand dollars a year. That's a minimum. Live where you want, work as frequently as you want, and refuse or accept any assignment. Are you interested?"

Based on his background? If you've accepted the fact that you can kill without compunction, if you can take someone's life with an analytical understanding, if you can divorce yourself from any human emotion when you eliminate someone's existence on this earth, then you are a good candidate for professional hit man. And apparently, Gallagher was. Deep inside he knew it. In most cases, he was simply eliminating a target. A target, not a human being.

And the money was a little better than working at a hardware store. One year, a million and a half, the next nine hundred thousand. It varied, depending on how hard he wanted to work and how many jobs were offered. Never less than five hundred thousand. As advertised.

His background was perfect for this job.

The year he joined the army, forty-six soldiers were selected for Sniper School at Fort Benning, Georgia. Forty-six out of hundreds that applied. Four graduated. Four in his class. A very elite group. That fact was not lost on him.

You had to be a stone-cold killer. And damned good at it. And the United States Army made sure that you were. The irony. The American taxpayers paid for his training. Thank you very much.

Stalking, tracking, engineering the situation, concealment, camouflage, observation, not to mention the shooting accuracy. Army-trained snipers, those who graduated in the top 10 percent or higher in their class, hit their primary target with their first round of ammunition 1.3 percent of the time. Their *first* round. It took the average soldier fifty thousand rounds to hit an enemy target. *Fifty thousand rounds.* After rifle training. A staggering number. Mind-blowing. To be fair, most rounds were fired as cover, into bush country, in bursts, not really aimed at a specific target. But still, no one understood those figures. So, go *figure.* Crazy numbers that no one would believe. And the average American taxpayer just kept on keeping on. They paid the bill. Did they know?

Paladin apparently only hired the best. Gallagher assumed there were others. He didn't know that, but it made sense that there was a network. He never asked. Never wanted to know. It was probably dangerous to know, in case any of them ever got caught.

When most soldiers retired from the service—when trained killers, elite snipers, walked away from that job—they reenlisted in the general population of the United States. That's when they started to freak out with flashbacks, with blackouts and mental problems. If they were one of the lucky ones, the government put them in institutions. Agencies gave them drugs, or the retired military employees turned to drugs themselves and were responsible for petty crimes and maybe a homicide or two. Possibly they turned to suicide. There was a lot of that going around. Getting back to sanity was almost out of the question. If sanity was even a possibility. Or, they tried to make a living selling toilets to eighty-year-old widows. God deliver him.

He was at his wit's end. Gallagher was ready to jump off the deep end. Ready to bail on the system. Go off the reservation. Turn to a life of crime, drugs—something to make up for the lack of stimulation, the highs that he got as a trained assassin. He desperately missed the rush, the focus, the thrill.

Until someone called and said, "Hey, we need someone with your experience. We need someone with your character, your drive and determination." *Paladin* needed someone who had been trained by the most sophisticated killing school in the country. Someone who had been programmed as the ultimate killing machine. Finally, someone understood him. It was good to be an American citizen, someone who had once defended the country. Killed at least thirty enemies. Averaging about one point three shots per kill. Pretty special.

"Look," he'd turned his attention to the wrinkled, white-haired woman, "the Toto Dual Flush at two hundred fifty bucks is probably the best deal for the money. I've got a toilet that goes for one thousand seven hundred fifty bucks, but excuse me, ma'am, it's a toilet. They all pretty much do the same thing. I'm going to turn you over to another employee. Hopefully, she will tell you the same thing." And he walked out the door.

How fortuitous. How fortunate that someone—in this case Paladin—called, offering a career that fit his skills so perfectly. Skills taught to him by a patriotic national treasure. Uncle Sam. The white-haired, pointy-chinned, bearded man dressed in red, white, and blue. Gallagher was one lucky guy.

So, here he was. *Have Gun—Will Travel.* Usually, he'd use a gun, but there were other ways to kill the vic. Poison him, knife him, run him over. Should have been a simple task. Kill Willy Anderson. This should have been easy. But they wanted it to look like an accident. An accident? Now, it got complicated.

He had learned, figuring out how this guy operated, that Uncle Willy had numerous affairs with married women. Screwing around with adventurous, adulterous, committed women was almost an obsession with the slightly overweight, balding, forty-five-year-old playboy. Obviously, celebrity had its privilege. Women apparently threw themselves at the devilish driver who tossed his hat into the ring. But this town was starved for entertainment and celebrity, so Willy played by a different set of rules.

It was so easy to dig up the dirt. He'd been in town for three days, and he knew more than most of the residents. Or maybe more than the residents cared to share or admit. And with his ear to the ground, looking for ways to take out the Camaro king, Gallagher also found out that there was one more evil in this city of sin. It personified as a five-foot-two, greasy-haired, sixty-year-old sleaze-bag named Norman "Shorty" Gozling who seemed to have a monopoly on that sin.

Gambling.

The short man, Gozling, was a bookie. A small-time, *small* by stature bookie, granted, but he'd set up shop because of the racetrack. People needed to take their racing obsession to the next level, so enter Norman from the Windy City, who was glad to take their bets, their odds, and, while he was at it, their money for larger events. Boxing, football, soccer, basketball, baseball, whatever you wanted to wager on, Shorty would help you out. He now had four employees, and they were busy around the clock. If you woke up at three in the morning and decided to invest one thousand dollars in a potential game-changer in your life (literally a game-changer, maybe the Jets and the Patriots), make that call to Norman or one of his associates. They could make the wager. And if your bet was on Uncle Willy, or Rodger Dodger in the blue Mustang, or the midget-car magic of Stevie Staple at the Prescott Raceway, Shorty could cover that too. The main reason he was in business. That racetrack.

Was it a legal business? Hell no. Georgia was waffling, the state government bordering on the issue. The next state referendum . . . you never knew. So Gozling skated, but any week, any day, any minute he could be shut down. Probably should be shut down. But he was wallowing in the cash flow and wasn't about to close up shop until the government demanded it.

And, as it turned out, Willy the Wonder was more than a race car driver and more than a lothario. The guy was also a degenerate gambler, an unabashed player who would bet on anything offered. He would bet on his own race results, on every race on the ticket, on the Super Bowl, on the Little League Championship. The end of the world? He'd give you odds. And, with some subtle investigation, Gallagher figured that Willy invested heavily in Gozling's business. Thousands of dollars on bets every month. And lately, he hadn't been so lucky. He'd gotten a little more adventurous with his odds. And the wonder boy of the racetrack was losing big time on a number of bets. And falling behind in his payments. Apparently, he'd been warned. Now, the research that Gallagher was doing went beyond what he wanted to do. He wanted to picture the man as a target. That's all. But he found out Willy had been severely beaten a month before Ginger arrived. He still had bruises and walked with a slight limp. While pissed-off husbands were a possibility, it was more likely that Norman "Shorty" Gozling was responsible. And, it was whispered in certain public places, there had been subtle death threats. And that, apparently, was where Ginger Gallagher came into the picture.

The subtle investigation that he did lasted for three days, hanging around Larry's, a local coffeehouse. People talked. The study involved hanging for two evenings at the Nasty Reputation, a sleazy saloon on the east side. Even more gossip. Willy was slippery. He'd slip out the back door rather than face the music. He had stiffed people in this town and others. As popular as he was, he was on a number of people's shit lists.

Gallagher listened to people and learned that Uncle Willy was deep into Gozling for thousands of dollars. Maybe hundreds of thousands of dollars.

Rule number nine in the hit man rulebook: "Do your homework." Rule number ten: "Don't ask why." It was a dichotomy. If you did your homework, if you studied the vic, you usually found out *why*.

So, it was women or gambling. Gambling or women. And didn't that go back to the beginning of civilization? The Roman empire? The winning of the West? Or East, or any other situation? Willy was in trouble with his sexual exploits or with his gambling escapades. There was a reason to kill him off. And lay the blame to Willy Anderson's excesses. And apparently, there were at least two of those.

And Gallagher figured the gambling was what would bring Anderson down. Someone was pissed off. Probably someone was being stiffed and wanted to make him an example. An example that if you don't pay up, here's what happens. It was only an assumption, but when forced to figure, Gallagher usually nailed the reason.

He seriously wanted to be emotionally unattached. Rule number two in the assassin's handbook: "Don't make it personal," but it sometimes motivated his end result. If the victim needed to be killed, he usually found out why. He didn't really *need* to know why, and he preferred *not* to know why. Rule number ten: "DON'T ASK WHY"! If you knew why you were killing someone, you started questioning your job. Not a healthy attitude. The job itself was so screwed up. So confusing. You either had some feelings for the situation, the vic, or you divorced all feeling. Be that stone-cold killer. For the money, that was the best avenue. Focus on rule number two. Focus on rule number ten. That didn't always work.

And as he drove the rental Chevy Spark, following Uncle Willy, he remembered following rule number three: "Rent a generic car." You didn't want to be driving a vehicle that anyone would recognize. There were ten rules on the hit man's list. Except for number one, they all alluded to blending in. Become a part of your surroundings. And so far, for five years, this had worked for Gallagher. Thirty hits a year, it amounted to about four and a half million dollars and change so far. Tax-free. Not a fortune, but he knew a lot of guys from the service who turned into bankers, plumbers, electricians . . . jobs that paid thirty bucks an hour, and then people who lost everything and some who were homeless. Some in prison and some who took their own lives. So, four-plus million seemed like a pretty good deal. He wasn't rich, but he was doing okay. He had friends, acquaintances, and people he brushed shoulders with who had no idea what he did for a living. If this was called a living. Confusing, risky, but it seemed to work for him.

The number one rule was a little different. He'd learned that first rule when he was in Sniper School. As simple as it seemed, it made more sense than almost any other rule.

"Be quick."

Once you came up with the solution, the idea, the way the vic would be killed, once you planned it, orchestrated the situation, be quick. Do it. The more you strategized, the more you agonized and thought about it, the harder it became. Be quick. Number one rule. Be quick. And in the case of Uncle Willy, he had to come up with the idea . . . now. Plan it and execute it. Be quick. He'd already waited much too long.

Once you set up your target, you knew where they would be, where they would walk, socialize, drive, hide, then you planned the rendezvous. You positioned yourself, waited till the vic appeared, and pulled the trigger. No second thoughts, no questions. Be quick. The setup could take forever, but when it came down to the kill, be quick. Rule number one.

***

Eleven p.m. The race had ended at ten. He stayed behind Uncle Willy's tricked-out Jeep Cherokee, the tan vehicle working around the traffic, and Gallagher's rented Chevy Spark keeping pace. The pale-yellow rental was rule number three. "A generic rental." But the tiny vehicle kept even with the race, and there was never going to be an open interstate where Willy could open up the engine, accelerating his Cherokee and losing the minute Chevy. In this small town, there were no open freeways, no broad expanses of highway. Gallagher was pretty sure he could follow the Cherokee. And it was definitely headed a different direction than home.

As if in an action movie, Willy's Cherokee swerved around corners, passed cars that were traveling a little too slow for his taste, and sped up on the straightaways. The Spark lagged behind but within sight of Willy's Jeep. Just keep it in sight. That wasn't hard to do.

He'd followed the Cherokee for three nights, each time to a different residence. He had waited an hour, an hour and a half, sometimes two hours, until the driver left. Never the same address, never a specific time. If he was having sex with the woman of residence, his routine varied. Whatever happened, it wasn't lengthy, but during those three nights, Willy never slept over. He always left within a two-hour time frame and drove home.

And what was troubling, as if the assignment wasn't troubling enough, was the black Cadillac sedan that followed every night. A CT6. The car seemed to be a message that he needed to complete his mission. It made no sense that the occupants were sent to kill Willy. It had to be a surveillance vehicle. They were probably checking on when and if someone was going to perform on this twenty-five-thousand-dollar contract, two-thirds paid up front, and they were following Willy, unaware of the Chevy Spark. If they were surveilling Willy, they wanted to know if and when he was going to be killed. There were only two people who knew Gallagher was the hired assassin. Paladin and Gallagher. So, this had to be someone who wanted proof that the hit happened. Probably someone who was going to film the attempt, then report back to whoever needed to know.

The Cadillac disappeared when he pulled into the lot. The luxury vehicle had to be parked somewhere on the site, but out of sight. He was sure of that. So now there were two sides to the contract. Kill Uncle Willy, and get rid of the Cadillac. He didn't appreciate monitoring. Gallagher was fairly certain that the vehicle was following Willy, not him. He knew that Paladin didn't check up on him. Paladin trusted Gallagher. And for five years, he'd earned that trust. Someone may have guessed that Ginger was the hit man, but only because he'd overstayed his welcome. Gallagher wanted no surveillance and certainly no video.

No, thank you.

The hit man stepped out of the Chevy, stretched, and did a visual. The dimly lit parking lot was bordered on two sides by dense foliage. He straightened up, ran a hand through his sandy-colored hair, and briskly walked through the parking lot, designed for thirty vehicles. Most assigned parking, some for visitors and maintenance vehicles. He was a maintenance car. That's where he parked. The Cherokee seemed to be a visitor car. He walked the area again, on the inside of the lot. And there on unit twenty was a black Caddy. He felt certain it was the same Cadillac that had followed Willy for three nights. Lights off, no sign of activity. He walked by the car twice from a distance. He could see someone in the driver's seat. The driver would be concentrating on the door of the building, not paying attention to someone walking the lot. And the driver had his hands up, a phone or some video unit held high. The operator was going to film any action.

Not on his watch.

Rule number four: "Be prepared." For anything. In this line of work, you always walked into situations that you didn't expect. All of your senses needed to be on alert. Ones you didn't even know you had. Be prepared. Maybe *he* was being followed, probably Willy was being followed, by the person who was paying Gallagher. The one who was paying Paladin. That needed to stop. No one was to know how or why this assignment was going down. No one.

Climbing back into the small Chevy, he was glad he'd taken the indoor bulbs out of the car. No lights to distract anyone. He texted the license plate number to Dead-Eye. Everyone in this line of work had an alias. Big Jimmy, the Fishmonger Al, Cadillac Mike. Underground sources, a black market of illicit contacts that could give you invaluable information. It took five years to build the list and it was still growing. He wasn't going to deal with anyone "checking up on him."

Dead-Eye, a person he'd never met. Someone who didn't know anything about Gallagher. And Gallagher had found him or her on the dark web. A risky place to be. A risky place to search. But Dead-Eye was simply a reliable source who could track down leads for a substantial price. And Ginger could afford to pay that price. Bitcoins. Something he'd never heard of five years ago. Now, it was the currency of choice.

There was no question that this person, whoever paid for the Cadillac, was playing outside of the parameters. Come on. All you had to do was hire someone, and let them do their job. Why send someone to monitor the situation? Hell, that someone, that surveillance person, could facilitate the kill themselves. Save the expense of an outside hit man. If they didn't trust him to do the job, call Paladin and cancel the contract. That's probably what he would have done. But people are strange. People are different. Some people don't want to get involved. They just want to observe. Keep their hands clean. Sort of.

Sometimes his mind got in the way. The smart move was to leave well enough alone. Do your job and move on. But, damn, someone was fucking with his end result and he needed to know who and why. Did someone tell the Cadillac driver that Ginger Gallagher was the hit man? Impossible. The worst scenario for a hit man was to be outed. Cover blown. Or did someone hire this driver to detail the time, the place, and the way that Willy was wasted?

Dead-Eye got back to him in ten minutes. The Caddy belonged to a syndicate. Of course. Hard to trace. But Gallagher was paying the premium. The syndicate was called Smart Money Inc., and surprise, surprise, fronted by Norman Gozling. The gambling king. Now it made perfect sense. Gozling's goons wanted to make an example of someone who didn't pay their bills. In this case, Uncle Willy. And they were following Willy to make sure the job got done.

Ginger sat in his car, pretended that the surveillance car wasn't there, and waited for his prey to leave the building.

There was a new perspective in the assignment. He didn't want to know that. But certain people made it impossible to ignore the reason. He would prefer just to kill the vic, walk away, and take the next assignment, but now, Smart Money Inc. had introduced themselves and they were shadowing his mission. Sending a driver to make sure that Uncle Willy was killed. Ginger had been a professional for over five years. To his knowledge, and he was pretty good at evaluating a situation, no one had ever tailed him. No one had ever questioned whether the victim would be killed. Ginger Gallagher always took care of business. Well, almost always. There were always a few misses. Too few to mention.

And just then, Uncle Willy walked out of the building. Almost swaggering, he walked to the tan Cherokee Jeep and backed out of the parking spot. So Ginger would follow Willy home, and the syndicate Cadillac would also follow Willy to his condo. Then, if Ginger decided to take Willy out in his parking lot, the Cadillac would have full view of the deed. The driver would probably have video proof of the killing, filming it from his phone, and be able to provide that to anyone interested. Gallagher prided himself on being invisible. No one knew who he was or why he was in town. If the syndicate had photographs, a movie of the killing, they could blackmail him, maybe Paladin, or turn it over to the authorities. He didn't need this kind of aggravation. All the money in the world wasn't worth it. Taking a deep breath, he remembered rule number six.

"Don't overthink the assignment." Yet how could he not? The driver in the Cadillac *could* incriminate him. And he wasn't about to let that happen.

Gallagher drifted a little into the right lane, a little into the left lane, and at one point let the Cadillac pull ahead of him. Finally, he pulled into the apartment parking lot. Willy had parked in his assigned spot and walked to the entrance. The man had won his race, probably had his ashes hauled and was going to bed. Ginger stayed in the Chevy for five minutes, until he saw the Cadillac pull in and park two rows back.

Gallagher opened the door of the Chevy, no light. Bending over, almost crawling, he approached the black beast. The driver was sitting straight up, a small camera in his hand, and Ginger could hear the music playing from the man's system. The guy was moving his head to Bruno Mars, "Uptown Funk." Waiting to see if anyone was going after Willy. The camera gave it away. Don't fuck with the small-town Gozling syndicate. A driver was on watch patrol.

If he had pictures, then Gallagher was toast. All the syndicate had to do was turn over the video evidence.

He was convinced that they hadn't figured out *he* was the hit man. And Ginger Gallagher definitely did *not* need a nanny. Someone to check up on him. Going back to the car, he reached into the glove box and pulled out a pair of brown leather gloves. He reached into his pocket, took out a thin metal wire, then slipped on the gloves.

Crouching low, he walked to the driver's side and hesitated, listening to the music. *"Don't believe me, just watch. Don't believe me, just watch."* Holding the wire garrote in his left hand, he stood up. "Always be prepared."

Gallagher tapped on the driver's window. The man spun around, surprised, and pushed a button lowering the window.

"What?"

Ginger hit him with a hard right, a strong enough blow to break his jaw. He grasped the driver by his hair, pulling his head out the window, then quickly forced the wire garrote around his neck. The driver was wheezing as Gallagher twisted and squeezed the device. The victim's hands grabbed Gallagher's wrists, desperately trying to relieve the pressure, to stop the thin wire from cutting through the skin and cutting off his air supply. The man's tongue was hanging out of his mouth as he gurgled, moaned, and in thirty seconds, he'd drawn his last breath. No lights highlighting the event.

"Don't believe me, just watch."

And that was one less problem Gallagher had to worry about. Collateral damage. He'd never had to do that before. Didn't bother him. Just another experience in the life.

Rule number four. "Be prepared." For anything. In this case, getting rid of an obstacle. He was tempted to call Paladin and make sure no one had outed him. Maybe someone had figured out that the stranger in town was a hired assassin. But he didn't. He'd figured it out for himself. The syndicate simply was watching the target. And getting evidence of someone killing Willy.

Gallagher reached into the man's rear pocket and took his wallet. Reached into the other rear pocket and took the man's phone. Then took the SiOnyx Aurora from his hand. A camera that could film at night as if it were day. He'd been right. The man had the perfect instrument to vividly capture any action in bright color as if it were daylight.

It could be tomorrow before they found him. Depending on who he reported to, it could be days. Maybe weeks. Gallagher hoped for the latter. He pushed him into a reclining position so no one would see his dead silhouette through the window.

Robert Roberts. Really? Who the hell would name their kid Robert Roberts? Two hundred bucks in cash. Added on to his twenty-five thousand. A small but nice bonus. The last call on the phone was to Smart Money Inc. He didn't relish collateral damage, but he also didn't relish having his cover blown. Compartmentalize your mission.

Everything you did worked toward the final mission. And that mission was all that mattered. All that mattered. Kill Willy. Tomorrow morning, he was going to kill the man. As soon as he left his condo. This was taking much too long.

***

You planned, and calculated, and set up the operation. Then executed it. But sometimes, you had to just let the situation dictate how and when. Sometimes it was serendipity.

Gallagher followed Willy, eight o'clock in the morning. His light-brown Cherokee weaving through early morning traffic. Ginger was hoping that last night's spy with the camera wouldn't be discovered for a couple of days. By then Gallagher would be hundreds, thousands of miles from the dirtbag town of Prescott, Georgia.

Let's get this over with.

Willy drove and drove, past gray, weathered tobacco barns, rotting tenant shacks buried in wild shrubbery and weeds, two dated roadside motels with the names Gordon's Motor Court and Ernie's Tourist Stop. Past cotton fields and sparse stands of ash trees. Thirty minutes later, he pulled into a large, circular drive. A brick-framed sign in front announced "Rainbow Connection Children's Center." Maybe Willy had a kid there. Maybe he was using the drive to turn around. But he parked to the side, got out of his vehicle, and limped into the large brick facility.

Ten minutes later, he walked out, stepped into his Jeep, and drove off. Gallagher didn't follow. Instead, he exited the cheap Chevy and walked into the lobby. The mousy receptionist at the desk smiled.

"Can I help you?" She stood up behind the mahogany-topped desk.

"Maybe."

Interacting was dangerous. Someone might remember the meeting, the conversation . . . they might remember him. The reason he dressed in jeans, a simple T-shirt, and sneakers, with a generic blue ball cap pulled low on his forehead.

"I'm sort of a friend of Willy Anderson, and I thought I saw him walk out of this building just a moment ago."

"Uncle Willy?"

"Sure. That's his nickname."

"Yes," she gave him a bucktoothed smile, shuffling papers in front of her.

"That was him, right?"

"Oh, yes. Thank God. Who are you?"

"I know him. I just wondered why he was here."

"Why are you here?"

"A friend."

"I'm sorry?"

"A friend asked me to check up on a . . ."

"One of our charges?"

"Sure."

"Give me a name."

"First of all, why was Willy here?"

"Uncle Willy wins at the speedway. We get a windfall. If you're a fan, if he's your friend, you know how kind he is."

He wasn't. He really didn't need to know.

"I shouldn't tell you this, but Willy donated a couple thousand dollars from last night's purse. I was actually at the race last night when he tossed the beret into the crowd. We love him to death!"

And Ginger Gallagher needed that death thing. It was why he was here.

"Wow. Is he always this generous?"

"Even more so."

"How so?"

"He visits the kids we place in foster homes. And, he sponsors a number of them. School supplies, clothes, whatever they need."

"Really?"

"You said you were a friend?"

"Well . . ."

"How much do you really know about him?"

"Apparently, not that much."

The girl dropped her smile and walked around the desk.

"You have a great friend. If he truly is a friend."

"He sponsors foster kids?"

Shouldn't have asked. Too much information. Damn.

"He had a child. Maybe twenty years ago. The girl died at one year. I'm not sure why. Something to do with meningitis, I think. But Willy has been involved with . . ."

Ginger shook his head, smiled, and walked out. Double damn. Number ten. "Don't ask why." He was being paid a lot of money to not ask why. He hadn't known anything about Willy's gifts, and now he knew too much. Yet, now he was intrigued. Not a good thing. Number two: "Don't make it personal."

And then there was Norman Gozling. The man who apparently had contracted to kill Uncle Willy. There wasn't much question. Gozling had to be the guy. Gallagher drove back to the Thunderbird Motel, logged onto his laptop, and started running searches on Norman Gozling and gambling operations in Georgia. He half expected to see that the gambling king gave all his money to a local church or senior citizen center. That didn't happen.

Several inquiries referenced the man. He'd been arrested and exonerated on charges of extortion, illegal gambling, and forcible rape. A story from ten years before mentioned a partner in Chicago, a financial investor in Willy's syndicate. He and his wife had disappeared under mysterious circumstances after completing a large business transaction.

Their car was found at Midway Airport, but their tied-together bodies washed up on the shore of Lake Michigan near Navy Pier. And that was only on the first link. Other links listed the short man as a small-time gangster, someone who was arrested for beating one of three wives and had skated on a charge of armed robbery. He laid that off on two friends. He had no idea they were going to hold up the convenience store and pistol-whip the clerk.

Ginger stared at the picture of the man: slicked-back hair and a pinched face with hooked nose. He looked up from the screen and shook his head. This guy was a bad dude, a hard-headed man, who had the means to dodge the charges. And now, he was paying big bucks to kill

Willy. All because Willy wouldn't pay his gambling debt. And Gallagher understood the need to send a message. However, some of that money was going to the welfare of displaced children. Foster kids.

Get the hell over it. He was being paid to do a job, not deal with some moral issue. This was his assignment, his fucking responsibility. Today or tomorrow, come hell or high water, he had to kill Willy and earn his salary. And he knew how he was going to do it.

Besides, Willy was no saint. He was sticking it to Gozling's operation and sticking it to married women in the area. Ginger was surprised he hadn't been taken out by a jealous husband long ago. Instead, the only thing he'd heard of was the beating Gozling's goons gave him.

Number six: "Don't overthink the assignment."

***

Smart Money Inc. was on Fifth Street, down from the stucco-covered 1910 courthouse with the old clock tower that was always stuck at one twenty-eight. Gallagher parked in front of the two-story brick building and stared at the second story, wishing he had X-ray vision, wondering if Gozling was inside and what he was doing at the moment. In reality, the guy was really his employer and he shouldn't be second-guessing the man who signed the check.

As he sat there, the blue cap pulled low over his face, a Jeep Cherokee pulled out from behind the building and he caught a glimpse of the driver. The vehicle was brown, but it wasn't Willy. Greased-back hair, a hooked nose, it could be Gozling.

Gallagher pulled out and followed the Jeep, about twenty minutes from the courthouse. A higher-end of establishments than his tailing of Uncle Willy to Rainbow Connection. A steak house, Asian restaurant, an upscale Holiday Inn, and finally a complex of townhouses. The Cherokee parked in a carport at the third building, and Ginger slowed down and watched as the short man stepped out of the vehicle. He'd seen pictures. There was no doubt this was Norman Gozling. The possible rapist, murderer, robber, and wife beater.

He pulled up behind the vehicle, got out, and walked to the front. Stenciled on the concrete parking curb was one word: Gozling.

***

He stopped before going back to the Thunderbird Motel. At the Auto-Zone store and the convenience store, where he bought an automobile headlight and a hammer, and at the convenience store a large jar of olives. Essential elements to take out his target.

Inside the sparsely decorated room, he opened his suitcase, the one that had been checked at the airport, and opened the coffee tin. French Market Coffee & Chicory. He loved the stuff. But this tin was filled with smokeless gunpowder. Not a drinkable beverage.

Pouring out the olives from the jar and draining the glass container, he jammed toilet paper into the briny jar, drying it out. Then he slowly filled it with gunpowder, pouring it carefully into the cavity, and with his pocket knife he punctured a hole in the metal lid. If he had tried to puncture it when the lid was back on the jar, a spark could set off the powder. He was too close to the finish line for that to happen.

Over the nearest wastebasket, he smashed the headlight with a small ball-peen hammer, eyeballing the wires and filament. He carefully broke them free from the base and shoved the small device into the slit in the olive jar lid.

He packed up the coffee tin, his minimal wardrobe, the Glock, a toothbrush, and amenities. Walking out to the Chevy he swore to himself he would never visit this godforsaken town again.

He knew where Willy lived. Knew his parking spot. Knew what hours he slept and pretty much when he woke up. It was the one reason he'd overstayed his welcome. He knew everything about Willy. He should have just killed him on day one or two. This was his decision. He was God. And only two people knew that. Paladin and Ginger Gallagher.

When darkness approached, he approached the Cherokee. There was no problem breaking in the driver's door. First of all, it wasn't locked. The sign of a cocksure egotist who didn't believe anything could happen to them. He loved these guys. People who owned the town. Bulletproof!

He leaned under the dashboard and with a swath of duct tape he secured the gunpowder-packed jar to the car's base. Using his cellphone flashlight he located the wires connected to the starter, cut them, and connected them to the olive jar. Gallagher wasn't a mechanic, but he knew enough about the ignition to realize that there was a good chance a turn of the key could ignite the powder in the glass jar. The glass jar would explode, sending shards into the car, the surrounding area, and of course the victim. The fire could spread to the engine and explode the gas supply.

Of course, something could go wrong. Even in Frederick Forsyth's book *Day of the Jackal*, the intended victim, Charles de Gaulle, bends down at the exact second the sure-shot Jackal pulls the trigger. The shot completely misses the target.

In this case, Gallagher figured there was an 85 percent chance that his quarry would be killed. He liked the odds. Message sent.

He wanted to be close enough to confirm the kill, not so close as to incur any of the damage. Ninety percent of the destruction should be inside the Jeep. He parked in an open spot by the street. A quick getaway spot, and he could still see where the Jeep was parked.

He closed his eyes, mental alarm clock set for seven a.m. It never failed him. Never. He didn't question it. No need to.

***

He snapped to attention, staring out at a misty Georgia morning. Gallagher was not sure exactly what time the target would walk to his car. Stretching, yawning, he kept his focus, and at seven forty-five, he watched the target exit his residence and walk toward the Jeep.

The man eased into the vehicle, apparently fastened his seat belt, and turned the key. One, two, three, four . . . BOOM!

The explosion rocked Gallagher's car. The bolt of red-hot fire consumed the vehicle in two minutes, and there was no chance anyone would survive. Mission accomplished.

Ginger waited for another sixty seconds as the flames subsided. Other than cars on either side, there was no collateral damage. He smiled. This needed to be done. Wasn't going to look like an accident. Didn't really matter.

***

An hour later, driving his rental to Atlanta, his cellphone pinged. Paladin.

"Tracker?"

"Paladin?"

"I haven't heard. Apparently, you haven't pulled the trigger?"

"I will. Today." He really wasn't into turning around and doing the deed. But . . .

"Cancel the mission. Our employer has met an untimely end. He paid for the job, but considering he's no longer with us, I see no reason to go any further."

"Paladin, I have it planned." He tried to sound concerned.

"No. Abort."

"Okay."

Rule number eleven, one he'd invented: "In a rare moment, do what is right."

WASTED TIME

JOHN GILSTRAP

"Be serious, Tony," Samira Carter said to me. "What you're talking about is a zoning matter. I can't get involved in that."

I squeezed my red rubber stress ball as I paced behind my desk. "Of course you can," I said. "You're the county executive."

"Exactly my point," she pressed. "I can't show favorites."

I laughed. "Don't bullshit a bullshitter," I said. "Showing favorites is how you got your job. You remember me speaking at your fundraiser, right? The one that brought in the record contributions? It wasn't that long ago."

"Of course I remember, Tony. And I am forever grateful. But—"

"This could be the time to refer to me as Senator Bayne," I said, cutting her off. "Or, if you prefer, Chairman Bayne, because I run the Finance Committee. You remember that, right?"

"Oh, come on, Tony—"

"What did I just say?"

Samira made a growling sound. "Seriously? Okay, *Chairman* Bayne, you're being unreasonable."

"Abigail Vanden gave two thousand dollars to your campaign," I reminded her. "And handed you an envelope with many other checks just like hers."

"You're telling me things I already know."

"Evidence to the contrary notwithstanding," I said. "Clearly, you have lost sight of the significance of her efforts."

My assistant, Tammy Miller, peeked her head in my door, but I waved her off. She didn't leave. She was wearing her this-is-important face.

"Dammit, Tony—*Chairman*—it's a restaurant, not world peace. Zoning says no. If I intervene, it will look like I've been bought by campaign contributions."

"It doesn't have to," I said. "You can handle that however you want, but Abigail is very special to me. That alone should be reason enough for her to be special to you."

"Is this really the most important thing on your plate right now?" Samira snapped. "I mean, for God's sake, the country is perpetually on the brink of war, the economy is fragile as glass, and you want me to pull strings for a pizza shop?"

"It's Italian fine dining," I corrected. "And yes, I do. Given your constituents' enthusiasm for the minor league ballpark you campaigned on, I think you'd be wise to see the world through my eyes."

That knocked her off her game. "What are you suggesting?"

Tammy still hadn't moved from my door. Her face looked dour, and she held a pantomimed thumb-and-pinky telephone receiver to her cheek. I underhanded the stress ball to her, and she snatched it out of the air effortlessly.

I continued with Samira. "As you said, the economy is fragile. I know we talked about some federal loan guarantees to support the construction, but under the circumstances, that might prove to be a problem."

She fell silent long enough for me to wonder if she was still there.

"Elections are not that far away, Samira," I said, sweetening my pot. "Abigail and I could just as easily throw our support behind Michelle McGarry as with you."

"This is extortion," she seethed.

"Oh, please. Extortion and politics are entirely different things." I changed my tone to emphasize the need for Samira to pay attention. "You've already pulled strings for Andrew Zimmerman. Don't think I don't know that." Samira had promised the property Abigail Vanden wanted to use for her restaurant to gajillionaire Andrew Zimmerman, who wanted the entire low-rise complex to be rezoned to allow him to build a much larger and more expensive monument to money.

I continued, "I even have the documents that prove your interactions with Zimmerman. You're foolish to write that stuff down, by the way."

"Look, Ch-Chairman Bayne." Samira sounded flustered. "I don't know—"

"Of course you do," I interrupted. "You can chase your tail on this all day, but you're going to do it my way. Otherwise, your emails to Zimmerman go to CNN. Best case, you get tossed out of a job, but the smart money says you'll get jail time."

Silence.

"And you know Zimmerman will throw you under the bus in the first ten words of his interrogation, right?" I pressed.

"Okay!" Samira nearly shouted it. "Okay, you win."

"I always do," I said, and I clicked off. To Tammy: "What?"

She returned the stress ball with a stylish behind-the-back toss. "Assholery becomes you," she said with a wink. "You have a phone call."

"No shit," I said, mimicking her pantomime. "I never would have guessed. From the look on your face, it must be the president."

Her eyebrows bounced. "Way better than that," she said. "Line four."

I lifted the landline and punched the blinking button. "This is Senator Bayne."

"Hi, Tony," an overly cheerful voice said. "It's your baby brother, brother." I felt the blood drain from my head as I sat hard in my chair.

***

At my brother Jordie's suggestion, we met at a Starbucks on Fifteenth Street, Northwest, only a few blocks from the White House. He'd chosen an outside table despite the chill. Spring hadn't yet arrived, but it was close. I figured if I stayed in the sun, it wouldn't be too bad. He waved as I approached, but he didn't stand, even as I shook his hand.

"Afternoon, bro," he said. "Excuse me. *Senator* Bro."

"Hey, Jordie," I said. Even with the passage of time, I had a hard time faking pleasure at seeing him. "How long have you been out?"

He smiled, exhibiting two missing teeth. "Gotta love them liberal judges," he said. "They said fifty years, but I guess they only meant thirty-five. I surely do thank you for all them visits."

"You were in Kansas, Jordie," I reminded. "That's not a place I get to very often."

"Christmas cards find their way to Kansas," he said. Three and a half decades in the slammer hadn't taken any edge off his homicidal sneer. If anything, the years had honed it. "Letters, postcards. Even the phones work there."

I knew when I agreed to this meeting that I was going to take a verbal beating. Now that we were seated across from each other, I knew it had been a *huge* mistake. "Why are we here, Jordie?"

"Let's call it a family reunion. Anybody I know still alive?"

To hell with it. "None that would want to talk to you," I said. And I believed that was the God's honest truth.

"Pretty harsh, there, bro."

"You're a murderer, Jordie."

He brought a hand to his chest, feigning surprise, and whirled in his chair. "What? Really? Who told you that?"

I didn't honor him with a response.

His face turned serious as he leaned into the table. I pulled back, concerned that he might lash out.

"My past worked out well for you, didn't it, *Senator*?" He seemed incapable of saying the word without mockery. "I seen how you campaigned as a justice warrior. I seen how you bragged that you wouldn't even come to the aid of your own kin. Televisions work in the joint, too."

I waited for him to work through whatever speech he'd prepared.

An employee with a hoop in his nose exited the main door and approached us. "Excuse me, guys. But you need to buy—"

"You need to kiss my ass!" Jordie yelled. "Leave us the hell alone!"

The employee blanched and dashed back inside.

"Not planning to stay a free man for very long, I see."

"I don't have to put up with his bullshit. I can sit wherever the hell I goddamn want."

Yeah, I thought. I'd give him three months back in society. Six months, max.

Jordie got back on point. "You know, I seen you once on the tube tellin' some big-hair news babe how you were ashamed of me."

"The whole family's ashamed of you, Jordie. What's left of it, anyway, after you were done."

Jordie smiled as if I'd stepped into a trap he'd set for me. "Aren't you all high 'n' mighty?"

Yet again, I decided to let him run.

"We both know that I'm not the only murderer sittin' at this table," Jordie said with a smirk.

My stomach knotted, but I'd been waiting for this and I kept my face passive. I said nothing, expecting that he might have a recorder on him. You never knew what angles Jordie was playing. Yes, a young man had died at my hand, but that was a long time ago, and it was mostly an accident. Jordie was the one who actually killed him, but I was a party to it, and in the eyes of the law, it didn't matter that I hadn't delivered the fatal blow.

"You remember Adrian Bowman, right?" Jordie pressed. "*Take what you want. I promise I won't scream. Please stop, please stop.*"

My breath caught in my throat. I'd stopped hearing those words a decade ago, about the same time I stopped reliving the horror in my dreams. My wife, Suzie, would wake me up from those screaming nightmares, but I never told her what they were about. Adrian had threatened to expose me as part of a cheating scandal at Northern Neck Academy. It would have gotten me thrown out and it would have disgraced me. I'd intended only to scare him a little. His body had never been found, so officially, Adrian Bowman wasn't even dead.

At one point, the Bowman family had floated a reward topping $25,000 for information on his whereabouts.

"Are you just going to sit there and sweat in the cold?" Jordie mocked with a satisfied grin. "Or are you going to say something?"

"I'm not your performing monkey, Jordie. I agreed to come and listen, not to talk."

"You think I'm wearing a wire, don't you?" Jordie said.

I answered with a shrug. There was no conceivable answer to that question which would not make me sound guilty of something.

"I'm not," Jordie assured.

My derisive smirk wasn't as honed as his, but I tried my best.

"Oh, I get it," he said. "My word's not good enough for you, is that it? You want something more dramatic? Well, it's too cold to strip naked for you, but how's this? For the record, whoever is listening to this, I'm the one who actually killed Adrian Bowman."

He said it loudly enough to make me whirl in my seat to look for witnesses. "Jesus, Jordie."

"Look, Tony," he said. "I swear to God, I'm not trying to jam you up. We've got a problem, you and I, and I'm here to keep you out of jail on this thing. How's that?"

There'd been a time when my brother had been a pretty decent guy. He always had a short temper, and he was always in trouble, but there'd been a softness in his eyes. Sitting there at Starbucks, I saw that softness for the first time in decades.

"Let's walk," Jordie said. "I imagine Sammy Snowflake in there with his nose ring is going to call a cop, and neither one of us needs that kind of publicity." He stood, and I followed him toward Farragut Park, uncomfortable at being so visible to the public. While the chairman of the Senate Finance Committee was not famous enough for the cover of gossip magazines, I'd logged enough hours on Sunday talk shows to be recognized by players in this town. And Farragut Park was ground zero for K Street lobbyists.

"If you take the rod out of your ass, you'll be less recognizable," Jordie said, as if reading my mind.

"Are we going to get to the point sometime today?" I asked. I'd grown tired of the tarantella of pretending to give a damn about what he had to say to me.

"Okay, here it is," he said. Along the edges of the park, the fleet of food trucks that sucked revenue from surrounding restaurants was beginning to pack up for the day. "For the last thirty-five years or so, you've truly believed that your shit doesn't stink. While I was rotting away, you were ruling the world, confident in the fact that you were untouchable."

I moaned. "And you wonder why I didn't visit?"

He continued as if uninterrupted. "You assumed your shit didn't stink because no one ever found Adrian's body. You know I could have buried you, right? I could have gotten a lighter sentence, maybe, and all I'd a-had to do was tell the cops where the body was. I didn't do that. You should give me some credit for that."

"You've always put others first," I said, hoping that the irony was palpable. He didn't tell anybody about Adrian because he didn't want to be tried for his murder, too.

"Didn't you ever wonder why nobody found that kid?"

My stomach churned. I *had* wondered that, in fact. Someone finding the body had been the central element of some of those screaming nightmares.

"Well, here's the thing," Jordie said. "When we jammed Adrian's body into the cave in Culpeper, we thought we'd fooled everyone."

This time, I knew my poker face failed me. "What are you telling me?"

"I moved him," Jordie said. "If he'd been left there to rot, he'd've been found for sure. That would have totally screwed up our lives, so I moved him to a safer place."

I waited for it.

"Don't you want to know where?"

"I don't know that I do." That was as honest a statement as I'd ever uttered.

"Well, you have to," Jordie said. "That's the reason I'm here. I moved Adrian's corpse from the cave to a hole under the boards of Gramma Bekins's barn."

"You took it all the way to Pennsylvania?"

Jordie shrugged. "It made sense at the time, what with the reward down here and everything. Nobody'd be looking for him in Pennsylvania Dutch country."

Some dots connected in my head, and they made me uncomfortable. "Tommy and Missy were from up there." Those were among the relatives Jordie had murdered.

"Yes, they were." Jordie cleared his throat and looked at the ground. "They found out what I was doing."

"That's why you killed them?"

My brother forced a laugh. "It's as good a reason as any, isn't it?"

"And Uncle Neil and Aunt Doris?"

"They wouldn't listen to reason."

I pulled to a stop, surprised by the emotion I felt welling up. "Jesus, Jordie. Are you telling the truth?"

He crossed his heart and raised his hand. "The God's honest."

"I had no idea."

"Of course you didn't. I didn't want you to. Why suck you into what was already a shit storm for me?"

I gestured to a bench along the sidewalk. "I need to sit," I said. "I'm so sorry."

Jordie sat next to me. "You didn't do nothin'." He laughed—a genuine one this time. "Well, other than killing Adrian."

In the moment, I had difficulty sorting out the significance of all this. He didn't seem to be circling a blackmail threat. Any doubt that he was wearing a wire evaporated with that testimony. "I-I'll be honest with you, Jordie. I don't know what to say, beyond thank you."

"I appreciate that," Jordie said. "But that's not what we need to talk about." He took a deep breath and turned sideways on the bench. "Gramma Bekins's farm has been sold to a developer."

I felt myself scowl. "We don't have any claim to the money from that. That's the other side of the family."

"It ain't about the money, big bro. Think about it. They're gonna tear down that barn, and they're gonna work the ground."

My blood turned to ice water. "They're going to find the body."

"Bingo." He emphasized the word with a forefinger poked toward my nose.

My head exploded with disaster scenarios. "It's been almost forty years," I said. "That's a long time—"

"There's no statute of limitations on murder, Tony." He spoke softly. "I'm not trying to rub anything in or make anything worse. That's just the way it is."

I stared. I no longer was able to form words.

"This is new for you, bro. I get that. But I've thought this through from one end to the other, and there ain't no gettin' around it. We need to move that body. The construction dudes are gonna find the remains, and they're gonna call the cops. The cops are gonna shut down construction and call the media. Neither one of us stripped Adrian naked before getting rid of the body, so there's clothes and shit that can be traced. DNA, too, maybe. I don't know when they started doing that."

I desperately tried to think of another way. "Perhaps—"

"No perhaps," Jordie said. I was just as glad he interrupted, to be honest. I didn't have any ideas. "You're a big honkin' senator, Tony. You're on television, and half the country is in the other party and they'd love to see you hang from a bridge span."

That image seemed awfully specific, but I didn't pursue it.

Jordie was right. If the body were found, it would be huge news. Parents never get past the death of their child. And if the parents were gone by now, the siblings would never get over it. Hell, *Northern Neck Academy* never got over it. I said, "If the body has any leftover DNA, they can match it to some degree after the fact. One way or another, they'll be able to determine that it's Adrian."

"Right," Jordie agreed, but he wasn't finished yet. "Remember, even at the time, some people thought you might have something to do with his disappearance. The way you clashed with him over who was King Big Dick on campus."

Back then, in that part of Virginia, having the last name Bayne carried a lot of deference. The cops had looked into me—I presumed they looked into others, too—but they came up blank and never even grilled me. Asked a few questions, but it never got heated.

"No one thought he was dead, though," Jordie went on. "At least, not officially. A seventeen-year-old kid got a wanderlust and disappeared. In the eighties, I figure that must have happened a lot. It's easy for cops to turn away from a cold case like that, but the body will change everything. It's gonna embarrass everyone. It's going to fire up the social justice whiners, and the media is going to go nuts. How long before History Channel does a special—"

"I get it, Jordie," I snapped. I didn't need to hear any more of the doom. He'd sold me. "All right, we need to do this, but we need to be careful."

"I think I figured that part out," he said.

"No, even more careful than usual," I explained. "People recognize me. They're going to notice a guy my age buying shovels and plastic bags. Whatever the hell we need to do this thing."

"They didn't notice me, I don't think," Jordie said.

Something in his tone put me on alert. "You already bought it?"

"Yep. Sulfuric acid, too. You know, for dissolving—"

"Don't say it," I said. "I watched *Breaking Bad*. I know what we do with the acid." I settled myself with a deep breath and rubbed the back of my neck. "How long do we have?"

"They've already settled on the sale," Jordie said. "Why would they delay the work?"

"You mean now?" I asked. I suppose it made sense, but I wanted more time to process it.

"How long do you need to change out of that suit and put on some shit kickers?"

***

"Seriously?" Jordie asked with a laugh as we met at the designated spot at Tysons Corner Mall. "That's what you're wearing?"

While he was dressed all in black, I was wearing khakis and a sports shirt under a light-blue windbreaker. This was as casual as my wardrobe got. "I'm not as prepared for grave robbing as you," I said.

"Not even a pair of jeans?"

"Not even," I confirmed. "I presume we're taking your car?"

"*My* car? Jesus, bro, I just got out of prison. My bank account hasn't built back to go-cart status, let alone car status. I had to take a cab to get here, and that was half my life savings. You got a rental, right?"

I felt my jaw tense. "Did we discuss me getting a rental?"

"I figured you were smart enough to figure out for yourself that it's a bad idea to drive your own car to a crime scene."

When I heard him articulate the thought, I saw that he had a point. I glanced at my Cadillac Escalade, wishing that I'd done a better job of thinking things through. "It's too late for tonight," I said. "Even if a rental place is open, grabbing a car at midnight is going to raise some eyebrows. Should we put it off till tomorrow?"

"I don't think it's worth the risk," Jordie said. "The only thing stopping them from being at work right now is the fact that it's dark."

So, we took my Caddy. The first stop was the barely habitable travel trailer that he called home in the far reaches of the worst corner of Alexandria, Virginia. It sat in a field behind an equally dilapidated house that had to be pushing eighty years old. "Why didn't you just have me pick you up?" I asked. "Why the double-travel?"

He gestured with a hand to the darkness past the windshield. "Do you think you would have found this place on your own? Your GPS would have taken you to that main house. You don't want to knock on that door."

"Why is that?"

I saw his silhouette pivot toward me, and I could feel him rolling his eyes. "Let's just say they're more accommodating to people in my line of work than to people in yours."

I interpreted that to mean the house was either literally or figuratively a den of thieves.

"I did time with one of the guys in there," Jordie explained. "We were cellies, and when he heard that I was on the homeless spectrum, he let me crash here in his backyard."

Accessing the ancient Shasta canned-ham trailer meant driving off the end of the driveway and across the backyard, which was littered with beer cans and assorted other trash. Jordie was correct that I could not have driven this route without him at my right, urging me on. Even with him there, it seemed like a good way to get shot.

We galumphed our way across the yard and stopped in front of the trailer, where assorted body disposal tools stood stacked and waiting. A plastic wading pool that would be resistant to the acid, two axes, two saws, two shovels. A bottle of bleach. A bag of lime. The corpulent cartoon fish around the circumference of the pool made me feel sick.

"How did you get all of this without a car?" I asked.

He pointed through the darkness back toward the house. "My buddy has an old pickup he let me use. And don't worry. I didn't buy everything at the same place."

I tried to say something pithy, but my voice wouldn't work.

"You gonna be able to do this, big brother?"

No. "I don't see a lot of options."

"That's because there isn't a lot," Jordie said. "I'm not bullshitting you when I say that prison is much worse for some people than it is for others. It would suck for you."

"Let's get on with it." I pulled the door release and opened it to the chilly air. Five minutes later, we were on our way.

As we drove into the night to unwrite history, my thoughts wandered back to that night in 1982 when everything went so horribly wrong.

***

I knew that Dr. Applewaite, the headmaster, would be returning to campus the next morning, so if I was going to get Adrian Bowman to stay quiet about the . . . *shortcuts* I'd taken during my math exam, I would have to do it that night. April 12, anniversary of the sinking of the *Titanic*.

Adrian was as OCD as anyone I'd ever known. He always walked the same route to go to the same places on campus at the same time on the same nights. Every evening started at the Commons, where we ate dinner, and then he was off to the library, where he'd study till 8:45 and then he'd be off for the dormitory.

The campus at Northern Neck Academy was nicer than many colleges, though I didn't have the frame of reference to know that at the time. Manicured lawns and mature trees, plus riding stables, outdoor swimming facilities, and an archery range. The main building was constructed to look like an antebellum plantation house, complete with tall columns and a grand staircase.

Adrian's nervous-tic habits limited my time frame. Each of us had a ten o'clock curfew, at which time we were to be in our rooms. Lights-out officially happened at eleven, but the house mothers and fathers didn't much care so long as you kept quiet and stayed in your room. The only exception was for bathroom necessities.

Whatever I was going to do had to be done between 8:45 and 9:45 if we were going to avoid demerits for being out too late. Too many demerits led to personal time with Dr. Applewaite and his famous butt paddle. If Applewaite ever needed a second career, lord high executioner would have suited his talents and personality.

Jordie had been kicked out of the Neck the year before, but I knew he had a head for fixing things, so I turned to him for ideas. After I shared my conundrum, he right away came up with the idea of nabbing Adrian and scaring the shit out of him. Once he told me the plan—which he seemingly pulled out of his ass, without any real thought—the whole thing seemed perfectly obvious.

Adrian's route from the library to the boys' dorm took him through a part of the campus that I always tried to avoid. The path ran parallel to Lee Creek and was always three shades darker at night than I felt comfortable with. There'd never been any muggings or other crimes committed here as far as I knew—though the routine discovery of condoms in the nearby woods told of other activities that, while not illegal in the Commonwealth of Virginia, would get your ass turned purple by Applewaite if he found out.

Color me a scaredy-cat. Certainly, that's what my old man would have called me. And frequently did.

Whether it was Adrian's own fear of the dark or some awareness of what was waiting for him, Adrian Bowman walked down the path as if he were nervous. Hands in his pockets, head down, strides shortened.

Jordie and I had been lurking there for over half an hour, not wanting to miss him, and making sure that our eyes would be fully adapted to the darkness.

Jordie took the lead as Adrian passed. We waited till we could see his back, and then went to work. Adrian apparently didn't hear us as we approached, because he made no effort to run or even to duck as Jordie slipped the pillowcase over his head and yanked back on it hard, causing Adrian to flop backward onto the path.

"If you yell, I'll break every one of your teeth and carve out your eyes," Jordie said. I didn't dare talk because Adrian would recognize my voice.

Jordie cinched the pillowcase tight under Adrian's chin and lifted him to his feet. "Be careful," Jordie said. "If you fall and I don't let go of the bag, you might break your neck."

"P-please," Adrian whimpered. "Take what you want. I promise I won't scream. Just please don't hurt me."

"I wish I could promise that," Jordie said, and he laughed.

We headed deeper into the woods, off the path and toward the creek and the neighborhood beyond. Northern Neck Academy had no fences. Not secure ones, anyway. The adjacent subdivision was dominated by thirty-year-old, old-money houses. The residents were mostly probably lawyers and doctors, I figured, so they didn't worry me. But if you were a bad guy and you wanted to kidnap a kid rich enough to afford Northern Neck Academy, there really was nobody to get in your way.

As we dragged him through the woods, Adrian started crying and praying. I didn't even know he was religious. He attended chapel on Sundays just like everyone else, but when everyone *has* to go, it's tough to tell if anyone *wants* to go.

I left it all up to Jordie. He said he had a place to take him, and I believed him. I followed, not wanting to know the details.

Adrian whimpered and whined the whole time as we pushed and pulled him through the woods. I wanted to ask where we were going, but I didn't dare let him hear my voice. I figured that one way or the other, I'd find out our destination when Adrian did.

Jordie led us to a dilapidated structure that looked like it might have been a garden shed in its former life. Made of plywood, the surfaces were delaminating in several spots, and the glass in all the windows was missing.

"Why are you doing this?" Adrian whimpered.

"Why are you such an asshole?" Jordie snapped back. He kicked the back of Adrian's knees, and our prisoner collapsed onto his butt.

"Please don't," he begged.

Jordie kicked him in the balls, and Adrian folded in on himself.

I smacked Jordie's shoulder. "Easy," I whispered. "He doesn't even know why he's here."

"Tony?" Adrian recognized me right away.

Jordie grabbed my arm and shook his head, urging me to say nothing.

"I promise I won't say anything," Adrian said. "I was just kidding about the cheating. I swear to God—"

Jordie kicked him in the stomach this time, and Adrian rolled himself into a protective ball. Then his breathing went wrong. He started heaving for air.

"What's wrong with him?" I asked.

"I don't know," Jordie said.

We both kneeled next to Adrian. I snatched the pillowcase off his head, and I saw the terror in his eyes. In the wash of my flashlight, I could see that his lips were turning blue.

"What did you do to him?" I asked.

"You saw!" Jordie said. "I kicked him. Maybe I broke—"

Adrian coughed out a wad of blood and his breathing turned into a kind of snore as his muscles relaxed and he wet himself.

"Oh, shit!" I said. "Oh, shit. Oh, shit."

I didn't know what to do. Neither of us did. Two minutes later, he was dead.

The rest of that night is a blur. I remember we found an unlocked car with the keys stuffed behind the sun visor on the driver's side. It was parked in a shadow, and we were able to drag Adrian's body into the trunk, and then I drove. We went all the way to Culpeper, every bit of ninety minutes away. I sort of remember the shallow cave where I off-loaded the body, but I also sort of don't.

I guess the gods were on my side that night, because I was able to get back to the dorm almost three hours after lights-out without being seen.

Then, when Adrian turned up missing, I thought for sure there'd be hell to pay. I lived in fear of the day when that knock would come at my door and I'd face cops and handcuffs, but it never happened.

Looking back on the good fortune that the body had never been found, I don't know why it never occurred to me that someone might have moved it—let alone that Jordie would have.

***

We made it to south-central Pennsylvania in what felt like record time. The last time I'd been to Gramma Bekins's farm—probably fifteen, twenty years ago—development as we knew it in the DC area wasn't even a possibility. Farmlands stretched in every direction, and the farmhouses themselves were separated by hundreds of yards, if not by miles.

Now, it was clear that suburbia was encroaching. Still far from the congestion of Northern Virginia or suburban Maryland, many of the farmers had gone the way that Gramma ultimately did, selling out the family homestead to developers of subdivisions. Way out here, the houses we saw were more of the modest three-thousand-square-foot variety than the hideous McMansions that dominated the DC market.

The driveway to Gramma's house had, for all of history that I could remember, been marked with a simple concrete post stenciled with the initials IDL, for Isaac Don Lettinger, Grampa's name. He always said that people he wanted to see would know what it meant, while people he didn't want to see had no reason to know anything about who lived there.

I recognized the long right-hand curve leading to the driveway, but the concrete post had been replaced with a giant construction scar that had taken down at least a hundred linear feet of old-growth hedges and trees.

"Holy shit," Jordie said, speaking my thoughts. "They've done all of this in two days? Good thing we didn't wait."

"What do you think we're going to find?" I asked. "I mean, it's been thirty-five years. Will he be more than a skeleton?" Hearing myself ask that question churned my guts. I was referring to a teenager whose parents had never known peace because of what I'd done.

"We'll find out together, big brother. And soon." He pointed ahead through the windshield. In the blue light of the moon, I could make out the silhouette of Gramma Bekins's barn behind the wreck of her old house.

"Did the house burn?" I asked. Stupid question, because clearly it had. Heavy charring and smoke stains stood out in the wash of my headlights.

"You see what I see. That's not how she died, is it?"

"No. She moved away from here a few years ago into a senior center. She had a thousand things wrong with her, but I think the official cause of death was a pulmonary embolism."

"Whatever that is," Jordie said with a wry chuckle. "I used to like coming up here."

I agreed. Gramma and Grampa's farm was a place of freedom. While our parents were hoverers, always trying to manage our days for us, those annual three months in Pennsylvania were all about staying out of Grampa's way. Want to fish? Fish. Want to take the .22 into the woods? Shoot till you run out of ammo. The only thing they wouldn't tolerate was staying up late or sleeping late. We'd grump about it, but I for one enjoyed the long days of nonstop adventure.

I pulled the Escalade to the far side of the barn, away from the road, which itself was easily three hundred yards away.

"I don't suppose you've thought up some kind of cover story in case we get caught," I said.

"I'm not sure that's possible," Jordie said. "Not getting caught is pretty much our only move."

I threw the transmission into Park and settled myself with a deep breath. "You lead, I'll follow," I said.

For the next long while, I don't think we said anything. We just went about the grisly job of shoveling up the dirt floor of the barn under the creepy illumination of two white-gas-powered Coleman lanterns. For reasons known only to him, Jordie had chosen to bury Adrian Bowman's body in one of the horse stalls, where once-stout plank fencing surrounded four rectangles that measured about ten-by-five feet.

The dirt was settled and well-packed after this much time, though I don't remember livestock ever being in this space.

Twenty-five minutes in, I was soaked with sweat, despite the chilly air, and filthy beyond words. I could smell dirt in my sinuses. We both stood shin-deep in separate holes. "Hey, Tony," Jordie said.

I looked up to see him holding his lantern under his chin, causing hideous shadows to bloom on his face. I yipped and jumped, triggering a laugh.

"You know I'm a murderer," he said. "Ever think maybe you're digging your own grave?"

I hadn't yet, but I did then.

He launched a huge laugh. "Oh, relax," he said. "I'm just shittin' you. You should see your face!"

Nothing about that was funny. "You're sure this is the spot?" I asked, trying to shift the focus away from my own fear.

"This is where I remember," he said. "If not this stall then one on either side."

I considered commenting that maybe we should have started digging in more than one stall at a time, but I didn't think that would help either the mood or the progress.

Tink.

I heard the sound and felt a vibration through the shovel blade at the same instant. "I found something," I said.

"I heard."

I lifted the shovel and thrust it again.

Tink.

"It could be a rock," I said, but I didn't believe that for an instant. I planted the shovel blade in the dirt next to the hole I'd started and moved the lantern closer.

At first glance, I couldn't make out what I had hit. I stooped low and then went down on my hands and knees to start scraping the dirt manually. The first thing I felt was fabric, and it made me jump. I don't know why. Maybe just the creepiness factor.

"I found clothes."

"Keep going." Jordie pulled out his cellphone and clicked on the built-in flashlight. Instantly, my workspace transformed from dull yellow to bright white.

"Don't you worry about the light shining through the slats in the walls?" I asked.

"We've got to get this thing done, big bro."

He was right.

As I pulled dirt away by the fistful, the horror revealed itself. I wondered if this was how a sculptor felt when peeling away rock or clay to reveal the image of what lay within.

The fabric was frayed and decayed, but still identifiable as cloth.

I took a break and sat up straight, my butt resting on my heels. I inhaled deeply and felt my breath catch in my throat. "I don't know that I can do this."

"Do you really see a choice?" Jordie asked. Something had changed in his tone. It sounded harsher. More direct.

But he had a point. No, I did not see a choice. We needed to move quickly.

I bent back over my work and pulled more dirt away. I jumped again when I saw my first flash of white bone.

"Oh, shit," I whispered. It looked like a finger. As I pulled more dirt away, the finger became a complete hand. I pulled on more dirt and the hand joined a skeletal wrist, which then disappeared up into a shirt sleeve.

"It's not archaeology," Jordie snapped. "We don't need to preserve the damn thing. We don't need to map it or mark it. We just need to dig the sonofabitch up."

I began to feel uncomfortable. This was the old Jordie shining through. The one with the homicidal attitude.

"Lighten up," he said, again reading my thoughts. "This is a goddamn crime scene, and you're moving in slow motion. We've got to dig."

I started to say something about showing respect for the dead but saw how stupid that would be. Adrian Bowman was only dead because we'd made him that way.

I rose back to my feet, grabbed the shovel, and got back to business. I no longer worried about *uncovering* the body. Instead, I concentrated on pulling it up out of the ground. I jammed my shovel blade below where I figured his waist to be, and I lifted, levering the handle to gain mechanical advantage.

As the body arched up out of the ground, dirt fell away, exposing more bone and fabric. I saw a plaid flannel shirt. A thick leather belt and decomposed denim trousers.

I froze.

Adrian hadn't been wearing denim. No one at the Neck wore denim. Chinos were about as casual as anyone got, unless we were on the athletic field, in which case the only option was one of the regulated school athletic uniforms.

"The body's wearing jeans," I said. "Adrian wasn't." When I looked to Jordie, I was horrified to see the smile on his face, though it was barely visible beyond the halo of his phone's light. He was enjoying this.

"What the hell's going on?" I demanded. "And get that damn light out of my eyes."

"Sure, bro. I've got everything I need." The light went off, and he slid his phone back into his pocket.

Panic bloomed like a ball of ice in my gut. "What do you mean?"

"Just what you think," Jordie said. "Your jury's going to have a hell of a lot to watch and listen to."

"What did you do?"

"You were right to worry about me wearing a wire," he said. "Didn't you wonder how I got out of the joint so early?"

Of course I had. But with all that had happened since he called me, my mind had been in a jumble. I could barely form words, let alone wonder about how my brother got out of jail.

"I don't understand," I said. The calmness in my voice surprised me. "This isn't Adrian."

"Apparently not," Jordie said. "But he's here somewhere."

"Who's *this* then?" I pointed to the corpse at my feet.

"Off the top of my head, I don't remember," Jordie said. "There's nine bodies in here. I'd have to look really hard to know which one is which. Adrian was the last, so he's probably near the top of the stack."

My ability to think evaporated.

"You look like you need to sit down, bro."

He was right. I sat. I ignored the discomfort of whatever was poking me in my butt cheek. "Are you telling me that you're a *serial killer*, Jordie?"

"Not anymore. I've *reformed*." He winked at me. "You should be proud of me, bro. You've always considered yourself to be the great nego-tiator, but I gotta tell you that you got nothing on me."

I couldn't wrap my head around the enormity. "When did you do this?" I managed to say. "And how?"

"What, these other dead folks?" He piffed. "Call it youthful exper-imentation."

"So, those nights when you wouldn't come home and Mom would get so worried . . ."

"Yep. Well, not *every* night, of course."

It was getting harder and harder to breathe. "So, you *intended* to kill Adrian?"

Jordie laughed. "No, and ain't that just my luck? The one I killed by accident—that *we* killed by accident—is the one that led to me getting caught."

"Missy and Tommy?"

"They saw me burying Adrian. The hole was open, and they saw another body. They freaked out and ran to tell Uncle Neil and Aunt Doris." He held his hands up in a full-body shrug. "What else could I do? I knew I couldn't get rid of four bodies at once before I got caught, so I turned my attention to covering the hole back up. I figure that saved me from a needle in my arm."

He went quiet for a bit, as if giving me time to process it all. "You talked about showing this to a jury," I said. I began to see the glimmer of a self-preservation strategy. "*My* jury. If you tell them that I was involved in Adrian's murder, I'll—"

"You'll what? Tell them that I killed all these other people?" He laughed. "They already know." He sat down at his end of the tiny grave and folded his ankles under his thighs. "And they didn't care. Dude, you've got some serious political enemies. They'll do anything if they get to perp-walk the Senate Finance Committee chairman out of a barn full of bodies."

"They're not going to just let you walk away from all of this."

"They already have. Because they get *you*." The old Jordie was back in full menace. "I served thirty-five hard years for murdering four people. My lawyer met with the very politically ambitious United States attorney and told him that he could deliver the great Tony Bayne on a murder charge, but that I would have to be let out and granted immunity for any other crimes that I might have committed."

"The US attorney *knew* about these other bodies?"

"He knew there might be other bodies, but he had no idea where they were. The only one he's interested in, though, is the one *you* helped to kill. This location was my hole card. If they gave me the deal, I would give them everything they'd need to roast you on a slow spit for years and years. They'll take everything you've ever earned, bought, or believed in."

"If that were true, you could have played that card ages ago," I said.

"You were only a kid then," he said. "We both were. I really didn't want to jam you up. Then I watched you disown me and apologize for me and disrespect me for thirty-five years. After I'd served enough time for prosecutors to save face, I knew it was time to pull the trigger on you." His smile showed genuine pleasure. "And here's the part that warms my heart. My time served is in my past. As I wile away my remaining years somewhere in the Caribbean, you're going to die in a concrete cage."

Suddenly, it felt as if there wasn't enough air in the room. "Oh, my God, Jordie."

"And part of the deal was that I got to make this speech before they shove you into the dirt and put cuffs on your wrists. You're going to the big house, big bro, where you can think about all that wasted time." He stood. "Okay!" he yelled.

"Wait!" I said. "Wait, I can work something out for you. The country doesn't need this kind of controversy right now—"

The darkness of the barn transformed into noon. Bright lights jumping to life all around me.

"Federal officers!" someone barked from behind. "Senator Anthony Bayne, you are under arrest for the murder of Adrian Bowman."

VICTIM OF LOVE

REED FARREL COLEMAN

THE KIOSK

Cashier at CVS. Stockman at the local Dollar Store. Checking IDs and sales slips at Costco. Stuffing mailboxes with "Free Estimate" flyers from unlicensed, uninsured roofers. Supermarket pack-out man. Picker for an auto-parts supply chain. Box folder for Giovanni's Pizza. Dominos delivery man. Crimson Tiger Chinese Dumpling Shop delivery man. Ice cream scooper. Office cleaner. Gas pumper. Car washer. Taxi driver. School bus driver. Uber driver. Lyft driver. Handing out political leaflets for candidates whose prospects were slimmer than his own.

Vincent Love had a thousand nondescript jobs during his forty-three years of nondescript living. He hadn't been born with a sense of humor or, if he had been, it was small and vestigial, like the tail we lost somewhere along the evolutionary trail. Maybe it was like the gill slits in embryos that become jawbones, voice boxes, and ears. Maybe he was still a fish. It would explain a lot. In any case, he was incapable of seeing the humor or the irony in either his family name or in his most recent career choice—working twelve hours a day at the Felicia's Face Masks kiosk at the Brixton Regional Mall.

His life, much like the cavernous mall, was empty. Empty as a third of the mall stores gone out of business. Empty as another third that would soon follow suit. Still, Vincent was required to wear a face mask. He didn't mind. Not minding was perhaps his only real skill. Besides, his face wasn't much to look at. He wasn't ugly. He wasn't handsome. Vincent was as memorable as a stick figure, as remarkable as clear plastic wrap. His boss, an unlikable man not named Felicia, forced him to wear a different mask every day.

"It helps show our wares, son."

That confused Vincent the same way it confused him that the man speaking to him was named Arlo and not Felicia.

"I'm older than you are, Arlo."

"Yeah, and so what?"

"Then why call me son?"

"It's an expression. Are you all right in the head? You autistic or just a fucking idiot or something, boy?"

"Boy?"

Arlo saw that calling him boy confused Vincent even more than calling him son. "Never mind, you dummy. Just wear a different mask every day and you'll have a job."

Arlo patted Vincent on the shoulder and walked away, laughing, shaking his head.

Vincent had had many unlikable bosses. There was the supermarket manager who called Black people the N word but had posters of nude Black women all over the walls of his office. He liked calling Vincent his own personal 'tard. Vincent didn't like that man, but he guessed he didn't mind. He didn't mind it when the manager fired him. He even understood. Vincent had caught the man pleasuring himself in his office, calling the women on his walls rude names. He'd been fired before and would get fired again. He had had to learn from a very young age how not to mind.

His high school public speaking teacher, the unfortunately named Miss Kuntzler, gave Vincent's class an assignment he would never forget.

"For next class, ladies and gentlemen, you have to do a three-minute presentation that begins with the line, 'My superpower is . . .' Be honest as you can be, but also give yourselves the freedom to be creative. That's all I'm going to say on the subject."

Vincent remembered being excited for the first time in his life about speaking in front of other people, even those kids who'd been merciless to him. Remembered asking the social worker at the home to help him pick out clothes the next morning. Remembered raising his hand to be first to speak. Remembered the nervous expression on Miss Kuntzler's face when she picked him. Remembered one of the few times in his life he felt joy at waking up. Remembered, verbatim, what he said in front of the class that day.

My superpower is being a punching bag. People have meanness inside them. All people do, even the nicest people like Mr. Martindale at the home. It's an orphanage, but they make me call it the home. Whatever that's supposed to mean. People need to have a place to put their meanness, and my superpower is that I can take that meanness in, sop it up like a sponge. I guess I don't mind it. It is the only thing that makes me special . . .

Vincent remembered Miss Kuntzler asking him to stay after class. Remembered her telling him how beautiful his presentation had been and how terribly sad it made her. Remembered her asking him if it was okay if she hugged him. No one at the home ever hugged him. He didn't recall anyone ever hugging him. Not anyone. Not ever. So he was more than a little afraid to say yes. He said yes because he really liked Miss Kuntzler. He remembered loving the feel of a hug. What he remembered most was Miss Kuntzler crying on his shoulder.

"Did I do something wrong, Miss Kuntzler?"

"No, Vincent. You did very, very well today. I'm so proud of you."

"Then why are you crying?"

"Because I've been a punching bag, too."

"Not you. How could that be?"

"I'm not a sponge."

"But you're so beautiful, Miss Kuntzler. Why would people be mean to you?"

He remembered her crying harder when he said that. She held him at arm's length, stroked his cheek, stared right into his eyes. That, like hugging, was another thing no one ever did with him. She said, "Thank you for saying that about me. But my last name, Vincent. People were cruel to me because of my name. They still are, sometimes."

"What about it, your last name, I mean?"

As confused as Vincent was by Arlo not being named Felicia or by Arlo calling him son and boy, he had been even more confused as a teenager by Miss Kuntzler. Confused about why her name made her a punching bag. Confused by the things he felt with her arms around him. Confused by the lemon peel smell of her perfume. Confused by the coconut scent and silken feel of her black hair against the skin of his neck and cheek.

He remembered those sensations and those smells because no one other than Miss Kuntzler would ever hug him. Even the prostitutes he was sometimes with refused to hug him. *Listen, John, you want hugs, go home to Mama. Take your pants off. I don't got all day.* He didn't understand why they called him John. Whenever he'd ask or say his name was Vincent, they'd laugh at him and take his money.

Miss Kuntzler hugged him once more, on the last day of school. His memories of that second hug were very different from the first.

"You won't see me again, Vincent," she said. "I'm getting married and we're moving to North Carolina. Be happy for me, Vincent. My name won't be Kuntzler anymore. They won't be able to hurt me anymore. No more punching bag for me."

His muscles stiffened. He pushed away from her. Turned his back and ran out of the classroom. Ran out of school and never went back. He remembered he felt something new that day: rage. He was feeling it again as he was reliving it.

"Yo, Vincent, what's the matter?"

Vincent came back into the moment, staring up from his metal folding chair at the security guard in front of him on the Segue. Andre had craggy, dark-brown skin, short gray hair beneath his helmet, and smelled of too much Old Spice. Vincent liked the peppery smell of Andre's aftershave. They had developed a kind of friendship born of shared boredom and necessity.

"Hello, Andre."

"What's wrong?"

"How could you tell with my mask on?"

"I was police for twenty-five years. Done this job for ten more. Man does those kinda jobs as long as I've done 'em, man learns to read all the signs of trouble and pain from the eyes up or from the eyes down."

Vincent smiled. "That's your superpower. That's what Miss Kuntzler would say."

"Who?"

"Never mind, Andre. Whatever it was is all gone."

"You say so. Okay." Andre nodded. "But you ever have any troubles, you know Andre is here to help."

"I know. Thank you."

"Okay, then, I'll catch you later, my man."

When Andre rolled away, Vincent could still feel the smile beneath his mask. That's why he liked Andre. Not many people he encountered in the course of his vacant life could make him smile. Vincent got up from his seat and gazed into the large rectangular mirror the few customers he'd had would use to see how they looked in this mask or that. Vincent had forgotten that he was wearing the Siamese cat nose, mouth, and whiskers mask today. He barely paid the mask any mind. Instead, he ran his fingers over the fabric of the mask to feel his smile beneath it.

He sat back down and thought about what Smart Meal he would nuke for dinner that evening.

MEOW

Thanksgiving Surprise was the Smart Meal he'd chosen. He read the promotional copy aloud off the back cover of the box: "America's favorite holiday in a single dish. White meat turkey, gravy, mashed potatoes, stuffing, candied yams, cranberry sauce . . . all kinds of yummy." Vincent shrugged his shoulders because although he liked turkey, he didn't have a favorite holiday. He had a least favorite one: Christmas. He thought of Christmas as the phoniest time of year. The time of year at the home when everyone pretended to be happy. When everyone at the home knew the rest of the world had families and they were here because they were unwanted. When they got gifts from beneath a donated tree, gifts no one else wanted. Gifts they were supposed to be happy about. That's when it was hardest not to mind.

He didn't want to remember. After he put the two one-inch slits in the plastic covering of the Thanksgiving Surprise tray, popped the tray in the microwave, he put his Siamese cat mask back on and thought about Andre's kindness. He went into the bathroom of his studio apartment across from the Brixton Bus Depot and looked in the medicine chest mirror. Thinking of Andre made him smile and once again Vincent ran his fingers over the feline nose and whiskers of the mask to feel the smile underneath. He liked the feel of it and thought smiles were amazing things. When you experience so few of them, it was easy to feel amazed by them.

It was only after he removed the cat mask to look at his smile that the world wobbled. When he gazed back at the mirror, the bottom half of his face was the face of a Siamese cat. He gasped. He shook his head. Rubbed his eyes red. Still his nose was a slightly moist leathery pink triangle with two tiny nostrils. His chin came to a sharp point. Whiskers extended several inches out from his now very tapered and brown furry cheeks. He felt like he was smiling, but he couldn't see it. Cats can't smile. *Even if they could*, Vincent thought, *they wouldn't give you the satisfaction.* He made a joke! That was almost as remarkable as his half-cat face. "Meow," he said to no one and laughed.

He held his left hand over the bottom of his face and stared in the mirror once again. Above his hand, Vincent's dull brown eyes, thin brown eyebrows, short sparse eyelashes, brown hair threaded with strands of gray, oddly furrowed brow all looked as they had always looked. The microwave timer sang its siren song of five monotone beeps. Thanksgiving Surprise was ready. Distracted, he pulled his left hand away and the half-cat face was gone. Same old Vincent. He told himself he wouldn't have minded either way, cat face or not. If he was going mad, he guessed he wouldn't have minded that either. At least it was a change.

Before eating, Vincent put on the Happy Freuds' third album, *Sigmund in Dreamland.* The Happy Freuds were the only band he ever cared for. The irony of their name was lost on him. Of course it was.

The darkness of their long instrumentals appealed to him in ways he could never have explained because he didn't understand himself. While that might've bothered most people, it never mattered to Vincent. Of course it didn't. Usually, he could lose himself in the Freuds' ethereal mix of strings and synthesizers, guitars and Thai xylophones. Not tonight. Tonight he was interested in another way to lose himself.

Even as he ate his turkey and listened to the music, Vincent could not get the half-cat image of himself out of his head. He put down his food before he was halfway finished and went back into the bathroom, mask in hand. He slipped the elastic bands of the Siamese cat mask over his ears and stared at himself in the mirror. As he exhaled into the mask, he noticed his breath smelled of turkey. That made him smile beneath the mask. *How long*, he wondered, *how long until it works?* He left the mask on for ten minutes before he couldn't wait any longer.

"Oh my goodness!" he said to himself aloud.

He said it because his face, from the middle of his nose down, was a blurry and bizarre conflation of the Vincent who had always looked back at him from the mirror and the cat face. It was like a bad drug movie from the 1960s with cheesy special effects. The Siamese cat face seemed to be superimposed over his own. And then . . . *Poof!* It vanished, leaving only Vincent's face in the mirror.

"I *am* losing my mind."

He folded the mask neatly in half, leaving it on the rim of the sink. He turned, immediately turning back, picking it back up. He found the small white label sewn into the left seam on the inside of the mask. His heart sank as it answered none of his questions. All the label said was: Made in USA.

THE MASK MAKER

The next morning the mall was emptier than usual. As Vincent made his way to the locked-up Felicia's Face Masks kiosk, the sounds of his footfalls bounced off all the hard surfaces. The Brixton Regional Mall was all right angles and hard surfaces. Even its name recalled a hard surface. The few people he passed were the masked and gloved old men and women who walked the mall for exercise. He wondered if any of them had envisioned walking around an empty mall as the way they would have been spending the mornings of their "golden years." He didn't see what was so golden about them.

His thoughts quickly moved on to other things, more important things, as he rolled open the kiosk, locked its wheels in place, turned on the cash register, and logged on to the credit verification system. That done, he had but one single fascination. He had worn the Siamese cat mask to work, forcing himself not to run his fingers across its fabric or peek beneath it. He supposed he was testing the limits of his sanity. It was a test to see if the cat face he had seen the previous night was in his head or in the medicine cabinet mirror.

Vincent checked his watch. Enough time had elapsed. He stood before the kiosk mirror, squeezing his eyes shut. Slowly lifting the elasticized fabric strap off his left ear, he let it fall away. He counted to three, took a deep breath, exhaled, and opened his eyes. The sight in the mirror made his next breath catch in his throat. Half-Vincent, half-Siamese cat peered back at him from the looking glass. He ran his fingers over the bottom of his face. It was no illusion. The bottom half of his face was silky brown fur and whiskers.

Then he heard it. A woman's gasp. It came from behind him. Without panicking, Vincent replaced the mask's left ear strap and turned.

"Amazing," he said. "Isn't it? Our masks are incredibly realistic."

The woman stuttered, "But, but, but . . . I saw, I saw—"

"What did you see?"

The woman was in her midseventies. Skinny as a blade of grass, she looked as if she had hollow little bird bones that would snap like twigs beneath her loose, brown-spotted skin. She had the old person turkey neck thing beneath the bottom of her N95 mask. Her limp, dull, steel-gray hair was damp with sweat. Her faded blue eyes were full of fear and confusion. They darted from side to side as she contemplated what to do next.

"I saw it," she said. "I saw your face."

"Before we were forced to wear masks, lots of people had seen my face. You're the first person who was ever kind of stunned by it. How do you think I should feel about that?"

"You . . . you can't fool me. I saw it."

"Yes, you said that."

"I saw your cat face."

"As I said, our masks are very realistic."

"No." She stomped her foot. "You can't fool me, mister. I saw your face while your mask was dangling from your right ear. You have a Siamese cat face."

Vincent laughed the kind of laugh he had only ever heard from other people: a sly, snickering, superior laugh. "Ma'am, do you realize how crazy that sounds? If I were you, I wouldn't go around telling people that. Disorientation is one of the symptoms, and you know the mortality rates in institutions is much higher than for the rest of the population. And at your age . . ."

That seemed to freeze the woman in place. Her confusion turned to fear. Still, she repeated, "But I know what I saw."

Vincent was too busy being startled by the language he was using, startled by his condescending laugh. Sarcasm and thinly veiled threats were very much out of character for him. He wasn't dumb, but he had never been quick-witted or any good at verbal fencing.

Then, as the woman decided she should move on and turned to go, Vincent called to her, "Oh, Miss . . ."

She about-faced. Vincent pulled down his mask. He raised his right hand, fingers bent as claws extended from a paw. He hissed at her as he scratched the air. The woman panicked, running, stumbling as she went. Vincent laughed that laugh again. When she was out of sight, Vincent removed the Siamese cat mask, carefully folding it in half and placing it in his jacket pocket. He kept checking the mirror. Within five minutes the cat face had faded. Certain the cat face was gone, Vincent chose the beagle snout mask to replace the Siamese cat mask. He let the beagle mask hang off one ear, donning it only when he saw someone coming his way. As soon as the person would pass, he'd remove it.

Good thing, too, because ten minutes later Andre came rolling up on his Segue, the old woman in the N95 mask trotting behind him to keep up. Vincent saw them coming and put the beagle mask on at the very last moment.

"Hello, Andre."

"Yo, Vincent. I know this sounds nuts, but this lady says you got a cat face under that mask," Andre said, nodding his head behind him. "She says you tried to intimidate and frighten her."

The woman caught up, panting.

"Me?" Vincent looked hurt. "You know me better than that, Andre."

The security man shrugged. "In any case, it's my job to check it out."

"He's wearing a different mask," the woman shouted, her voice muffled by her N95. "He had on a cat mask. Now it's different."

"Ma'am," Andre said, turning to face her, "he's got about two hundred different kinds of masks there. I know for a fact, Vincent here is under orders from his employer to wear a different mask every day."

"Check his face. It's a cat face. Check his face!" She insisted. "He hissed at me, clawed at me."

"I'm sorry, ma'am, but I have no authority to do any such thing unless—"

"That's all right, Andre. If it will make your job easier and satisfy this woman, I'm happy to do it voluntarily," Vincent said, tugging off the ear straps of the beagle snout mask. "Only me under here."

"See, ma'am, that's just Vincent's face there underneath the fabric. Same face I been looking at since he got the job here a few months back."

"But I swear to you, officer, he had a Siamese cat face under there. I saw it."

Andre was blessed with the patience of the Dalai Lama. "I believe you, ma'am, I do, but it's not there now. And truth be told, even it were there, I don't see what I could do about it. Nothing illegal about look-ing like a cat, far as I can tell."

The woman scowled, first at Andre and then at Vincent. "Are you making fun of me, officer? I'm not happy about this, not at all."

"Life is like that more often than not," Andre said. "None of us is very happy all the time."

"Well . . ." She wagged her finger, but was at a loss for what to say next. She retreated, still facing both men.

Andre waved. "Have a good day, ma'am." When she was gone, he turned to Vincent. "Man, this virus has got people all kinds of crazy. I heard plenty of insane shit in my lifetime, believe me, but just lately . . ."

"I know."

"Do me a favor, though."

"If I can."

"Put on that Siamese cat mask. I'd like to see how real it looks."

Vincent hesitated. He knew he shouldn't have, but deception and lies were never his strong suits. They never had to be. He was Vincent the sponge, the punching bag, a repository for other people's meanness. That when he wasn't being picked on or fired from some menial job, he was invisible to the rest of the world. In that moment of hesitation, it dawned on him that when he wore the mask and the half-Siamese cat face imposed itself on his, he felt different. That the Vincent Love he had always been would never have hissed and clawed at the old lady. He would have absorbed her accusations like a sponge. He more than looked like the cat. He had become the cat.

"You saw it yesterday," Vincent said, reaching for the mask in his pocket.

"I know, but—"

"No problem, Andre, but that lady shook me up." He was hoping Andre would say he understood and just drive on. He did not. "Okay," Vincent said. He replaced the beagle mask with the Siamese cat mask, and the second he put it on, he felt the change. "Meow. Meow."

Andre laughed. "Sorry, Vincent. People are all kinds of crazy. All kinds. Catch you later."

Vincent quickly swapped masks, again neatly folding the Siamese cat mask and placing it in his pocket. Oddly, the beagle mask changed him not at all. He had no desire to hunt rabbits or sniff everything in sight. He didn't want to wag his tail or play fetch or chew on sneakers. And after an hour, when he removed the mask, he was disappointed to see his own face in the mirror.

Maybe Andre is right, people were all kinds of crazy. Himself included, Vincent thought. But his curiosity got hold of him and he began searching through every box and piece of paper in the kiosk. It was nearly closing time and he had just about given up when he found what he was looking for. It was jammed in one of the kiosk roller wheel wells.

New Salem Custom Tailoring
74 Cauldron Lane
Brixton, West Virginia 24777
Amount Per Unit Description Total Due
30 12.00 USD Three Ply Fabric Masks 360.00 USD

The date at the bottom of the invoice showed the bill was long past due and that gave Vincent an idea. Problem was, Vincent often had ideas. He very seldom acted on them. As he remembered who he had always been, his enthusiasm waned. Still, as he rubbed the fabric of the pocketed Siamese cat mask between his fingers, the fire in him quietly smoldered.

CAULDRON LANE

When Vincent got home that night, he broke his routine. Instead of putting on the Happy Freuds and selecting that evening's Smart Meal, he ran into the bathroom and removed the beagle snout mask he had worn on and off throughout the day. His heart sank at the image in the mirror. It was him, just him. Then he pulled the Siamese cat mask out of his pocket and laid it on the sink ledge next to the beagle mask. The fabric felt similar if not exactly the same, but Vincent was no expert on fabric or anything else for that matter. The stitchery, too, looked similar.

He held both up close to the over-cabinet fixture and could detect no difference in how the masks reacted in the light. He was once again deflated and then . . . he noticed it. The country of origin tags were different. The beagle snout mask was made in Vietnam. His heart swelled.

Suddenly, the smoldering fire of the idea he'd had earlier in the day flared up. He grabbed his keys and wallet off the nightstand. With the beagle mask on, he was most of the way out the door when he realized he had forgotten two very important things: the Siamese cat mask and the overdue invoice. Having retrieved them, he was off to the ATM outside the bus depot and Cauldron Lane beyond.

***

Cauldron Lane was on the very outskirts of Brixton, the part of town locals referred to as Hades. Hades bordered the coal mines. With nearly all the coal pulled out of the ground, the mines were dormant. Dormant in terms of mining activity, anyway. Like in Centralia, Pennsylvania, one of the old mines had caught fire years ago and whatever coal remained slowly burned beneath the earth. Acrid smoke from the fire rose up through cracks in the roads and fissures in the surrounding woods. Even the name Cauldron Lane was a kind of lame joke. In a misguided attempt to draw tourists, all the paved streets in the area, which had once borne mundane tree names or Indian names, had been rechristened with names more befitting Hades. For instance, what had once been Sachem Street was now Caldera Lane. Cauldron Lane had once been Live Oak Street. The tourists never materialized, but the new names stuck. Vincent parked his 1988 Plymouth Reliant at the corners of Brimstone and Caldera, because Cauldron Lane was in the area of Hades where only bicycle and foot traffic was permitted. The pavement was deemed too unstable to support the weight of motorized vehicles. The moment he got out of his car, Vincent was overwhelmed by the stench, a noxious cocktail of hot roofing tar and rotten eggs. The beagle snout mask did nothing to lessen the impact of the fumes.

Vincent was undeterred. He walked up the hill. Cauldron Lane's sidewalks were mostly large chunks of rubble overgrown with vines and weeds. Little puffs of steam were visible through the cracks in the blacktop. Vincent touched his toe to the asphalt, and it was soft from the heat below. Hardly anyone lived in the area anymore. Mostly just artists looking for cheap workspace and the poor who had always lived in the area. Vincent had no idea into which category the inhabitant of 74 Cauldron Lane fit. He didn't care because he was nearly as excited as he was that day in front of Miss Kuntzler's class.

The wooded lot around number 74 was really eerie. The old-growth trees behind it that hadn't already toppled were dead or dying. The newer trees were tiny and misshapen. All were covered in ubiquitous thorny vines, moss, and a hideous bloodred fungus. The house itself was unremarkable. A light-green, aluminum-sided L-shaped ranch right out of a 1950s American suburban dream. Neglected? Yes. Creepy? Not so much. The little part of the L was an attached, one-car garage with a wooden door that looked like it hadn't been raised since the second Reagan administration. The bottom of the door was rotting away where it touched the driveway, and its white paint was peeling down to the bare wood beneath. Its windows were opaque with dust.

Vincent stepped onto the rectangular concrete stoop. The wrought iron support holding up the overhang was so rusted it seemed to still be standing only out of habit. As he approached the front door, his hands were shaking. His palms were sweating. He rubbed them against the thighs of his pants to dry them off. He raised his right fist to knock. He hesitated, turned, turned back. He knocked. A bare-bulb porch light snapped on and he turned again. This time to run, but he could not. He wanted to, tried to. His mind was running, not his legs. It was as if his feet had become part of the stoop itself. Behind him he heard the door open.

"Please, come in." It was a woman's voice, a voice possessing a sultry rasp that made Vincent's legs weak. "Come in."

His feet moved again. He about-faced and beheld an open door. He stepped through it as if he were floating. The living room was large, its worn oak flooring partially covered with Persian rugs dyed in deep crimsons and indigos. The mismatched furniture was a jumble of midcentury modern, colonial, oriental, and rococo. But Vincent knew nothing of rugs or furniture. Two things captured his attention: the pervasive, cloying scent of burning incense and the otherworldly beauty of the woman standing at the center of the room. He was weak at the sight of her raven feather black hair falling over her shoulders to the cinched waist of her flowing black robe. Her green eyes flecked in black seemed to glow. They held him in place as if he were a specimen pinned to a board. The skin of her triangular face was a flawless light brown. Her slightly upturned nose came to a gentle point above lips so plush and red that lipstick was beside the point.

As enrapt as he was by the woman's unearthly appearance, Vincent could not get past the patchouli and clove-scented smoke from the little brass incense burner on the end table next to the sofa. Her eyes followed his. She smiled. Her smile was white neon, and he nearly keeled over at the sight of it.

"I'm sorry," she said, nodding at the incense burner. "I'm so used to it. I can't tolerate the smell of the burning coal and its gases. Won't you please have a seat?"

Vincent sat as if an invisible force pushed him down onto the rough orange fabric of the sofa. He reached into his pocket and took out the past due invoice for the masks. "I'm here about—"

She stopped him midsentence. "You're here about the masks. I have been waiting for you. Well, not you specifically, but I knew someone would come knocking. I'm very pleased it was you." She stood very close to Vincent, stroked his hair, lifted his face up by the chin. "This mask . . . this beagle mask, it isn't one of mine." She gently pulled it off and tossed it to the floor.

"But . . . but . . ." he stuttered.

She smiled that smile again. "No masks are necessary. You have nothing to fear as long as you are here with me."

He didn't doubt her. He wouldn't have doubted anything she might've said. There was something powerful and reassuring about her voice. If she had told him to fly, he thought he would have gone up to the roof and tried flapping his arms.

She took the receipt from his hand, crumpled it up, and tossed it to the floor. "Consider it paid. What is your name?"

"Vincent."

"Vinnnn-cennnnt," she repeated as if it were a prayer. She stroked his cheek. "Which mask of mine did you wear?"

Again he reached into his pocket. This time he held out the Siamese cat mask to her. She rubbed the mask to the skin of her face, breathed in the smell of the fabric.

"Yes, Vincent, a favorite of mine."

"The mask . . . my face . . . I—"

"I know, my darling Vinnnn-cennnnt."

She leaned over and pressed her lips to his. She opened her mouth. He opened his. But instead of pushing her tongue into his mouth, she inhaled. He was frozen, as unable to move as he was on the stoop. She seemed to be inhaling him. It went on for what felt like an hour. Then, suddenly, she blew hard into his mouth. That was the last thing he remembered.

He woke up on the sofa, feeling strangely light-headed. When he stood, he stumbled. He had never been drunk but figured this was what it must have felt like. There was a noise, a droning mechanical noise. He followed it through the house like a siren's song to a door that led from the house into the garage. He didn't hesitate. Opening the door, he saw the woman, back to him, at a sewing machine. She paid him no mind, not bothering to turn to him. His attention was drawn to the bolts of fabric stacked on shelves pushed up against the garage door. Unlike the incense in the living room, the garage stank of acrid-smelling liquids bubbling in pots atop several camping stoves.

"Those are my special dyes," she said, her eyes still focused on her work. "The dyes that make my masks like none other. See the bubbling white pot. That is my most special dye."

He stepped around to face her. "You're making a mask now?"

"For you, Vincent. My most special mask of all, dipped in my most special dye. It is the mask you need, the mask you have wanted your entire life." She still did not look up from the machine.

"I have the money Arlo owes you and—"

"I have no need of your money."

"But how do you know what I want and need?"

She looked up, finally. Vincent gasped because for the briefest of seconds, the woman looked not like she had in the house, but like Miss Kuntzler. "I know, Vincent, because I have tasted you. I have breathed you in and breathed you out. And now there is a little bit of me in you. I am the hands that will wring out the sponge you have always been. I will deliver the punches you have absorbed."

He didn't understand. The machine went silent. She handed him a large mask. Vincent looked at the mask and was more confused than ever.

"It's blank and it's too big."

She got up from behind the machine and stood close. "No, Vincent, it is not blank. It's white and perfect for what you need. Go home tonight and sleep in it. It will cover your entire face, but it will not interfere with your breathing. In the morning, take it off. Look in the mirror and see if it isn't what I promise. If it is anything less, come back to me."

"But—"

"Shhhhh, Vinnnnn-cennnnt." She put her finger across his lips, removed it, and kissed him.

Once again, her breathless, sultry voice and a kiss made him forget. When he stirred, he was back behind the wheel of his Reliant, the big white mask in his right hand. He drove home to his little studio across from the Brixton Bus station. Everything was as it was when he left. Everything but him.

IT BEGINS

He did as he was told and slept with the mask covering his face. She was right about the mask not interfering with his breathing. He had had vivid dreams of the home, the orphanage in which he'd lived until he was eighteen. Only when he got to the bathroom did he realize he could see through the mask as if it wasn't there at all. It was when he removed the mask and looked into the mirror that he became as frightened as he had ever been. The face staring back at him didn't belong to him. It didn't have whiskers or a snout. It was the face of Jim McClure who had worked for four years as the assistant manager at the home. McClure was Vincent's chief persecutor at the home, a man who took sadistic delight in making Vincent's life miserable.

Vincent rubbed his face—well, not *his* face—with the tips of his fingers and the palms of his hands. His hands and fingers confirmed what his eyes saw in the mirror. One of the reasons McClure had been able to persecute Vincent with impunity was his good looks. McClure had tousled dark-brown hair, hazel eyes, and a strong chin. He remembered how all the women who worked at the home would act around him, how they would always hang around when he was there and whisper to one another after he left. Normally, Vincent would have stayed in his studio all day, waiting for the effects of the mask to wear off, but there was nothing normal about anything anymore.

He called in sick to Arlo. "Hey, Arlo, I can't make it to the kiosk today."

"You can't make it today, don't bother making it tomorrow. You're fired."

"Fuck you, Arlo."

"What did you say to me, you weasely piece of—"

"You deaf, asshole? I said, fuck you. You need me to spell it for you or sound it out phonetically?"

Arlo hung up.

Vincent's chest swelled with pride and his skin was hot with rage. He remembered rage from the only time he'd ever felt it. He liked it. He liked everything he'd said to Arlo. And now he knew how he would test the power of the mask.

***

Dressed in his best suit and tie, Vincent walked into the Brixton Regional Mall through the west entrance instead of the employee entrance. He waited by the fountain just outside the temporarily closed food court.

This was where all the seniors who walked the mall liked to congregate. Oh, they socially distanced, sitting far apart, but old people needed to run in packs as much as teenagers did.

"They need someone to listen to themselves whine about their aches and pains and prescriptions, about how their children ignore them," Vincent whispered to himself.

Goodness, he thought as he sat on the cool black granite fountain ledge, *it was so liberating to feel hate. No wonder McClure tortured him. It was like a drug.*

Then he saw her, the old woman, coming his way. He slipped on a blue paper mask.

"Excuse me, ma'am," he said, stepping into her path. "I'm Jim McClure from the company that runs the mall."

It dawned on him that although he looked exactly like Jim McClure, he might still sound like Vincent Love.

She twisted up her eyebrows in confusion. "What's this about?"

Now Vincent couldn't be sure if that confusion had to do with his voice or with what he was saying. There was only one way to find out.

"One of our security staff reported that you registered a complaint about an employee at Felicia's Face Masks kiosk. Is that correct?"

"It is indeed, young man."

"We're very sorry, ma'am. We know how trying life can be during these times. We'd like you to know that employee has been let go. As a token of appreciation for your patronage, we would like to send you a fifty-dollar gift card to use at any of the stores or kiosks in the mall." Vincent took out a notepad and pen. "Please give me your name and address and we'll send that right along to you."

"Why not hand me the card—"

"Rules, ma'am. I'm sorry. It's that personal contact thing."

"Hettie Walker, 2121 Marchand Park Street, apartment 4C—"

"I know it. Again, Mrs. Walker, we're very sorry."

He stepped out of her way. As Vincent watched Hettie Walker leave, he felt that rush of self-satisfaction. He really liked the new Vincent. His former incarnation would never have figured out how to trick the old biddy, but somehow he knew that apologizing and offering her something for free would do the trick. He'd passed the first part of the test with flying colors. Now, heading away from the food court fountain, he moved on to the two most difficult sections of the test.

"Excuse me, sir," Vincent said to the barrel-chested man unfolding the sections of the mask kiosk.

"Yeah, what can I do for you?" asked Arlo, not yet facing Vincent. "We ain't open."

"Please, sir, I'm looking for a job and—"

"A job, huh?" Arlo stopped what he was doing. He turned, staring right at Vincent. "Can you start tomorrow?"

"But you don't even know if I'm qualified or not."

"Can you breathe and walk at the same time? If you can, you're qualified. You should have seen the mutant moron you're replacing. What's your name?"

Vincent's skin burned with anger, but he kept a smile plastered on his face beneath the blue mask. "Jim McClure."

"Okay, Jim McClure, I got today covered. Tomorrow morning, same time."

"Thank you, sir."

"Arlo."

"Thank you, Arlo."

"Forget the thank-yous. Just show up."

Two parts of the test down. One to go.

He found Andre back by the fountain, giving directions to the bathrooms to some new morning mall walkers. Vincent waited until the old people were out of earshot before approaching.

"Excuse me, were you giving those people directions to the bathroom?"

Andre spun his Segue around. He stared at Vincent, but just like Hettie Walker and Arlo, there wasn't an ounce of recognition in him. "I was."

"I missed the last part about after turning left by the entrance to Sneaker Nook."

"No problem, sir. After turning left at Sneaker Nook, you go half-way down the corridor and the restroom entrance is on your right."

Vincent nodded and thanked Andre. *A shame*, Vincent thought, *but by the same time tomorrow, Andre's job was going to take a very ugly turn.*

VICTIMS OF LOVE . . . SORTA

Hettie was first. He had wanted her to be second but figured she wouldn't answer the door to him after nightfall. She died with relative ease. Even as his knees held her arms to the floor and he pressed his gloved fingers tighter and tighter around her fragile little bird-bone neck, he wasn't sure why he was angry enough at her to want to snuff out her life. All she had done was see his Siamese cat face. He supposed that would have been all right had she not gone to Andre and made a fuss. The why was moot because he seemed unable to control his rage or to stop himself from enjoying the power surge he felt as the life drained from the old lady. The mask maker's words came back to him as Hettie Walker stopped struggling.

"I am the hands that will wring out the sponge you have always been."

But his were the hands wringing the life out of Hettie Walker. He just squeezed and squeezed and squeezed until there was a snap and the old lady went utterly still. No more wriggling, no more choked cries for help, no more gasping for air. Nothing. He stood, wiped his brow on his sleeve, and left without looking back.

***

Vincent watched as Arlo came out the vendors' door at a little past ten. Before the virus, it would have been impossible for Vincent to do what he was about to do, but now, with fewer open stores, reduced hours, and skeleton crews, the cars in the parking lot were few and far between.

Vincent didn't know which car was Arlo's, so he had to follow him at distance. Only when the Escalade's lights flashed and Arlo turned toward it, did Vincent approach.

"Arlo!"

The squat man turned and looked at Vincent. "You! What the fuck is your name again?" Arlo snapped his fingers, trying to remember. "McClure. That's it. I'll see you tomorrow morning. Now get—"

Arlo didn't finish his sentence because he was preoccupied by the black handle of the eight-inch chef's knife Vincent had plunged into his liver.

"I'm not Jim McClure, Arlo." Vincent pulled the knife out of Arlo's liver and stuck it into Arlo's belly. "I'm the mutant moron. I can walk and breathe at the same time just like how you can die and be confused at the same time."

And Arlo was both of those things, profoundly so. Vincent made sure of the dying by sticking the chef knife through Arlo's throat and severing his windpipe. The devil would have to see to the resolution of Arlo's confusion. When Arlo finished dying, Vincent removed the dead man's watch, rings, and wallet.

SO SORRY

The knock was expected. Vincent had made certain to stare up at the CCTV cameras at the mall and he'd left a breadcrumb trail the police could follow to the vicinity of his apartment building. Vincent had also made sure to wear the magic mask to bed. It was a risk old Vincent would never have taken because he couldn't've been sure what he would dream of or whose face would stare back at him from the mirror. That morning, perhaps for the first time in his life, he was pleased to see his own face looking back at him.

"Vincent Love?"

"Yes. Who's asking?"

"I'm Detective Adam Martin," said the man in a surgical mask at the door. He held up a silver star with the words Brixton Detective written across it in block lettering. "May I come in?"

"What's this about?" Vincent opened the door and gestured for Martin to enter.

"You are employed by Arlo Wiley at Felicia's Face Masks?"

"I was until yesterday. Arlo fired me and said he had hired someone new. Why?"

"Mr. Wiley was murdered last evening."

Vincent shrugged. He had never been any good at lying and figured now wasn't the time to test whether his skill at it had improved. He was sure Jim McClure would have been a much better liar.

"You don't seem very broken up about it."

Vincent confessed, "I'm not. Arlo was a mean man, and he fired me just because I didn't feel well yesterday. But I didn't wish him dead."

Martin took out a series of somewhat blurry photos of a man with Jim McClure's face. "Do you know this man?"

Vincent stared at the photo. "No, Detective."

"Would you please remove your mask, Mr. Love?"

"Why?"

"Please." Vincent removed the mask. Martin shook his head. "Thank you. You can cover up again."

"Is that all?"

"We traced this man in the photos to the area of your building," Martin said, pointing to the photo.

"Do you think I might be in danger?"

"I can't say, but I'd be careful for the next few days . . . just in case. So sorry to bother you."

"I understand. Maybe I'll get out of town for a while."

"Not a bad idea if you've got someplace to go."

Detective Martin left without any fanfare, no last-minute, unexpected questions. Vincent had questions of his own, but was careful not to ask them. He realized they hadn't yet found Hettie Walker. When they did, the cops might be back, and he didn't know if he could evade suspicion as easily during their next visit. Vincent thought it was time to move on from Brixton, but he had a stop to make on his way out of town.

HADES REDUX

He parked his Reliant where he had that first time. The area was scarier in the daylight. Everything, all the decay and the destruction, the vines and red fungus, the fires and smoke seeping through the fissures, were there to plainly see. In the light, he took note of several houses that were collapsing beneath the weight of vines and weeds and wildly growing vegetation. It was, he imagined, what the world would look like after man had perished and nature reclaimed the planet for its own. He didn't generally have those kinds of "big" thoughts, but he had never been a murderer before either.

Although he was mostly his old self, looked like his old self, he was not completely his old self. Once again, the mask maker's words came back to him.

"I have breathed you in and breathed you out. And now there is a little bit of me in you."

The door to 74 Cauldron was open, and she was there waiting for him just inside. This time, though, her beauty left him cold. His reaction was not lost on her.

"I can be any woman or man you desire, Vinnn-cennnnt," she said in that breathless, sexy rasp. "I know who you want, who you have always wanted."

She turned her back to him and when she turned again to face him, she was Miss Kuntzler. She looked as she had looked all those years ago. She even smelled the way Miss Kuntzler had smelled—of citrus and coconut. He remembered the feel of her hug when she held him close. The mask maker took Vincent by the hand and led him into a bedroom.

"You've done well, my darling," she said in Miss Kuntzler's voice, pressing her finger to his lips. "As long as you leave a trail of blood, I will be here for you." She let her black robe fall to the floor and laid herself down on the bed.

Vincent remained standing, silent.

"I understand. This can't be easy, wanting me so badly for all this time. Let me help," she said, turning on her side, facing away. "Come lay next to me when you're ready. Put your arms around me."

But the mask maker had misunderstood, because the thing he wanted most from Miss Kuntzler was not her love and affection, not an apology. He wanted her to hurt how he had hurt after she abandoned him. He reached down to where the mask maker had let the robe fall to the floor. He removed the silken black sash from around the waist. He wrapped the ends of it around his hands. He slid into bed with the mask maker, then looped the belt around her neck and pulled. As he pulled tighter, he whispered in her ear, "There is a little bit of you in me."

When Vincent left the bedroom, he turned to see a pile of gray ash shaped like Miss Kuntzler, a black silk sash around its neck. He lit the bed on fire, thought about tossing the white mask into the pyre, and reconsidered.

With the white mask in his pocket, he drove west into the future. There were countless pores in a sponge, thousands of menial jobs to be had, and an untold number of potential victims of Love.

PRETTY MAIDS ALL IN A ROW

HEATHER GRAHAM

The bus veered to the right, but Shauna MacMillan was accustomed to standing by the driver when she spoke to a tour group on the bus. Marty Guidry was driving, and he had driven the same route daily for almost twenty years.

She knew when the bus was going to swerve, and she had a good grip on the rail. He smiled at her briefly. "You got it, kid. You're the best. Anything for you."

He wrinkled his nose toward her fellow guide, Jace Tremaine. Shauna just smiled and shook her head.

They had left the French Quarter and business district and ventured toward Uptown. They'd started in the French Quarter, and she had told her group the usual stories about Madame LaLaurie and what was *believed* about the murders at the Sultan's House, the Axeman, and more.

But now they were on the way to the grand site for Tremaine Tours.

She started her speech on the haunting of the cemetery they would now visit. This is the "unique and special" part of the Tremaine Tour Company's "unique and special" tours.

"When the night is dark and a fog arises, locals and visitors alike swear they hear the screams of Louise LaBelle, the woman who styled herself as a priestess and called herself the Queen of the Underworld. Her 'reign' on earth lasted from 1843 until 1859. To understand what went on, of course, I first need to explain that the true practice of voodoo comes from a mix of Catholicism and African and island religions, and those who truly practice would do no harm to others. Any harm done to another soul comes back on the one who caused it three times, and as in most religions, it's a sin to hurt others. Louise LaBelle was despised by the true believers in New Orleans and the surrounding areas. She promised the unwary she could cast all kinds of spells."

Shauna looked over her tour group, gratified to see all fifteen people in her group on the little bus were staring at her, listening, wide-eyed.

No one was talking or whispering—or even playing with their cellphones—through her speech.

She smiled and continued.

"Louise LaBelle could see that evil befell her clients' enemies; she could create love potions that never failed, break up marriages, in fact, do anything required of her. In truth, she had a small army of servants who were terrified of her—and ready to do anything for her, including poisoning others, creating 'accidents,' or causing other havoc. When she began her reign, she saw to it that when a young man failed to do her bidding, he choked and died before the other servants. A subtly delivered poison did the deed and cemented her power over her people. We know this from her diary. But to all who watched, he stood before her and explained that to kill was wrong—and then choked and died on his own words."

"Oh, Lord!" A woman in the third row of the bus whispered. "How horrible!" She was older and appeared to be on the tour with a teenaged grandson. Agnes Butterfield was written on her name tag. The boy, Ted Butterfield, was watching Shauna with amazement.

The nice-looking man behind the woman, dressed in a short leather jacket with dark-brown hair and blue eyes—a businessman taking a break possibly—with Ashton Williams written on his name tag, asked, "Wouldn't he be the one screaming in the cemetery?"

Shauna grinned, happy she was entertaining people. She knew she told the tales well, and it was rewarding to see every member of her tour group staring at her and listening intently.

"Some say it is her victims, those interred here, who scream at night as well. As once it was assumed their ghosts cried out after her death when it was later discovered they had been sealed in a vault and the living were screaming, seeking a way out. They perished in that vault long before they were discovered—"

"A vault? Underground? What about the water table?" someone else asked.

Shauna looked toward the back of the bus. This time the speaker was a young man, and though she couldn't see his name tag, they'd spoken briefly when they'd made stops in the city, and she knew he was Duke Weston. He appeared to be in his early twenties, with long brown hair and a lean face. He had his arm around a young woman, Carrie Saunders, though Shauna thought they had just met at the tour offices.

Maybe they were matchmakers, too, she thought with some amusement.

Duke had worked fast! Carrie was an attractive redhead—and looking a little fearful as she listened to the stories. Fearful and ready to cuddle up to a brave, strong man.

"The cemeteries here were made the way they are because of the water table—but also because the Spanish were ruling the city when St. Louis Number One was opened in 1789. So it was created in the Spanish design. Now, many are an amalgamation of French, Spanish, Creole, and American styles, but . . . Yes, floods have caused coffins to rise and float, and the 'cities of the dead' do ensure a loved one's body does not float down the street. And that was part of the tragedy of what happened. Louise LaBelle owned many slaves but also had many poor immigrants in her employ as indentured servants. To prove her power again, she built the vault with her lover, Jorge Gonzalez, and in one of her 'mystic' rituals warned that those who didn't follow her decrees would disappear. People were terrified. She created beautiful dolls—dolls resembling those who had angered her. When someone saw a doll that had been crafted in their image, they were terrified. And those who she had threatened did disappear, leaving others to believe she was a queen of the underworld. The bodies were discovered by accident a year after the 'disappearance,' and the water rising in the vault along with a lack of oxygen killed all those sent into it. And so, it is said, once screams sounded from the living—but then from the dead. Still, it's the ghost of Louise LaBelle that is seen in the mist at the cemetery. Because when those bodies were discovered—drowned and not mystically sent to a dark universe—the people had endured enough. They rose against Louise LaBelle and didn't just kill her."

"What did they do to her?" a woman, Kiki Myers by her name tag, asked.

"They skinned her alive before chopping off each of her limbs and then her head."

"Oh, Lord," Carrie murmured, inching closer to the long-haired young man.

Shauna wasn't surprised when her co-guide, Jace Tremaine, broke in, rising to talk to the group—and managing to step around Shauna to be front and center.

"We're moving toward an area in the city called Uptown. On the way to your hotels in the French Quarter, you passed through Metairie, and while there are massive cemeteries there—which you might have seen—Tremaine Tours takes you to a special cemetery, one you can't visit on your own! You see, it's still a private cemetery, but it belongs to the family of Jacques Tremaine, our CEO, and, as you've heard, it has some of the most fascinating interments and stories in the area!"

Shauna listened with patience as Jace gave his speech. Jace didn't know any of the stories. He was Jacques's great-nephew, and that was why he had a job. He was home now on a break and would be returning to his Ivy League school soon enough. He was here to look good so his uncle would continue paying for his schooling. Jace was truly a golden child—beloved by his family. To be fair, he was handsome, with amazing bone structure; eyes a true, brilliant green; dark hair; and a physique honed daily at the gym.

He was in finance—and intended, he had told her, to take over the stock market one day.

Shauna didn't resent him for it. Jace was likable. She was sensible enough to keep her distance from him, but he was funny, cute, and complimentary with his pickup lines. She just knew better than to ever accept any of his invitations.

She loved her job and was delighted to be a licensed guide and working for Tremaine Tours. Their groups were limited. Never more than fifteen people, and there were always two guides and a bus driver.

"And we are about to arrive!" Jace said, glancing at the gates of the cemetery and smiling at the bus driver deftly wielding his way through the narrow entrance.

Marty was a good driver, a man who had been at it for twenty years. He was quiet. He just drove the bus. Shauna had been working for the company for nearly a year, and she knew little about him except he had been married, his wife had died, and he had no children.

He parked on a trail near the site where Louise LaBelle had been executed and the marker that stood there. Supposedly, her remains had been burned after her death and rested below the marker.

"Wait!" the redhead asked as they were about to announce that the passengers could roam the cemetery. "If it's a Tremaine cemetery, why is LaBelle here?"

Shauna looked at Jace.

He shrugged, grimacing to the crowd.

"Ah, well. So, kind of obviously, LaBelle was made up, but she had no problem calling herself 'the beautiful!' But her real name was Louise Tremaine. She was a great, great—I don't know how many greats—aunt of mine, I'm sorry to say!"

"Oh!" The sound seemed to rise from everyone on the bus.

"But . . . you have no problem showing us all this horrible stuff about an ancestor?" the man with his arm around the redhead asked.

"I'm with the famous philosopher George Santayana on that. He said, 'Those who cannot remember the past are condemned to repeat it.' Oh, not that I think my family is going to go crazy and start killing people. I just mean we must remember to be good and decent human beings to one another. If we don't remember evil that was done, we can become evil again."

As everyone left the bus, Jace looked a little desperately at Shauna. Was he sorry he had spoken?

"Really?" she asked him quietly.

He knew a hell of a lot more about the stories than he had ever admitted!

He nodded; his smile was sheepish.

"Yeah."

"I can't believe I didn't know that!" she told him.

"It isn't in the books anywhere," he said. "My family was always rich—blood money, maybe. Anyway, one of my forebearers made sure her name was erased from all family history."

"And you just gave it away!" Shauna marveled.

He shrugged. "She was evil. I'll bet every family traces back to those who were good—and those who were bad. Just some were . . . very, very bad. Anyway . . ."

Shauna and Jace stepped out of the bus.

"Walk around and we'll talk again!" Shauna called out cheerfully. "We'll meet at the marker and talk again. There are simple aboveground tombs and many beautiful mausoleums. Over the years, the Tremaine family opened the cemetery to friends and then other residents, and they built a mausoleum where those who couldn't afford a family burial might be interred. There are exceptional statues and monuments here. Enjoy—"

She never finished the sentence.

A high-pitched, terrified sound came from the rear of the cemetery, behind the large mausoleum, where there were many aboveground, single tombs.

Shauna looked at Jace, stunned and frowning, and they both turned to run in that direction.

And they saw them.

From a distance . . .

It could have been a scene from a toy store display.

They were lined up, just like dolls on a shelf, all different, all beautiful, dressed to a T, with sophisticated makeup and all . . .

Dolls . . .

Except they weren't dolls. They were—or had been—human beings.

Pretty maids all in a row.

There were five of them.

Seated together atop an aboveground tomb in the shadow of several of the historic, elegant, and atmospheric family mausoleums that made the cemetery so unique, fascinating, and haunting.

The women's bodies had been balanced together, corpse against corpse.

Shauna stared, unable to scream.

It was Jace, behind her, who swore softly and managed to pull out his phone, dialing 911 and stuttering out what they had discovered.

***

Detective Clark Thoreau stared at the scene in silence. He had gone so far as to assure himself the "dolls" were real.

And that each was dead.

Two medical examiners had now arrived and he was receiving sketchy, preliminary information.

The corpses had been set there sometime during the night. They had been dead for different amounts of time—and kept refrigerated.

Pete Harrison, the beat cop who had first arrived on the scene, cleared his throat and said, "Sir, I saw to it the passengers on the tour bus were returned to it immediately. I've kept the reporters out. The first passengers to see the bodies were Duke Weston and Carrie Saunders. They thought at first they were props—something set up by the tour company to enhance all the ghost stories they tell about the place. When they went closer and saw they were real, Carrie screamed. Some of the passengers never wandered this way. I ordered everyone held in the bus anyway. The bus driver is Marty Guidry, and the guides are a young lady named Shauna MacMillan and Jace Tremaine—a great-nephew or something to the fellow who owns the cemetery. The young woman, Shauna, has a manifest of the passengers with all their names, and oh, they have name tags! Apparently, the tour asks people to wear them since they make stops for refreshments, and that way, people chat with each other and have a better experience—so they believe."

"Thanks," Clark told him.

He stared at the dead women again, shaking his head.

Pretty maids all in a row.

He was accustomed to the bizarre in New Orleans. Besides being a cop, he'd lived in the city all his life. He loved his city—the history, the beauty of the architecture, the museums, and the vibe that people were people, no matter where they came from or the color of their skin.

But this . . .

He studied the victims. Serious work had gone into the appearance of each corpse; the eyes had been painstakingly sewn open. The lips had been sewn shut—and forced into forming macabre smiles.

He left the corpses to the medical examiners and made his way over to the bus, followed by Pete Harrison. The passengers weren't all on the bus—many were standing around beside it, anxiously talking to one another as if they'd known each other forever.

Maybe the name tag thing worked.

He produced his badge as he approached, taking in the group. They were mixed, older, younger—but no small children, thankfully. An attractive young brunette was talking to a group, trying to speak calmly. She was in her early twenties, slim and lithe, and speaking gently. A man about her age was just behind her, letting her do the talking. He appeared shell-shocked. A man of forty-five or fifty was near them, watching as he perched atop an aboveground tomb.

"It's your family!" a woman suddenly cried, pointing at the young man. "You did this! Someone in your family did this! How horrible, you killed people and made dolls out of them just to enhance your story about Louise LaBelle!"

"What?" the accused man said, stunned.

Clark hurried forward. In truth, it wasn't such a bizarre theory—no more bizarre than the discovery of the victims.

But it needed to be nipped in the bud.

As he hurried closer, the young woman started speaking.

"No, no, Mrs. Butterfield!" the young woman said. "Please, we knew nothing about any of this, and the Tremaine family are good people. Jace would never do anything like this!"

"Would I be on the bus this morning if I knew anything about this?" the young man asked.

The brunette continued. "Please! This is the work of a madman or a crazy person—people don't kill to enhance stories. The cemetery has been used by a psychotic killer, possibly because a killer could get over the low stone wall and because it is away from the busy areas of town. Please! I know you're upset, but—"

Clark stepped forward. "Please don't throw out accusations without any kind of evidence. That's how rumors start, and it's difficult enough to find the truth without battling rumors," he said.

The brunette looked at him gratefully. She had enormous brown eyes and an exceptionally pretty face—drawn right now with horror and worry.

"Detective Clark Thoreau," he continued, showing his badge around the group. "I'm sorry you all came upon this. I'm going to get you all out of here as quickly as possible. Who first came upon the scene?"

A woman with a tag identifying her as Chrissy Miller answered first.

"I never came upon the scene—and I don't intend to!"

A man with his arm around a redheaded girl stepped forward.

"It was us, Detective. I'm Duke Weston and this is Carrie Saunders. We wandered that way, looking for the stone that supposedly sits over Louise LaBelle's ashes. And—"

"I screamed!" Carrie said.

"Did you see anyone else in the cemetery? Or anything unusual?"

"More unusual than doll corpses?" Carrie asked.

She wasn't trying to be sarcastic—her question was sincere. And she had a point.

"I'm sorry. Anything else left behind. Someone possibly there or near the scene," Clark said.

Mrs. Butterfield stepped forward again.

"Please, please, please, let us go! We were just on this stupid tour!

I have my grandson with me, and he shouldn't be . . . he's going to be so upset!"

"I'm fine," the boy said.

"We're going to let you all go, I'd just like to make sure we can contact you if we need you for anything," Clark said. "Except . . ." He paused and turned to the tour guides and the bus driver. "I'll need you to stay. If the rest of you want to head to the entry arches, patrol cars will bring you back to the French Quarter. Officer Harrison is going to get all your information, and then you're free to go. Of course, if you think of anything, please let me know immediately."

"We were just on the bus," a man whispered.

"Who were they?" another murmured. "Who were they?"

"We don't know. And we'll need to inform first of kin, so . . ."

He wanted to ask them not to talk to the press yet. That would be an effort in futility, he knew. And even talking to them now was an effort in futility. They didn't know who the victims had been; they didn't know the cause or method of death, or even if it was the same for all. They didn't know how the corpses had arrived; though unlike many of the historic cemeteries, this one had a low stone wall a two-year-old could crawl over.

If any of the passengers had been involved, they were unlikely to run up to him and explain what they'd done and why.

He stepped back as Harrison took over with the group, motioning to the guides and the bus driver to follow him just a few feet from the others.

"Far-fetched, and far from others and cameras here, but . . . this is your family's cemetery."

Jace winced. "I know that! But we weren't looking to make anything more 'haunted' or bizarre. If anything, my great-uncle wanted to close the tour business. He's tired, his son and grandchildren live in NYC and they're not leaving, my dad is a stock market guy, and my great-uncle is just worn out. He'd never want this!"

Clark thought the kid was earnest, but he'd be researching it all himself.

"You're a detective?" the young woman, Shauna, asked.

"Yes?"

"I'm sorry. You're just—young."

"Older than I look," he assured her. "I'm with Orleans Parish. A cop since I got out of the military, a detective the last three years. So. You haven't heard about anything else going on in the cemeteries anywhere? Anything unusual from other tour guides?"

Shauna MacMillan and Jace Tremaine looked at him solemnly and shook their heads. Clark glanced over at the bus driver, Marty Guidry.

Marty lifted a hand to him. "I just drive. I don't talk to anyone."

There was little else to do with the small group until Clark had been able to do a lot more research. He could see a forensic team had arrived, and he hoped they—or the medical examiners— could give him something.

"Thank you. I'll be in touch," he told them.

"That's it? We can go?" Shauna asked.

He nodded. But he looked past her and said softly, "The vultures will be descending."

Officers were cordoning off the whole cemetery.

Reporters had already gathered just outside the gates. Of course, any of them at any time could just crawl over the short stone wall. He hoped they respected the police presence.

Clark turned back toward the tombs where the human dolls had been set.

He felt a wave of growing anger. His city. He loved it. The true history was rich; the people here were amazing. New Orleans had come into the contemporary world kicking and screaming—then the city had turned about. Always international, New Orleans welcomed everyone.

People were still people. He had a job because man could be damned inhumane to his fellow man. Most murders were perpetrated by some-one close to the victim. Serial killers, however, could choose victims at random. This one had chosen pretty women. He hadn't appeared to have had a type, other than young and pretty. Two victims appeared to be African American, two Caucasian, and one of the young women had been Asian.

Clark walked over to Dr. Paul Andre, senior ME on-site, and looked at him hopefully.

Andre shook his head with a grim look on his face. "Overdose of pills on the lot, I'm going to say. Strange. The last girl there—the blond in the baby-doll nightie—was killed recently, I believe. The latest victim. But they were kept in a freezer. I don't know if that helps you or not. None suffered apparent violence. I haven't been able to find a scratch or a bruise on them. I'll know more after autopsy, but I'd say you're looking for a killer with a large freezer."

"Thanks. I'll get a canvass going in the neighborhood, and I'll get someone at the station to start a search on freezers that large."

"Restaurants?" Andre asked.

Clark winced. He thought of slabs of meat hanging beside . . .

Human beings.

"Try a human finger along with your gumbo," Andre muttered.

"Are any of the women missing parts?"

"No, I'm just . . . I'm just being bitter. This is too sad, and I'm an ME. You know, we're supposed to be callous, eating our sandwiches right on top of corpses. And to be fair, when I have a heroin pusher on my table, I'm not worrying about his chances of heaven. But this . . . they couldn't have all just committed suicide in the same place in the same way and . . ."

"No," Clark said flatly. "No."

He looked around. Dusk was coming.

"Dr. Andre, when you can, let's move the victims to the morgue. We'll have every news outlet and gawker known to man out here trying to get video and pics of these poor girls."

"I'm ready."

He made a loop in the air, letting his second and their assistants know they were ready to move the women to the morgue.

Clark stopped to talk to Officer Harrison. He wanted a house-to-house canvass started. Surely, someone had seen something when a killer had brought five bodies to a cemetery in a residential neighborhood.

The corpses were taken to the morgue.

He paused and looked out over the cemetery one last time before leaving.

The bodies had been left by the memorial stone that supposedly stood over the ashes of Louise LaBelle, the scourge of her time.

He glanced at the forensic team. They hadn't made it to the stone yet, and he was careful as he approached it.

The cemetery was maintained well, but it didn't have high walls. Kids came at night, some to smoke pot or drink beer and tell tall tales; and some came to try to scare a potential companion, to get them cuddling up and close. They'd gotten strict in the city, and with several of the outlying cemeteries, but this one just had the little wall, and policing it was a hell of an effort.

Gum wrappers, cigarette butts, even empty cans were often left behind.

But as he approached the stone, he saw something.

His hands were already gloved but he dug in his pocket for an evidence bag.

A note had been left on the ground just before the marker on a thick piece of cream-colored paper. Four words had been written on it.

"For you, my belle."

Maybe the woman's accusation against the Tremaine family hadn't been so crazy.

Was a Tremaine trying to appease a long-dead ancestor?

Shaking his head, he walked back over to the leader of the forensic team and handed him the note.

The guy nodded dully. The scene had gotten to them all.

"Most people just leave flowers," he muttered.

Clark nodded and headed to his car.

It was going to be a hell of a long night.

***

Shauna, Jace, and Marty returned to the tour offices on Royal Street.

Marty, as usual, had just silently driven.

Shauna and Jace were silent as well for most of the trip, both shell-shocked.

"I just . . . I just don't believe what we just saw," Jace said at last. He winced. "And that woman—she thought that I or someone in my family could have done that!"

Shauna touched his arm. "Jace, she was just frightened and freaked out. I know your great-uncle and he isn't a psychopath! Someone with a sick mind did this."

He glanced her way with an appreciative smile. "You know, they should have built a wall around that place years ago. Things have happened before. People who don't understand voodoo trying spells and such, drug pushers meeting up with teens . . . but nothing like this."

"Jace, you all are going to quit the tour business?"

"There's no one to run it," he said with a sigh. "I like figures. I want to work stocks. And now . . ." He paused, shaking his head. "We can build a wall and keep people out. But other tours will go by it. They'll say that the soul of Louise LaBelle entered a murderer's body or some such thing. They'll make more money off someone's suffering. I mean, I guess that's what we were doing, but LaBelle committed her murders more than a century ago, but now . . . wow."

"They'll find who did this," Shauna said with confidence.

He glanced at her with a crooked smile. "GQ cop is going to find the killer?"

"He's young—that doesn't mean he's not a good detective. Besides, they'll have a whole task force working on this. The papers will be all over the police."

"Hey. You liked GQ cop, huh?" he asked her.

"What?"

"You didn't see the way he looked at you? Now, I understand. I'll bet he calls you for more information."

"Jace—"

"Hey. I'm heterosexual, and I thought he was cute as hell! Those hazel eyes, bronze skin—and muscles. Tall. Imposing."

Shauna shook her head. "I was too freaked out to notice."

"What? You're suddenly blind?"

She laughed. "No, but totally freaked out! Besides!" Jace was feeling down. It wouldn't hurt to be a little honest with him now. "You're GQ material yourself."

"If I'm not a crazed murderer!" he told her. He was quiet a minute. "So, how come you would never go out with me?"

"Self-preservation," she told him.

"What?"

"You're a busy man. You move on quickly. I love it here. And I'm more into . . . well, I'm more into commitment. But that doesn't mean . . . doesn't mean you're not a great guy and you haven't the right to be all into figures—"

"Female figures!"

They were both startled when Marty spoke.

"Hey!" Jace protested. But he and Shauna both laughed; it was good to hear Marty talk.

They lingered in the courtyard a few minutes after Marty dropped them off to go and park the bus.

"I'll be in touch," Jace told Shauna. "I want to check on my great-uncle. The cops were already there. He's horrified and worried and . . . I think I should see him."

"Of course! I'll, uh . . . I'll be at my place if you need me," she told him.

He smiled. "I may come by."

Shauna nodded and watched him go then turned to walk the few blocks to her apartment in an old house just on the other side of Esplanade. She saw people paused in front of an electronics store—they were watching a newscast on a television screen in the window.

And the Tremaine Cemetery was in the background as the anchor spoke about the horrible, tragic, and bizarre murders.

She kept walking.

Her apartment was on the ground floor. The building had been erected as a grand mansion in the early 1800s. Now, it was four apartments. Her apartment was accessible through the courtyard—it had once been the carriage house.

She was grateful that she didn't run into any of her neighbors as she entered. Inside, she leaned against the door.

Then she locked it, closing her eyes.

She opened them again quickly. The image of the dead women seated on the tomb seemed to be printed on the back of her eyelids.

She didn't tend to be fearful, but she turned and made sure her door was locked.

Darkness had come. And she was suddenly afraid. She thought about running out and back to Bourbon Street where tourists and music bursting from a dozen clubs might still her fear.

But she'd have to come back. Alone.

She checked the lock again. And frightened or not, she was going to shower. She felt as if . . .

As if she needed to wash death away from her skin and hair.

As she walked to the bathroom in the little apartment, she winced.

Visions of Alfred Hitchcock's *Psycho* flashed through her mind.

"Stop it!" she told herself out loud.

She needed a shower. She was going to take one.

***

To Clark's surprise, IDs on the victims came back quickly. Maybe he shouldn't have been so surprised. He was still saddened. All five had been "working girls." That made their identities easy through their fingerprints because each had been arrested at least once for soliciting.

Talking to Dr. Andre on the phone, he learned they had been known to work in different areas, from New Orleans and then east as far as Biloxi and west as far as a border town in Texas.

But it was easy for a killer to pick them up.

"I won't start the autopsies until tomorrow, but I'm willing to guess they were killed with recreational drugs laced with fentanyl."

"So, it was easy enough for the killer to pick up the women. Easy enough for him to kill them as well, especially if they had a history with drugs," Clark said.

"In my experience, people working on the fringe do tend toward drugs—a way to make getting by a little easier," Dr. Andre said.

"So, we know the victims, and we can guess how they were lured. Now I just need to find a freezer," Clark said thoughtfully.

"I'll let you know if I get anything else," Andre told him.

Clark thanked him. As he hung up, Lieutenant Godfrey tapped on the door and walked into Clark's office.

"You've got a . . . well, you've got one hell of a mess going. The department is at your disposal. The media has gone wild—no way to stop it. Press conference in the morning. You'll be ready."

"I'll be working through the night," Clark promised.

The lieutenant left him.

Clark put a call through to Jacques Tremaine, family patriarch. He didn't know if he was surprised or not that the man immediately came to the phone. He was horrified—and eager for Clark to find the truth. "Those women . . . those poor women!"

"Is there someone you know of who might have a grudge against you—who might be using this as a way to get to you?"

"I—I guess anyone can have an unknown enemy. But I have fought against the old evil in my family with everything in my power. I am good to employees; I am fair in all business dealings. I—I'm old and I'm tired. I oversaw the tour company myself, and I don't know if Jace mentioned it to you or not, but I'm ready to close the company and try to enjoy being an old codger until . . . well, I'm almost eighty. I'd like to spend some time on a small beach somewhere," Tremaine told him.

"If you think of anything, of anyone, please. I'll come by tomorrow just in case you've thought of something."

"One of your men brought the news to me and talked to me today—"

"Yes, we wanted you informed immediately, and we needed to let you know we were cordoning off the cemetery until we're certain we've gotten everything we can."

"I'll think, yes, I'll think."

Clark started by arranging his notes. He gathered his crime scene photos, and he reimagined the scene. He used every possible research option to find out more about the Tremaine family. Nothing suggested any member of the family had engaged in anything more dangerous than illegal parking in the last hundred years.

He took out his list of "guests" on the tour bus. They came from all over the country.

Eleven of the fifteen had just arrived last night. That left four of the people on the bus, the beautiful young guide, the Tremaine kid, and the bus driver . . .

Which could all mean nothing. But killers often liked to return to the scene of a crime—to watch the horror and shock of those who came upon the victim or victims.

Officer Harrison tapped on his door and poked his head in.

"Door-to-door, sir. And I have written reports for you. I'm assuming the setup was done in the middle of the night, but there are a few things in there. One woman saw a long-haired guy with an 'I'm hungry' sign walking around. Another saw a white van in the vicinity. It's all there. A few people didn't answer their doors. Of course, we've got a tip line going, and they'll see that anything relevant is given to you. But so far, we have a guy who is convinced the ghost of a toy manufacturer has returned and joined up with Louise LaBelle to create more pretty dolls."

"Thanks," Clark told him. He stood to take the sheets with the reports from the residents of the neighborhood.

He put them together with everything he had.

He looked at the crime scene photos again. As he did, he saw the forensic lab was calling him. Vickie Quinn was on the phone.

"You've got something?" he asked her.

"Well, you know, it's a lab. It will take time to go through every-thing, but I found something really strange on the note you found."

"Oh? What?"

"There's more writing—strange. The paper is like a kid's playbook with images appearing with something as simple as water. There's more written on it underneath the words in pen."

"What? What's written?"

"I don't know if it means anything or not, but I thought I should tell you right away."

"Yes, yes, thank you—what is written?"

"'The best is yet to come. True homage, my Queen.' I'll text a picture with the words showing."

"Thank you."

They ended the call.

He looked at the text the minute he received it. He put it with what he knew, and what notes he had received from the officers doing the door-to-door questioning.

And he thought about the Tremaine family. And again, he thought about people, about watching expressions and the way people behaved.

And as he sat at his desk staring at what coincided with what, he couldn't believe what he was seeing. Impossible. It just couldn't be this . . . evident! And maybe it wasn't. Maybe he was seeing something that wasn't there. But he couldn't take chances.

He stood up, suddenly desperate to get back out on the street.

Desperate.

Because he didn't want to see another woman become a pretty doll, an addition to the pretty maids already in a row.

***

Shauna was unnerved.

She managed to get into the shower—but nearly slipped and fell onto the tile floor when she heard someone knocking at her door.

She leaped out and grabbed a towel and managed to slip into her underwear and a knit dress while she was still dripping. Why? Whoever was there might have just gone away.

But it might have been Jace.

Or the detective.

She hurried to the door and checked through the peephole.

It was Jace.

She quickly opened the door.

"Hey," he said dully.

"Hey."

He grimaced. "May I come in? I mean, you've been great, but if you're afraid of me—"

"I'm not afraid of you, Jace. Come on in."

She opened the door for him, wishing her apartment were a little more luxurious—or at least comfortable or clean. It wasn't a terrible mess, but she'd left laundry to be folded on the table by the sofa, and there on the coffee table was the bag of chips and tea she'd indulged in earlier in the day.

"Um, have a seat," she said. "Can I get you anything?"

He shook his head and sank into the sofa.

"Are you all right?"

"Yeah." He winced. "I've been with my great-uncle. He's taking this badly. Well, I guess . . . I guess as human beings we should all take it badly. Maybe I will have something."

"I have fresh iced tea—"

"Anything stronger?"

"Um—bourbon?"

"A straight shot would be great."

She went into the little kitchen. He seemed to be staring blankly at the air.

She brought him a shot glass of bourbon.

"Aren't you going to join me?" he asked her.

"I . . . uh, sure."

She left him to pour another bourbon. Then she joined him in the little living room and sat on the edge of the sofa. She was happy he was there, but she was feeling awkward.

"Look, what was done was horrible . . . those poor women. I mean, we don't really know what was done to them yet. If the police know, they haven't said. And I suppose they will do an autopsy on each victim. And . . ."

Her voice trailed. She didn't know much more.

He gave her a sad look. "I'm going to say they didn't make themselves up and hop on the tomb together to just die," he said.

"No."

There was another knock on her door and she almost jumped a foot off the sofa.

"Uh, just the door," she said lightly.

She managed to stand up and head to the door, trying not to look quite so awkward and wondering who would be visiting her at that time of night.

It was the detective.

"Detective Thoreau," she said, blinking. She'd thought she might hear from him again. Just not that night.

"May I come in?" he asked.

"Yes, of course. I mean, I'm sorry, my place is not big, but . . ."

He stopped, staring at Jace. "Having a drink?" he asked.

Before Jace could answer, she was surprised to hear another knock at her door.

"I'll get it," Detective Thoreau said politely. He moved to open the door.

To Shauna's surprise, it was Marty Guidry, the bus driver who was never social in any way, shape, or form.

"Come in," Thoreau told him.

Marty looked at the detective suspiciously. "What are you doing here?"

"Follow-up," Thoreau said briefly.

"What are you doing here, man?" Jace asked. "Marty, I've known you for years and have never seen you anywhere but work!"

He didn't answer at first but then stood very straight. "I came to look after Shauna. To protect her!"

"Protect her from what?" Jace asked.

Marty didn't answer.

"From what?" Thoreau asked as well.

Marty gave himself a shake, then pursed his lips and looked around.

Then, as if he were in a sci-fi movie, he stretched out his arm and pointed a finger at Jace.

"Look, Marty—" Jace began. "I didn't—"

"What are you drinking?" Detective Thoreau asked Jace.

"Bourbon. I think I deserve a shot," Jace said defensively.

"All right. And Shauna has a bourbon?" the detective asked.

"Yes, I have a bourbon," Shauna said. "But—"

"Jace, drink Shauna's bourbon," the detective said.

"What?"

"Drink her bourbon," Thoreau repeated.

Jace rose, shaking his head. Marty took a step back, staring.

Lord, what was going on? Did they think Jace had put something in her drink? That—that he was going to do something to her? Had she been naïve? Was he here just to kill her . . . poison her? Had the "dolls" in the cemetery been poisoned? Was she a total fool?

Jace had always been rich.

He'd gotten everything he'd wanted in life.

He was just home for a while . . .

"Okay. Whatever."

Jace reached for Shauna's drink. He lifted it to his lips and swallowed the shot in a gulp.

"So—" he began to say.

He never finished his sentence.

Sensing movement behind him, Detective Thoreau spun around and to Shauna's stunned surprise, he drew out a gun and shot Marty Guidry.

Marty . . .

Who held a gun in his hand, his fingers releasing it as he gasped and choked on his blood, trying to speak.

Thoreau was on his knees by the man, pulling out his phone to dial 911.

"Marty?" Shauna whispered in horror.

He was still alive; his eyes were on her.

"She wanted you. Louise LaBelle wanted you. You are the one who knows the stories and the history, and you are a beautiful doll. She was only slightly appeased by the sacrifices I gave her . . . She wanted you. She wanted you!"

"Why were you behaving as if Jace—" she whispered.

"Jace is a monster! He just wants to use you!" Marty cried.

Shauna was afraid she was going to pass out cold. Instead, her knees buckled, and she landed in a sitting position back on the sofa.

Sirens ripped through the night. More police came, an ambulance came, Marty Guidry was taken away, and all that remained was a blood stain on her floor.

And still . . .

It was hours after she had given a statement, after Jace had given a statement, after all the other police had come and gone that she was able to speak with Detective Clark Thoreau again.

"I don't . . . how could you have known? I mean, how . . . where did he have the bodies? I can't begin to understand . . . You made Jace drink my bourbon as if you thought he might be poisoning me, but you knew . . ."

"I had to be sure," Thoreau said. He let out a breath. "It had to be someone local. Someone who knew the cemetery and could store the bodies. That still could be dozens of people. But there was a note left by the memorial to Louise LaBelle. It honored her and later proved to also inform her that the best was yet to come."

"But—but what made you think I'd be in danger? I was in danger. I could have been dead. Jace and I could have been dead. You were just in time. If you hadn't been here, he intended to poison us both I imagine."

"I can't say what would have happened. I didn't know he had a gun, but . . . guns are easy enough to acquire," Thoreau said.

"But—" Shauna began.

"Hey, we can be pretty thorough. I researched the criminal records of everyone, and I also did a spot check on recent purchases." He grimaced. "After the note, I was afraid the killer wanted you. And I saw the way Marty looked at you, Shauna. It wasn't a sexual thing. It was more like a man standing before an idol. Then there was the clincher."

"Which was—?" Jace asked.

"One that didn't take Sherlock Holmes to solve. He bought a

giant freezer about six months ago and kept it at his property in Tremè, where he owns several acres. I don't know why, except somehow, he lost his grip on life, and maybe he needed to believe there was a ghost haunting the cemetery, one who might make his life better if he honored her. I don't know—it will take someone who knows a lot more about human psychology than me to really explain." He paused. "Anyway, I'm grateful. I spent part of today thinking we'd never catch this guy, or it would be forever and I wouldn't look so good to my peers or the public. And thanks to your help—unwitting as it might have been—we found the killer within twenty-four hours of his display."

Jace walked over to him and shook his hand. He gave Thoreau a crooked grin.

"No big deal. Happy to help. And, um, thanks! You saved our lives. Seems to me you know plenty about human behavior!"

Shauna thanked him, too.

The detective left them. It was almost morning.

Shauna looked at Jace.

He grinned and said, "I am not leaving you alone. And I'm not the monster Marty seemed to think, I swear it. And I don't want anything at all. I'll just sit here. I . . . I really want you to have dinner with me. Dinner. No strings."

"We can have dinner," she told him.

"What? Really?"

"Sure. Except, it's morning. How about breakfast?"

"Beignets and café au lait!" Jace said. "The best in New Orleans!"

His smile faded, and he looked at her seriously.

"How about a museum?" he asked her. "Um, I don't want you to go away, out of my life. What if we opened a museum? Story time—but with no corpses. Old or new."

Shauna smiled. "Why don't we start with breakfast?" she asked him. And she was glad. She'd always liked Jace. She just . . .

She'd always been afraid.

And now she wasn't.

She wasn't afraid to take a chance, to maybe have things go well, and maybe have them not go badly.

She knew two things:

She'd always be grateful to Detective Thoreau.

And she'd always be grateful to be alive. And so, she would take a few chances.

And she would live.

TRY AND
LOVE AGAIN

AMANDA FLOWER

"Ernie, I know that you took the money." I leaned my back against the bar and watched the thin, sixtysomething man tap the side of the beer glass with his blunt fingertips. It was in the middle of the day, but you wouldn't know it walking down Catawba Street in the village of Put-in-Bay, located in one corner of South Bass Island just five miles from Ohio's Lake Erie coast. The village was notorious for drinking and having a good time. Hundreds of thousands of visitors crossed from the mainland on the ferry to get away from it all every year. Fewer than two hundred of us live here year-round.

Not many people outside of the Great Lakes Region or outside of Ohio knew there was such an island in Lake Erie. I'd known all my life since I was born and raised here. I loved the island and didn't want to leave. That wasn't the norm. Not many people stay. If you don't want to work at a bar or a bed-and-breakfast, there isn't much for you here. However, I found my niche as a private investigator on the island. There was a need for it. A startling number of people crossed the water and lost their common sense. I can't find that for them, but I look for the people, money, and other belongings they might have misplaced while visiting. I was excellent at finding those, both in person and online. During the summer months, most of my work is face-to-face with people like Ernie, but in the winter when the island's population shrank, I took my business almost exclusively online and trolled the dark web for digital criminals while sipping hot cocoa. The face-to-face stuff is more my speed; the computer stuff pays the bills.

Ernie squinted and scrunched up his face. "I don't know what you're talking about, Jay-Jay."

"Ernie," I said. "Come on. If I didn't know you were guilty already, I would by looking at your face. If I tapped 'guilty expression' into my phone right now, your face would come up."

Ernie tried to force his mouth into a neutral expression, but it came off as pitiful.

"Ahh, come on, Jay-Jay. Give a guy a break. I thought we were in this together."

"In this together" was a phrase I heard often from year-round islanders. It was like it was us against the tourists—and sometimes worse than the tourists, the "summer people." The summer people tended to think that the island was theirs because they stayed up here for three months of the year, usually June to August. Not one of them would survive January on the island, no matter what their claim of ownership was.

"I'm happy to give you a break, Ernie. I'm doing that by not calling the police department. Besides, you know they don't want to have to arrest you again. No one in the department wants to take in a local if they can avoid it. Just hand over the two hundred dollars you took from the tip jar at the Music Box, and I'll make this go away."

The Music Box was a piano bar at the other end of Delaware Street just before the park that held the Perry Memorial began. The piano bar attracted a little different crowd than the usual Put-in-Bay merrymakers. The piano player reported the money stolen from the tip jar last night. Video surveillance caught Ernie red-handed taking the money. The owner, Val, was another local of the island and didn't want Ernie to be arrested for the crime, but he did want his money back. That's why he called me instead of the PIB PD.

I removed my cellphone from the back pocket of my jeans. "Val said if I couldn't make you return the money, I should call the police on you. I don't want to do it . . ."

"Jay-Jay, why would you want to go and do that? Haven't I always been nice to you? Can't you return the favor?"

"Ernie, you are nice to everyone, but you have sticky fingers. You have to stop taking things that don't belong to you." I tapped my foot. "It's not a good look."

"Do you think I care about my looks?" He gave me a hound dog face. On second thought, his loose jowls reminded me of my neighbor's old mastiff.

I folded my arms and waited.

He sighed, reached into his jacket pocket, and came up with a wad of cash. He handed it to me.

I counted the mostly small bills that would be found in a tip jar and saw it was all there. "Thanks. Glad to see you didn't spend any of it. That would make things so much more difficult."

"You didn't even give me a chance," he grumbled.

"I'll take this straight to the Music Box."

He grunted. "If you want to be a real private eye, Jay-Jay, you need to get off this island and live a little. Making old men pay back a few dollars isn't worth your time."

"In my world, two hundred dollars is a lot more than 'a few dollars.' That would pay for enough ramen to feed me for a year."

He turned back to his drink without another word. I knew that we would be having this conversation again when he stole from another bar in town. If nothing else, Ernie was consistent.

I headed out of the bar. When I wasn't working a job, I tried to stay as far away from Catawba Street as possible. The rabble-rousing got old after a while. I had been around it my whole life and saw every possible kind of drunk from silly to mean. There wasn't much there that interested me.

"Miss! Miss!" a man's voice called.

He had to weave around a group of tipsy college students dressed all in green. St. Patrick's Day was months ago, but there were at least two bars on the island that celebrated it every weekend during the summer to keep the luck of Irish in perpetual swing. I wondered if St. Patrick would be happy to know his legacy was living on through green beer and gaudy synthetic orange wigs in the middle of July.

"Can I help you?" I asked, eyeing the late-middle-aged man who called my name. To the best of my knowledge, I had never seen him before. I certainly had never investigated him. I never forgot those faces.

"Yes, I think you can. You're a private eye? Did I hear that right at the bar?"

"I prefer the term private investigator, but yes, I am."

"I have a case for you then. I'm looking for someone. A woman."

"Okay. When was the last time you saw her?" I asked, expecting him to say an hour ago at the Mad Hatter Saloon.

He surprised me by saying, "Twenty-one years ago."

I stared at him. "I don't know how I can help you if you misplaced her on the island so long ago. The cases I work are a tad more recent. I don't search for birth parents or things like that, if that's what you're looking for."

"I'm not looking for anyone like that. The person I want to find is Janelle Roper."

As soon as he said the name I knew who he meant, but he was going to have an awful time finding Janelle Roper.

"And who are you?" I asked.

"Oh, I'm sorry." He held out his hand to be shaken. "I'm Arthur Kheeler."

I obliged. His grip was dry and firm. It was a surprise to me, considering his mousey appearance.

"Well, Arthur, you will have a hard time finding Janelle," I said, repeating my own thought.

"Why's that?"

"Because she's dead."

Arthur fainted clear away. A tipsy coed tripped over him. "Gross, a dead guy."

"He's not dead," I said to her back as she stumbled down the street with her friends. I knelt beside Arthur, and he opened his eyes.

Arthur sat up. "What happened?"

"You fainted. Can you stand up?"

He placed a hand to his forehead. "I think so."

I helped him to his feet as more and more people on the sidewalk flowed around us. Two stopped to offer help, but I told them we were fine. I wasn't surprised more people didn't want to get involved. People didn't come to the island to help lend a hand. They were there to have fun and forget about their lives on the mainland. I got Arthur to his feet and, holding him by the arm, led him away from the street toward a bench in DeRivera Park that faced the water's edge of Lake Erie. He sat, and I let go of his arm.

The cool breeze coming off of the lake seemed to revive him. "I'm sorry about back there. What you told me came as such a shock. I expected to come to the island and have no luck finding Janelle. It's been twenty-one years, after all. But I never expected to learn she was dead." He shook his head and then winced as if the movement pained him.

He was going to be even more shocked when he learned the rest of it.

As expected, he asked, "What happened to her?"

The lake lapped at the break wall. Two children and a Labrador played nearby. The children threw the ball to each other, playing keep-away from the dog; the Lab seemed to love every second of it, even when he was thwarted in catching the ball. I thought about how to tell this stranger something that every local on the island knew. There was no way to sugarcoat it, so I simply said, "She was murdered twenty years ago."

"Oh my God." He sucked in a breath, and I kept a close eye on him from where I was standing to make sure he didn't faint again. He looked like he might have if he had been standing up.

"Murdered? What happened?"

"No one really knows." The case remained unsolved. Janelle Roper's murder was the most notorious crime on the island to date. "Tell me about you and Janelle." I thought distracting him was the best chance of avoiding another fainting episode. He was very pale.

"We met when I was on the island one summer in college for work. I was a bouncer at the Music Box."

I raised my brow.

"I know that I don't look like much now, but I had bone cancer. It did a number on my body. I'm proud to say I'm here today."

"I'm sorry to hear that," I murmured. "How did you know Janelle?"

"She was a waitress at the Music Box. I think when I saw her, it was love at first sight. We spent every free moment together that summer. We were in love."

"But you didn't stay in love." My tone was matter-of-fact.

He frowned. "I went back to school in the fall. I asked her to come with me, but she didn't want to leave the island. She claimed the best time to live on the island was during the off-season. We lost touch. It was a different time before social media exploded. Life got busy. I moved on, but I never forgot her."

I had to agree with Janelle about that. When the hourly ferries stopped coming, the days grew colder, and the bars shuttered their doors and windows. That's when the true islanders were most alive. We took a breath. We made less money. Saw fewer people. We were happier.

"After all this time, what made you come back now?" I asked.

"I recently got divorced. After surviving cancer and a horrible marriage, I promised myself that I would come back and look for her. Perhaps I was being naive to think she was here. I just couldn't imagine her off the island. The island was everything to her."

I nodded. That wasn't an uncommon sentiment among the islanders that I knew.

"But I'm too late." He bent at the waist and pressed his elbows into his knees. Cradling his head in his hands, he said, "I'm twenty years too late."

I wasn't sure what to say. I wanted to pat him on the arm, but what would that really help? It seemed to me that this man had been through hell and back and came to the island for something. What? I didn't know . . . redemption . . . closure . . . a second chance. Maybe it was all three.

"Do you want to meet with anyone who knew Janelle?" I asked.

He looked up from his arms. Black circles lined under his eyes, and the skin on his face seemed to be thin.

"Would it do any good?" he asked.

I shrugged. "I don't know, but the Music Box is still in operation. I could ask around." I removed my business card from my jacket pocket and handed it to him.

"What would your fee be?" He held the card in his hand with the tips of his fingers.

"Nothing for now," I said. "I can ask questions for free. Trust me, I'm good at it. Give me your cell number, and I will call you when I learn more."

He rattled off a number, and I typed it into my phone under the contact 'Arthur Kheeler.'

"Are you staying on the island?"

He nodded. "I have a room at Sue Ann's B&B. I'll be there a couple of days."

"I know where that is," I said, although it wasn't necessary. I knew where everything on the island was. "I'll touch base with you before you leave."

"Thank you." He stared in my eyes a moment longer than was comfortable.

I walked away. After a few steps, I looked over my shoulder and saw he was still watching me. I tried to shake the creepy feeling that crawled down my spine.

The murder of Janelle Roper was the most infamous case on the island. One that I had looked into before. If I solved it, people would notice. Solving the cold case could change the course of my business if I let it. I would be even more in demand with my online and in-person customers. Maybe this is what I needed to give the mundane work of convincing small-time criminals like Ernie to give money they stole back some meaning.

I went back into the throng of people well on their ways to being three sheets to the wind. That was how my late father would have described their condition. He would know. He had owned a bar on Delaware Street for nearly thirty years. He was the one who taught me the kinds of drunks I would run into on the island, especially in the summer. He knew them all: the ones who would be fun, the ones who would be stupid, and the ones who would be dangerous before they took their first shot.

The Music Box was at the end of the street not far from the ferry dock. It was a prime location because people usually started barhopping there. At least they did in my father's heyday. An old-school piano bar wasn't exactly what the coeds of the new millennium were looking for. Lots of them went straight for the sports and tiki bars. The new dance bars on the island were becoming more popular too. However, there were enough middle-aged folks coming back to the island to relive their wild days to keep the old piano bar afloat.

As soon as I stepped into the building, I was accosted with a gust of cigar smoke. I tried not to gag. Cigar smoke was a smell I abhorred. I didn't care how quality the cigar was or where it came from, the smell was suffocating to me.

Val, the owner of the Music Box for the last forty-some years, knew how I felt about the smell, but he puffed away at his stogy like he was the big boss in *The Godfather*.

"I got your money," I said, and removed the cash from my pocket. I held it out to him.

He accepted the money. "Thanks for this." He folded it and tucked it into the breast pocket of his shirt. "Did Ernie take it?"

I nodded and waved the smoke from my face. Looking up, I saw the giant chandelier that seemed to be made by a thousand crystals that hung over the empty dance floor. The piano's bench seat stood empty, but piano music played softly over the PA. There were a few elderly gents sipping cocktails and smoking cigars in the corner of the grand room. The room was grand, but it showed its age. Cracks appeared in the marble floor, the brocaded fabric on the chairs and sofas was worn. The Music Box's heyday had been many decades before.

Val bit down hard on the cigar between his teeth. "I hate to see that. Ernie isn't that bad. Can't let him in here no more though."

"That's probably wise."

"You're worth keeping on retainer, Jay-Jay, you know that?"

"Glad to hear I'm a good investment."

He cocked his head and removed the cigar from his mouth. "Why aren't you running off? Usually, when you finish a job, you can't wait to get out of here. If I had a dime for every time you complained over the smell of my cigars, I could have bought this island by now."

"I'm looking for some information." I stepped out of the worst of the smoke cloud.

"Oh." He stuck the cigar back into his mouth. "Business should be good if you already have another case. This place is littered with pickpockets in the summer."

"I'm not officially on a case. I just have some questions for myself."

"Shoot." He wriggled his bushy eyebrows that looked like black-and-white raccoon tails on his face.

"What can you tell me about Janelle Roper? She worked here, right?"

"Janelle Roper. Now, that's not a name I've heard in a very long time." He leaned back against the bar. "I'm no dummy. The only reason you would ask is if you were looking into her murder. Who hired you?"

"No one hired me."

He laughed. "You stick to that story. In any case, I hope you don't think you can solve Janelle's murder."

"Why's that?" I asked.

"Because you won't. Many have tried and failed. Why would you be any different? You think you can solve a twenty-year-old crime? In all likelihood, the killer isn't even on the island anymore. Not many people who lived here twenty years ago are still here."

"You are."

"I'm an exception." He eyed me. "Like you."

I scowled. "Tell me about her. What was she like? I think I know how she died." I didn't add that this wasn't the first time I had been interested in the case and a former Put-in-Bay police chief had let me read the murder file. Truth be told, there wasn't much to go on, and I didn't have much memory of it since I was just a child when the murder took place.

He shrugged as if it was my funeral. I really didn't care if that's how Val thought of it. "Janelle was a waitress here. She grew up on the island. As far as I know, she always lived here. She's one of the rare birds that never flew the coop." He paused. "Like you."

Another "like you." I didn't say anything and waited. When I was quiet long enough, I knew he would say more. He proved me right.

"She was pretty. A popular waitress and made great tips. The men liked her because she was flirty, but not in a way that would ever make them believe they had a shot with her. She was charming and used her charm to make more money. She really wasn't interested in them. She and they both knew it. Even so, they tipped her well, and a lot of the regulars refused to be served by anyone else while they were in the Music Box."

"So she never went on dates?"

"There was only one man I knew she dated in the whole time she worked for me. It was a young bouncer who worked for me the summer before she died. I was afraid that she would leave with him when he went back to the mainland after the summer. Thankfully, she didn't. The island was more important to her than some guy," he said dismissively.

"Was his name Arthur Kheeler?"

He stared at me. "How did you know that?"

"I heard it around town."

He scowled at me. "So you haven't been looking into this case for a while," he said sarcastically.

"I haven't." And that was the truth whether he believed it or not.

"Janelle surprised everyone by staying after Arthur left," he said. "She said she couldn't leave."

"Why not?"

He shrugged. "I don't know. Why did you stay? Maybe it was for the same reason."

My answer couldn't be Janelle's answer. I knew that much. My answer didn't bear repeating even to myself.

"Did you see her the day she died?" I asked.

"I sure did. She worked the day shift that day. That was unusual for her. Typically she worked nights because you could score the biggest tips. She was my best waitress, and she had the pick of all the shifts. I always scheduled her on nights because I knew that's what she liked. I remember that day she told me she was on the day shift because she switched with another waitress."

"Who was the waitress that she switched with?"

"Does it matter?" He folded his arms.

"It could."

"I don't remember, and there's no way to find out. No one who was on staff at the Music Box today was on staff back then. I don't keep the shift records. I would have thrown them away years ago. This was before it was all on the computer. I used to schedule with paper and pencil."

I frowned and wondered if the police department would know. I knew it must have been a question they would have asked all those years ago. If a murder victim suddenly changed her schedule, that was telling. She could have even switched her shift so that she could meet her killer, not that she would know the culprit's intentions at the time.

"She worked until four that day, and that was the last I ever saw her," Val added. "The next morning when the sirens went off, I learned that she was drowned at the ferry docks."

I nodded. From what I had read in the case file and heard through island gossip, she died by drowning. A heavy chain had been tied to her feet and she had been pushed off of the pier. It brought more *Godfather* references to mind. It was a terrible way to die. According to the coroner's report, which I had reviewed once before, she was alive when she went into the water. There was blunt force trauma, too. The coroner at the time couldn't determine if it happened before or after she went into the water. The murder occurred in October. The water must have been shockingly cold. I hoped the cold numbed some of the pain as she went down.

Her body wasn't found until the next morning when the ferry came in. In the fall, ferries were far less frequent, so she would have been in the water for hours at that point.

"Janelle was a good kid. It was a blow to the whole community when she died. We islanders have affection for the young kids who decide to stay on this rock. We had the same affection for her that we have for you."

"Was she having any trouble at home? With a boyfriend? Other than Arthur, since he was out of the picture by then? Anything like that?"

He shrugged. "Not that I know of, but I was her boss. She wouldn't have said something like that to me if she had."

"You said there isn't anyone working here today that worked the same time she did, but is there anyone still on the island who worked at the Music Box back then?"

He tugged on his goatee as he started to think this over. "Becca Dutton worked here at the time. She left the island for a long while, but came back last year to run the family B&B."

"Becca of Sue Ann's B&B?"

He nodded. "She stopped in here after she moved back just to say hello. Asked me to send folks looking for lodging her way. I said I'd help if I could."

It was interesting to note that was the same B&B where Arthur was staying.

"Thanks, Val," I said. "At least that gives me a place to start."

I left the piano bar considering what I should do next. I had other cases that I should be working on, but nothing this big or interesting. Most of my PI work was done behind a computer screen. I had no interest in it. It paid well, but it wasn't why I went into this line of work.

Still, it didn't explain what I was up to. Why was I bothering trying to track down what happened to Janelle? I wasn't getting paid for it. Maybe it was because no one else had been able to find the truth about her death. Maybe it was because I had tried and failed before. There was nothing I hated more than failure.

I decided to walk to the pier where Janelle would have drowned all those years ago. I didn't expect to find anything there to help my case—it had been decades since she'd died—but I needed to visualize what that night must have been like for her. Perhaps then, the questions that I needed to ask Becca Dutton would become clearer to me.

In my mind's eye, I thought about that night. Janelle was still alive when the killer tied the chain around her feet. Was she kicking at him? Was she unconscious from the trauma on her head? Was she hit with something and tossed into the water like a forgotten ragdoll? I could see it all a little too vividly in my head. I shivered and stepped back from the edge of the pier.

I would talk to Becca Dutton and see where that led me.

Sue Ann's B&B was on the other side of the island, as far away from the public dock and the bars as someone could get without leaving the island. This side of the island was tranquil. It was the place where the elderly and young families came to get away from the mainland and from the crowds by the pier.

The B&B was right on the water, and even though I couldn't see it, I knew the Canadian coast was just forty or so miles away.

I went inside the B&B. The decoration was strictly nautical with ship bells, rope, and boat wheels a major part of the decor.

"Jay-Jay, I haven't seen you on this side of the island for a long time," Becca said. She stood behind the registration desk with a bright smile on her face. She was a friendly woman with a welcoming face and rosy cheeks. If I was to think of a B&B owner in my head, Becca's face would be the first to come to mind.

"The bars are keeping me pretty busy with cases. There are always plenty of cheating spouses on the island in the summer."

She shook her head. "I keep my distance from that area until winter when we get the island back again."

I nodded. A lot of locals talked about the winter in reverent tones like that. Winter on the island was harsh. We were in the middle of a turbulent lake off the north coast of the country with Canada not too far away. We got the worst wind, snow, and sleet. However, we also got peace, as it was too rough for any mainlanders to make the crossing to the island even if they wanted to. In case of major emergencies or injuries that happened in the worst weather, islanders had to be airlifted off the island to the mainland.

"Is there something I can help you with?" Becca asked.

"Maybe. Do you have an Arthur Kheeler checked in here?"

She frowned. "You know that I don't have to tell you who is or who isn't checked in to my B&B."

"You don't, but you can."

"Did Arthur do something?"

"Not that I'm aware of."

"Then why are you asking after him?" She arched her brow.

"I met him down by the bars earlier today, and he mentioned that he was looking for someone. I said I might be able to help."

"If anyone could, it would be you. Who was he looking for?"

"Janelle Roper." I said the name and waited for her reaction.

She didn't disappoint. She gave a quick intake of breath. "Is that why he's here?"

I nodded.

"I thought he was familiar," she said, barely over a whisper. "Did he used to work at the Music Box?"

I nodded again.

She pressed a hand to her forehead. "I think I need to sit down." She came around the side of the desk and stumbled into the adjacent sitting room. The room was a sun porch and was surrounded by windows that allowed for a perfect view of the lake. Becca sat on one of the two floral loveseats.

I sat on the other. "Are you all right?"

She dropped her hand from the forehead. "I think so, but I haven't thought of Janelle in such a long time. So many memories came rushing back. It took the wind out of my sails, as my grandfather would have said."

"Were you close?"

She settled back in her seat. "We were work friends. Nothing more than that. I can't think of a single time I spent with her outside of the Music Box. We were both waitresses, but she made a lot more money than I did. She was better at flirting. It's not my strong suit. That could be the reason that I'm still single at my age." She gave a self-deprecating laugh.

I ignored her last comment and said, "What can you tell me about the summer you, Janelle, and Arthur all worked at the Music Box?"

"Nothing."

I stared at her.

"I mean it. I was twenty, and all I can remember about that summer was trying to earn enough money to get off of the island. I had no intention of staying or coming back." She held up her hands. "But look where I ended up—right where I started, and I'm very happy about it. If you'd told me twenty years ago that I would ever say that, I'd have laughed in your face."

Becca wouldn't be the only one who didn't remember what had

happened twenty years ago. As much as I would love to bring Janelle's killer to justice, I had to admit to myself that this was going to take time. Cold cases like this take years to solve, if they are ever solved at all. Who was I to think I could wrap it up in a few days?

"Janelle and I talked about it all the time," Becca said.

I looked back at her in surprise. "What did you talk about?"

"How much we wanted to leave the island."

This was news. "Janelle wanted to leave the island?"

"She talked about it constantly, more than I did even, and I actually left." She frowned. "I suppose she never got the chance. She made good money working at the Music Box, but like just about everyone else born here, she wanted to leave and see what the rest of the world was like."

"When I spoke to Val at the Music Box, he said she never wanted to leave the island."

"Oh, there is no way she would have told Val she wanted to leave the island. He would have been devastated. Honestly, I think she brought in half of his sales. People just loved her so much. However, with the friendly personality she had and the way that she could read people, she needed to do something bigger than waitress at some piano bar for the rest of her life." She said it like it was the worst possible fate she could imagine. "He believed that if Janelle left, the bar would go under. Even with Janelle on staff, the bar was struggling. This was close to the turn of the millennium. Piano bars were out of fashion. Business was slowing. Turnover was terrible. People came and went all the time. I stayed on because I knew I was leaving. Janelle must have stayed on for her own reasons that we will never know."

Something felt off about all of this. Both Val and Arthur told me that Janelle had no plans to leave South Bass Island, and here was Becca, who admitted to not knowing Janelle well, saying Janelle *did* want to leave.

"Does she still have any family on the island?"

"Not that I know of. I think she had a couple of brothers who left in their teens, and I think her parents died when she was a kid."

"Who took care of her?"

She shrugged. "It wasn't something she talked about. The thing I most remember about Janelle is that she was way more interested in the future than in the past. She always avoided questions about her past. I stopped asking. We were both young. The future felt exciting."

It was exciting until someone put Janelle in the lake.

"Is Arthur here right now?"

She shook her head. "He borrowed one of our courtesy bikes and went for a ride. I offered him a map of the island, so he knew where he was, but he said he didn't need it. He remembered the island from when he was younger. I would have asked him about the last time he was here and been able to place him if I could have spoken to him more about it, but another guest came up to the desk and interrupted us."

I nodded. "I'm sure I will catch up with him eventually."

"No one can hide from anyone on this island."

It sounded like a threat.

I tried to shake off the odd feeling that I had now gotten over Janelle's death as I climbed onto my moped and rode to the other side of the island. The moped was the only transportation I needed to get around the island. It was easy to store, and I could take it to the mainland by ferry if it needed repairs beyond what the mechanic on the island could handle. I tucked my hair into my helmet, and I was off. As I went to the other side of the island I passed the Perry National Monument, an obelisk that commemorated the War of 1812 Battle of Lake Erie with the British. It was a stately and dignified national park monument, which stood in stark contrast with what happened on the island the majority of the time. I slowed as I passed the monument because a man was standing at its base who looked a whole lot like Arthur.

I turned into the parking area, parked the moped, and walked over.

Arthur was reading one of the informational placards on the grounds. He looked up at me when my boots made a click, click, click sound on the stone walkway. He tensed when he saw me. I found that to be an odd reaction. He had asked me for help, hadn't he? I hadn't been looking for a new case that was clearly going to be impossible to solve. He had come to me. Now, he looked like he might regret it.

"Have you learned anything new?" he asked. "About Janelle?"

I studied him for a moment and wondered how much I should

share with him. He hadn't hired me, and nothing I had learned about Janelle's death was earth-shattering. There were conflicting thoughts on whether or not she wanted to stay or leave the island.

"You said that Janelle wouldn't leave the island with you at the end of that summer."

He nodded. "And she didn't, clearly, since this was where she died one year later." He walked around the monument and looked out into the water.

Today the lake was calm, but it was well known on the island that the temperament of the wind and waves could change in an instant.

"Did you remember that Becca from the B&B worked with you two at the Music Box?"

"I thought she looked familiar, but it was over twenty years ago."

"She told me something about Janelle that contradicted what you said."

He looked at me. "What was that?"

"Janelle wanted to leave the island." I studied him for some sort of reaction.

He didn't have one. At least, he was very careful not to have one.

"That's not true. Janelle told me she never wanted to leave the island. If she ever wanted to leave, it would have been with me. She loved me. I know that. I also know if she left with me, my life would have been different. I would have been happier."

"Your lack of happiness was her fault?" I arched my brow.

"I didn't say that."

But he kind of did.

"I'm not sure you're going to find the answers you're looking for this weekend," I said. "It seems that very few people on the island have thought about Janelle in a very long time."

"And I have thought of her every day." He stood up. "Thanks for trying to help. It was kind of you to reach out to a stranger like that." He cleared his throat. "I should get the bike back to the B&B. I told Becca that I would only need it for an hour."

The bike leaned against a tree. Arthur walked over to it, got on, and pedaled away without another word.

I decided that I would give myself one more chance to learn something about Janelle. I climbed back on my moped and rode the short differ-ence to the dock where her body was found. The dock looked much the same as it had twenty years ago. The signs had been refreshed and now there were automatic booths where ferry tickets could be bought, but the place where Janelle Roper's body fell into the lake remained as it always had. Dirty water lapped up against the weathered wooden pylons.

"Are you down here looking for me again?" a gruff voice asked. "I already gave you Val's money back."

I turned to see Ernie standing nearby in a pair of bibbed orange waders, a stub of a cigarette hanging out of his mouth. When I saw him, I remembered he worked at the fish processing plants near the ferry dock. "I wasn't," I said.

He moved his cigarette to the other side of his mouth. "You look-ing for Janelle Roper then?"

My eyes went wide. "How'd you hear about that?" I asked, not even bothering to deny it.

"I went to the Music Box just to make sure there were no hard feel-ings between Val and me, and he said you asked about her." He removed the cigarette from his mouth and tossed it into the water.

I bit my lip to stop myself from snapping at him over it. It was people like him who ruined our lake.

"I saw you talking to a mainlander too," Ernie said. "I'd watch myself if I were you, Jay-Jay. He's not who he seems."

"Why do you say that?"

"Working down here, I see just about everyone who comes to this island. That man has been here before and not too long ago, too. He may not be who he seems."

"He said that he hasn't been to the island in over twenty years," I protested.

"Are you surprised that people lie to you, Miss Detective?" He walked away. Lake water dripped from the cuffs of his waders as he went.

I frowned at his back. Had I just wasted my whole day? For what? For Arthur Kheeler to tell me a lie that he'd not been back to the island for twenty years? What was his game, and did it even matter to me?

Wouldn't it be better to wash my hands of it? It was time to get back to work on my paying jobs. Shaking my head, I left the dock.

And I really tried. I spoke with a hotel manager that wanted me to check in with an employee that called in sick a little too often. I did some searches for a money-laundering scheme at a microbrewery on the island. I followed leads, but I didn't care about a single one of them. All the time, my mind was occupied with Janelle Roper. What had happened to her? And had she wanted to stay or leave the island?

The thing about me, when I had a question in my head and couldn't shake it, I knew it was going nowhere until I gave the question its due. Janelle Roper's case wanted that.

By evening, when the bars were at their most lively, I gave up fighting it and walked back to the Music Box.

When I walked inside, I was surprised at the silence. No piano played. The place was empty. All the lights were on, but no one was there.

The swinging door behind the bar swung open and Val came out.

"Hey, Val," I said. "Where is everyone?"

"My crowd is older. They already went to bed."

I raised my brow. It was eight p.m. in the middle of the summer. The sun wouldn't set for another hour. Val's crowd wasn't *that* old.

"What brings you back?" he asked.

"Janelle," I said.

He grimaced. "I knew you wouldn't let it go."

"I spoke with Becca, and she told me something that you didn't."

He paled slightly. "What's that?"

"Janelle was going to leave."

He glowered at me. "I know."

"You knew? Then why did you tell me the opposite?"

He stepped forward behind the bar. I could no longer see his hands. That was worrisome.

"The bar was struggling," Val said. "Everyone wants these loud tiki bar places with gaudy plastic cups. Whatever happened to class? Janelle did tell me that she wanted to leave, but I told her she couldn't. The place would die without her. She brought in the most business."

"But you're still in business today. Your bar didn't die," I said. "She's gone, and it didn't make any difference to your business whether she was here or not." I still couldn't see his hands. That was a problem. "What happened when she told you she was leaving?"

His body shook. "I lost my temper. I picked up the first thing I could find. It was a thick crystal decanter. I wasn't thinking and threw it at the back of her head. She went down."

I swallowed a gasp.

He lifted his hands above the bar, and I saw the gun. I should have known that Val had a handgun within easy reach in his bar.

"I wasn't thinking straight when I threw it. She just crumbled to the ground. I thought she was dead right there. I tried to wake her up, but she didn't give me any signs of life. If she had, I would have called for help. I promise."

It was hard to believe such a promise from a man holding a gun, and "I wasn't thinking straight" wasn't a plea that was normally accepted by the court system. "You took her to a pier. You tied a chain around her feet and put her in the water."

"I wasn't thinking."

"According to the coroner's report, she died by drowning. She was alive when she went into the water."

"I didn't know she was alive. She looked very dead to me. She wasn't moving." He waved his gun over his head.

"You didn't take her pulse?" I asked.

He stopped waving the gun and pointed it at me. He held it steady. I realized being aimed at was a lot worse than him waving the gun around in the air. His chances of hitting me, especially this close, were so much higher.

He stared me in the eye. "I panicked. I panicked. The only excuse I have is that I panicked. I've had to live with that for the last twenty years. Do you think that is something that I'm proud of?"

"Are you panicking now as you threaten to kill another person?" a deep male voice asked.

I took a chance and glanced over my shoulder to see mild-mannered

Arthur Kheeler standing in the doorway holding his own gun. He didn't look as mild-mannered and weak as he had before.

"You know, I always thought you killed Janelle," Arthur said with an angry twist to his mouth. "You wouldn't let her go. You had her trapped here. She told me that. I begged her to come to the mainland with me, but she refused. She said she promised you one more year working for you on the island. She was going to honor that, even if it meant losing me. She was a person of high morals, unlike you. She kept her word. You broke yours. I even called the PIB PD telling them my suspicions, but what they told me, again and again, was you had an alibi."

Now that he said that, I remembered reading that in the police report as well. Val had been questioned but five people said he was at another bar that night. He even had a tab working at the bar. In hindsight, that should have caught my interest because Val had a bar of his own. I had never known him to go to another on the island.

"It is amazing what people will say for a summer of free alcohol," Val said.

I shivered and said to Arthur, "You knew she was dead?"

"Of course, I knew. Do you think I've been living under a rock? This is one the biggest unsolved cases in Northern Ohio."

I narrowed my eyes, well aware that Val still had his gun trained on me. "Who are you?"

"Arthur Kheeler. I just didn't tell you that I happen to be a retired police detective. I had spent my whole life wondering what happened to Janelle. When I retired and survived cancer, my marriage fell apart." There was an angry twist to his mouth. "It seemed the wife rather liked me working long shifts, and having me home was a little too much. When that was all over, I decided that I would spend the rest of my days finding out what had happened to Janelle. I thought about her every day when I was in treatment and wondered what might have been. I have been on this case for years, working every angle I could. I came back to the island whenever I could to follow the clues but always under a false name. This time, I thought I might have more luck if I used my real name, and it's been proven true. I never thought some petty theft

PI would lead me to the killer, but there you are. Something I learned in all my years of police work: how to use people to my advantage."

Ernie had been right about Arthur.

"You are supposed to protect and serve, not use people."

He shrugged. "Sometimes you have to use one person to save another." He turned to Val and leveled his gun. "I will ask you to put that down now."

"I can't. I'm too old to go to prison. If I go, I will die there."

"That's something you should have thought about before you took another person's life."

"I didn't take her life, not on purpose. It was an accident. I would never intentionally kill another person!"

His words stood in contrast with the gun he had pointed at my chest.

"I've had to live with that guilt for the last twenty years," Val said. "Do you even know how much pain that has caused me?"

I stared at him. How could he worry about his pain after he killed another human being? I would imagine after twenty years, he had had a lot of time to make up excuses in his mind to cope with the guilt over what he had done. Even so, I couldn't feel sorry for him. Janelle had been a young woman with so much potential. He took her life. There was no excuse for that.

"Put the gun down," Arthur said again. This time the tone of his voice convinced me that he hadn't been lying about being a retired cop. He said it with so much authority.

"No," Val said and lifted his gun. He shot the chandelier that hung in the ballroom. There was a spark as the electric current was cut, and the crystal chandelier crashed to the marble floor. Arthur and I jumped away.

I lay facedown on the marble floor and covered my head as tiny crystals showered my back. Slowly, I sat up and brushed the glass off of me the best that I could without cutting myself. Arthur was already on his feet and running out the door.

Outside, I saw Val run from the bar into Delaware Street, which was buzzing with activity. Without looking, he ran into the street. He wasn't halfway across when a speeding golf cart hit him, sending him sailing into the air. He landed in a heap on the asphalt. People in the street shouted.

Arthur and I ran to him.

The woman who had been driving the golf cart was screaming that she killed a man, but she hadn't. Val was very much alive. He lay on the asphalt holding his leg. His gun was five feet away. I grabbed a red T-shirt from a rack from one of the sidewalk sellers.

"Hey, you have to pay for that shirt," the shop owner cried.

"Bill me," I said, and then I bent down and used the T-shirt to pick up the gun.

Within a minute, police were on the scene—much like Bourbon Street in New Orleans, they kept a presence in this area—and the golf cart driver was arrested for driving under the influence . . . and for hitting Val.

The lone EMT on the island knelt next to Val, who complained about his leg.

Arthur saw me standing a few feet away holding Val's gun wrapped in the red T-shirt. The red shirt made it seem like I had blood on my hands. Perhaps I did.

Arthur walked over to me and took the T-shirt-wrapped gun from my hands.

"Why did you get me involved at all? You had the case well-in-hand," I said. "You suspected Val already."

"Because people on this island trust you. Had I asked half the questions that you did, they would have clammed up. You got answers from both Becca and Val. I used your home field advantage to my advantage."

I frowned. I knew in detective work that manipulation to get the information that you needed was sometimes how you played the game. I had been known to do it too. Ernie came to mind. Was my conversation with him just that morning? It seemed like it was years ago.

"Thank you, Jay-Jay, this would have taken me much longer without you."

I stared him in the eye. "I didn't do it for you. I did it for Janelle."

"So did I," was his only reply.

THE LAST RESORT

RICK BLEIWEISS

ONE

Walker's last job was one of the few that didn't go exactly as planned. He conducted all his usual surveillance, chose the right time and place, and dressed in his lucky suit and tie, but something went wrong. In retrospect, Walker believes he was given some bad information, either because he was working for a new boss who didn't know how he operated, or because it was a setup and he was the real intended target. Whatever the reason, nothing went right.

He crouched behind a timeworn green dumpster in the alley at the rear of the Bizzazz nightclub waiting for its owner, Smokey, to come out the back door as he did every morning at five a.m. Walker picked the spot because of Smokey's daily routine and because of the club's off-the-beaten-path location in a commercial area of Manhattan's meatpacking district where his gunshots would not be heard by any apartment dwellers. He knew the time of day was ideal for a hit as well—the only people who might be out that early in the morning in that area of town would be sanitation truck drivers, and the noise of their vehicles would probably drown out the sound of his gunfire.

When Walker saw the slightest movement of the doorknob, he stood up with his gun hanging in his right hand alongside his pant leg, waiting for Smokey to open the door and come into view.

But instead of the door slowly opening, it burst open and three large guys, each holding a piece, rushed out, looked directly at Walker, and started firing.

Fortunately, Walker still had fast reflexes ingrained in him from his combat training and war action with the Marines, so he dove behind the dumpster as the bullets whizzed above where his head and chest would have been if he were still standing. A few harmlessly clanged into the dumpster, thudding into it while the other shots pinged and rang off of the sides of the buildings lining the alleyway. While this ineffectual barrage was missing him, Walker peered around the dumpster and fired off two shots of his own. When he heard, "Holy shit, I'm hit. My arm," he knew he got one of the thugs.

Walker didn't wait around to find out how bad the guy was wounded. He'd lay odds on one-against-one, but up against three—or more?—at this close of range . . . he'd leave to live another day.

He stayed low and began inching backward, aiming his gun in front of him with both hands. Then he got up and started running zigzag down the alley, blindly shooting behind him as bullets harmlessly flew past him into the positions he had been in seconds before. Walker safely made it to the end of the alley, and once he got there, he turned past the building—hoping there weren't reinforcements waiting for him to appear.

But no one was on the sidewalk except an earbud-wearing sanitation man throwing garbage bags into his loudly rumbling truck, so Walker raced down the street still holding his gun in his hand. He looked back and saw the thugs come out of the alley and chase after him, but he was already halfway down the block before they emerged, and he was fast and able to stay well ahead of them. When he turned the next corner, he kept running and considered his options. He knew he couldn't go to his apartment or anywhere else he'd normally be because someone else might be waiting there for him, so he figured he'd better get out of town for a while.

As luck would have it, at that very moment a vacant taxi was coming up the mostly deserted side street looking for a fare. Walker hailed it, and when it pulled to the curb, he holstered his gun, jumped in, and told the driver, "Get me to Newark Airport. Fast." As the cab took off, Walker looked out the back window and saw two of the thugs turning the corner. *Too late for them. Good for me.*

When he arrived at EWR, Walker headed to United Airlines, and fortunately, no one was in the first-class line, so he walked right up to the counter.

"Where are you going to?" the woman standing behind the station inquired.

Walker had no idea. He only knew he had to get out of town immediately.

"What's the next plane out?" he asked. He looked at her name tag and added, "Sandy."

Sandy gave him a kind of funny look, "You mean you don't have a specific destination in mind?"

"No, I don't. Just get me on whatever plane leaves next."

Sandy gave Walker another funny look, "Whatever you say, hon."

She searched the computer for what seemed like an eternity. "Next one goes to Maui. It'll be boarding soon, but you can make it with no problem. I've got a seat in first available. Ever been to Hawaii?"

Walker was really in no mood for small talk. If the thugs had jumped in another cab and followed him to the airport, he'd want to get on the plane as quickly as possible, and he realized that if he wanted to make the plane, he'd better make things happen, so he sweetly said, "Nope. This'll be my first time," and then added with a little more urgency, "I'd really like to get on that plane, darlin'. Can we move this along?"

When Walker handed Sandy his driver's license and credit card, he realized that he'd be traceable to Maui, so he'd have to quickly get a new identity once he got there. That didn't bother him since he knew how things like that could be done.

Sandy gave Walker back his items and a boarding pass and told him what gate to go to.

Before he reached the security area, Walker ducked into a bathroom, which he judged to be empty except for a person sitting in one of the stalls noisily turning the pages of a newspaper. He wiped his gun clean with the handkerchief that had been neatly folded in the breast pocket of his suit jacket and wrapped it and the holster in paper towels and then placed them both in the bottom of a trash receptacle. He was confident that with no serial number and no fingerprints on the piece, no one would be able to trace it back to him. He did feel a bit naked without it, but he knew there was no way he was getting it through the TSA people.

Walker also considered depositing his cellphone in the trash but realized he would need it to book a place to stay in Maui and could get rid of it either on the plane or once he landed, and then get a new one on the island.

Walker made the plane with five minutes to spare before they closed the gate, all the time checking behind and around him for anyone suspicious. Because of the nature of his work, he had become skilled at identifying people, and to him, the passengers all looked like vacationers, families, honeymooners, and a spattering of business professionals.

As he entered the plane from the jetway, the somewhat attractive, middle-aged, lei-wearing blond flight attendant welcomed Walker with a smile and a question: "Are you going to Maui, sir?"

"I am . . . Phyllis," he replied, once again looking at a name tag. "Why do you ask? Isn't that where this plane is going?"

"It is," Phyllis answered, "but we make sure every passenger is going to the correct destination." She leaned in closer to him and said more playfully, "Plus, they've been having a heat wave there, so I hope you have some lighter clothes in your luggage you can change into at the airport."

"Thanks," Walker responded. "I'll do that, but probably when I get to the hotel."

Walker had no idea what hotel he was going to, so when he sat in the seat and gulped down the mimosa Phyllis brought, he leafed through the United magazine hoping to find some lodging ads. There were quite a few, but the one that caught his eye was the Surfland Resort in Kihei. The advertisement pointed out that it had secluded grounds and was at the far end of South Kihei Road. It billed itself as "The Last Resort in Kihei." Exactly what Walker was looking for.

Walker called the property before the plane started taxiing and booked, under the name Cashman, a one-bedroom suite that was at the front of the resort—overlooking the street and the ocean—one that would give him a great view of anyone coming to Surfland. Coming for him.

As the plane started rolling toward the runway, Walker lay the magazine across his lap and took stock of what he had on him. Other than his wallet, burner phone, and keys, he had his usual emergency roll of hundreds. He never had to use it before but was surely glad that he carried it at all times—just for an occasion like this. It would last him quite a while, even if he started paying for everything in cash.

Walker knew he'd also be able to tap one of his hidden accounts if he had to. They had a lot of money in them; he'd set things up so that if he ever got into a situation like this very one, he'd have access to as much cash as he needed—and the anonymity that goes with not using credit cards.

He then reclined his seat and started to think about the morning's events.

Damn. What the hell went wrong? Even though I've never worked for him before, Franks told me he got my number from Scotty Jamieson, and I've never had a problem with anyone he's recommended. Somebody was playing someone, and when I get back, I'm gonna find out of it was Franks playing Scotty or Scotty playing me—whichever one of them it was is going to pay for it. Big-time. But that still leaves me wondering, why'd someone want me dead? And what's their relationship to the target, that guy Smokey? He was probably in on it, but how? Why?

I'll get to the bottom of this when I'm back in New York, and before I accept another job, I'll take care of whoever set me up. But being shot at felt good in a weird way—haven't felt alive like that since engaging with those Taliban creeps. Man, I didn't realize how routine my job had become until today. No rush, no blood surging through me, no endorphin surge. It felt good to be back in action. I didn't realize how much I missed that feeling. I'm looking forward to going up against whoever they send after me to finish the job. I'll be in full combat mode and ready for him. And when I eliminate him, then I head home and get my answers. And my revenge. And that Smokey—he's one dead man walking right now.

While Walker let his adrenaline decay as much as it could, he lifted the magazine off his lap and leafed through the rest of it to see what was in store for him in Maui. One ad in particular caught his eye. It was for a shave ice stand, also on South Kihei Road. He had loved snow cones since the days that he and his father would go to the Puerto Rican Day parade in Manhattan and the July Fourth Parade in Staten Island. His dad would always buy both of them snow cones to mitigate the heat of the summer as they stood and watched the balloons, floats, horses, and other parts of both parades go by. Walker ripped the ad out of the magazine and put it in his pants pocket. *If this place's syrups are as good as the endorsements in the ad say they are, that is something I'm going to try for sure.*

When it was safe to stand up, Walker put the magazine into the seat-back pocket in front of him and walked the few feet to the first-class bathroom, where he removed the battery from his burner phone and then dumped the phone in the trash bin, putting some paper towels over it.

TWO—BACK IN NEW YORK

"You want me to stay calm," Smokey raged, "when that bastard murdered my brother and had the nerve to show up at his funeral and kiss him in the coffin? I couldn't believe it when I saw it on the video. And then you three couldn't take him out? You blew a simple setup that my mother . . ." Smokey crossed himself, " . . . rest in peace, could have taken care of."

Al "Smokey" Challow, the owner of Club Bizzazz who, using a contact a friend had given him and an assumed name, Willy Franks, had hired Walker to purportedly take himself out, continued screaming at Jimmy, Jake, and Bobby. "And one of you idiots got shot and he got away? You want me to stay calm about that?"

As the three men shuffled their feet looking for something to say, Smokey reached into the humidor on his desk and pulled out one of the expensive Cuban cigars he was always smoking, hence his nickname. Just as the flame from his lighter lit the tip of the Cohiba Behike 52, the door to Smokey's office opened and Sammy and Lou walked in. Sammy stood next to the others while Lou went to the coffeepot and poured half a cup of lukewarm java into one of the off-white ceramic mugs sitting next to the carafe. Smokey exhaled a large puff of smoke and turned to the two newcomers. "You heard what happened? How these three mooks botched an easy job?"

Sammy responded somewhat sarcastically as he distanced himself from the others by a step or two. "We did, boss. That's what happens when you send amateurs to do a professional's job."

Lou added, while downing the coffee in one large gulp, "Sammy and I wouldn't have blown it. Hell, either one of us could've taken Walker out by ourselves."

Jimmy looked at Lou with fire in his eyes and anger in his voice. "That's easy for you to say. I never seen a man move as fast as he did when we started shootin'. He was movin' like a commando."

Lou walked across the room and got within six inches of Jimmy's face. "So tell me, mister genius, why wasn't one of you comin' at him from behind? Why were you all in front of the target? Don't you know anything about strategy?"

When Jimmy didn't reply, Sammy piped up. "Boss, let Lou and me go after Walker. We'll find him and do what these three schmucks couldn't do."

Lou added, "Guaranteed. In fact, I don't even need Sammy with me. I can do the job myself. Easy, peasy."

Smokey thought for a moment before responding, "You really think you can do it alone, Lou?"

Without any hesitation, Lou responded, "Of course I can. Smokey, I just got to town a few months ago after living on the coast my whole life. Walker doesn't know me and has never heard of me. That'll give me a decided advantage. He'll never see it coming when I get to him."

Smokey stood up from his desk chair and smiled for the first time that day. A sly, evil smile. "You got it, Lou. Make it happen. Whatever you need, just ask and it'll be there for you—money, transportation, cover, information. Just get the bastard and make sure he knows that I sent you." After a slight pause, Smokey addressed the others. "Get outta here and let me and Lou talk about things."

As the men started to walk to the door, Lou grabbed Jimmy's arm. "Is there anything else you can tell me that might help move things along faster?"

Jimmy stopped and thought for a moment before answering, "Yeah. We saw the cab he got into. I made sure to remember its number."

Smokey handed Jimmy a pen and a piece of scrap paper. "Write it down. At least you did *something* right today."

After Jimmy wrote the number down, he, Jake, Sammy, and Bobby left. When the door closed behind them, Smokey raised his right arm, waggled his finger at Lou, and harshly said, "I'm countin' on you." Then he lowered his arm and softened his tone. "My cousin in LA said you'd be a real asset to my drug business, but doin' this for me is a real bonus. I won't ever forget what you're doin' for me, Lou."

"My pleasure, Smokey," Lou replied. "Actually, I'm gonna enjoy it."

Smokey was a bit taken aback by that. "You are?"

"Yep," Lou responded. "I'll show the braggart who's really the best. It ain't *him* now that *I'm* here. I'd love to stay and chat some more, but I'd better get moving and find out where he is. One thing though, can you get me a picture of him, so I know exactly who I'm lookin' for?"

"I never seen a photo of Walker," Smokey replied, "but I'll have a still made from that funeral video. They got a shot of the bastard kissing my brother. I know a sketch artist who used to be with the cops who can draw you a real good likeness from it and what I remember him looking like. Walker's face is carved into my memory, so between the still and the sketch, you'll have what you want by tomorrow morning."

As Lou gave a thumbs-up and started to walk to the door, Smokey called out, pointing to the cigar, "Hey! You want one of these? Like you, they're the best."

Lou responded, "No thanks, I don't smoke. It's not good for your health. They're gonna kill you one day."

Before Lou closed the door, Smokey admonished, "You just kill Walker. I'll worry about what kills me."

THREE—ON THE PLANE

Walker was unable to sleep during the nearly thirteen-hour flight; he was too wound up and edgy from the events of the day. He had nothing to read, the millennial sitting next to him never took off his earbuds, and after watching one movie, Walker couldn't find any others he was interested in seeing, so he started thinking about his life and his job.

He revisited his childhood—how his parents ceremoniously named him Burton Ashley Walker, after both of his grandfathers, but everyone just called him Walker starting as far back as he could remember. After he got out of the Marines, there was no one who even knew what his given names were.

He capitalized on that and the privacy it brought—he was always paid in cash and didn't do anything online. He reveled in the knowledge that it was almost impossible to find someone when all you had was their last name and there was no internet presence for them—unless they wanted to be found.

In Walker's line of work, the only people he'd want to locate him were potential employers, and they all had the ability to contact him, and regularly did when they had an assignment—because everyone knew he was the best at what he did. No one else even came close. Everyone understood that.

Walker recalled what his mentor, fellow ex-Marine and hit man supreme, John Hanks, drilled into him: "When you're engaged to go after a target, observe what your quarry does—how they act, where they go, what they do. Learn their patterns and behaviors; that's the key thing." And Walker basked in the knowledge that most of his competitors, if anyone would even call them that, just went barging in, trying to eliminate the pest they were sent to eradicate; they often didn't succeed because they didn't prepare adequately, whereas Walker always got the job done. *That's why I get paid the biggest bucks.*

Walker was also proud that his successes earned him a nickname. On the streets he was called the Solution. He liked that, but he once told Hanks that if it were up to him to choose his own nickname, he'd prefer to be called the Last Kiss.

He had explained why to John a few months before Hanks had a stroke caused by his excessive drinking—which Walker fruitlessly had warned him to cut back—"A kiss is a beautiful thing. A way of people connecting. What's the first thing a mother does with her new baby? She kisses it as she holds it to her bosom and in her arms. And what does someone who loves you do? They kiss you. A kiss is a means of expressing love, or friendship, welcome, warmth, sexuality. Or, in my case, death. I know that if a kiss is the last thing in a person's life, they will die happier. Nothing can be more personal and beautiful to remember as you pass away."

As a result, when Walker killed his prey, he always kissed them. Most times they were still alive, and it was the last thing they remembered. But sometimes he had to wait until well after they were dead. He recalled the numerous times he went to a funeral home, pretended to be a friend of the deceased, and then planted a small one on their forehead in the open casket, or the occasions he went to a morgue to give a last kiss. It was so easy to do. *I'd just pick up a lab coat and wait until the coroner went on a break.*

As much as Walker hated the vermin he eliminated, the ones he called the dregs of society, he still tried to give each of them their last kiss, even though he often threw up after doing it.

Walker felt a tinge of sadness that he was thinking about murder and death in New York while sitting on a plane heading to the tropical paradise known as Maui, Hawaii.

FOUR—HELLO, MAUI

After the plane landed in Maui at the Kahului Airport, Walker was tempted to stop at one of the clothing shops that lined the arrivals concourse, but he wanted to get to the resort and establish his base there as fast as he could, so he loosened his tie, opened the top button of his shirt, and walked straight to the taxi area. He knew that cab drivers accepted cash, whereas Lyft and Uber used credit cards, so he got into one of the vacant taxis standing outside the arrivals terminal and told the driver to take him to South Kihei Road.

"Exactly where on South Kihei do you want to go?" the driver asked. "It's a long street."

Walker knew he didn't want to be traced to the resort, and when he remembered the ad for the snow cone stand, he told the cabbie, "Beach Street Shave Ice."

"The best on all the islands," the driver proudly proclaimed as he pulled away from the curb.

When they were leaving from the airport on the appropriately named Airport Road, Walker noticed a huge plume of gray smoke rising from the ground about what he estimated to be a mile away. "What's that?"

"This heat spell's made everything dry as tinder. That's one of the bigger brush fires burning here," the cabbie told him, then added, "They're working on containing it."

"Damn," Walker responded, "I thought they only had those in California and Oregon."

The cabbie momentarily turned around. "Nope, we get them here too. Not that often, but when it gets hot like this, we get 'em for sure."

"Damn," Walker reiterated, as the driver turned to look back at the road.

Thirty minutes later they reached the shave ice stand, and as soon as

Walker left the air-conditioning of the taxi, the oppressive heat engulfed him. *Glad I decided to get a snow cone. Man, this is too damned hot.*

Walker strode up to the service window of the Beach Street Maui Shave Ice, the self-proclaimed best shave ice stand in South Kihei, and scanned the board that listed the myriad of flavors and combinations. As he stood there, Walker swore under his breath, "There are too damn many choices. Why can't they make it simple, like in New York—just red, blue, or yellow syrup. I don't have all day to decide." Then he chose coconut mango.

The three bronzed, bikini-clad young women sitting together at one of the stand's three outdoor tables watched Walker place his order and pay for it. One of the girls giggled and whispered to the others as they all leaned in to keep their comments from being heard past the table. "He sure looks out of place, doesn't he?"

Walker overheard what she was saying despite her desire to keep it private, and assumed she was referring to his yellow silk tie and tailored dark-gray pinstripe suit which was causing sweat to profusely stream down his pale face in the ninety-plus heat and humidity of that unusually warm October afternoon.

One of the girlfriends added, "It looks like he hasn't shaved in a couple of days," and then the third girl observed, "But I'll bet he cleans up good for an old guy. How tall do you think he is? Six one? Six two?"

Walker was, in reality, six foot, three inches. He worked out with a trainer regularly, so as the teenager properly observed, he was in good shape. In fact, he was in superb shape.

The third girl called over to Walker, "Hey, you. Mister. You just get here? You okay?"

Walker ignored the questions and didn't respond while he began to eat his shave ice and slowly walk toward the street.

She asked again but in a much louder voice. "Hello. You. Silent guy in the fancy suit. You unfriendly?"

Walker stopped moving and pivoted to face the three girls whose gazes were instantly mesmerized by his ice-cold steely-blue eyes. He wanted to tell them that they should be afraid of him and to forget they ever saw him, but instead, he said, "Nah. Not completely unfriendly. Just tired after the trip from the mainland. What're you, locals?"

The first girl proudly announced, "We're seniors at Kihei Charter."

The second girl added, "And cheerleaders."

The third girl finished by bragging, "And we're the ones everybody wants to hang with."

Walker leaned in toward them. "You do look like a group of fine young women, but right now, I don't have time to socialize." He put his shave ice cup down on the table, took his tie off and neatly folded it in his suit pocket, and opened the second button of his shirt, exposing a bit of his muscular chest, which the three girls silently admired. Then he picked up his melting shave ice cup again. "It's a bit too hot to be standing out here with this suit on. And, unfortunately, you're a few decades too young for me. I'll see you around, though."

Walker turned and began walking away at a brisk pace down South Kihei Road toward the Surfland Beach Club, that last resort at the south end of Kihei Road. As he left, the first girl stood up, cupped her hands to her mouth, and shouted at him, "I'll bet my mom would like you."

Walker put the shave ice spoon straw in his mouth, transferred the cup to his left hand, raised his right arm, and gave her a wave without breaking stride or turning around.

By the time he reached Surfland, after a short ten-minute walk, there was no shave ice left. He had eaten most of it, and the heat had melted the rest, so he held the paper cup up to his mouth and drank down the remaining liquid before tossing it into a garbage can at the bottom of the knoll that the resort sat upon. Before walking up the path to the resort's office, he stood next to the trash barrel for a moment, sizing up what he'd see when he was in one of the front units looking down on the street.

"Not bad," Walker confirmed to himself, assessing that any of the front units at the top of the hill, one of which he had booked, would have a clear view of anyone down below on the street or sidewalk.

Satisfied he wouldn't be taken by surprise, Walker looked around to make sure no one was following him and then walked up the path to the office. He checked in as B. A. Cashman, paid for two weeks in hundreds, got the key to his unit, and was told which parking spot—that he didn't plan to use—was his. When the slightly overweight, sunburned, forty-something woman, whose one-piece bathing suit was evident under her flower-patterned shift, finished registering him, she commented that not many people paid in cash, told him his unit would be cleaned in two days when the housekeeping crew came, and then handed him a book-let that proclaimed on the cover, "The Best Maui Maps."

Walker took the pamphlet and started to leave, but he stopped and turned back to the woman. "What's the best place to get some clothes around here?"

She smiled. "Mr. Cashman, there's a map somewhere in the middle of that booklet I gave you that shows all the businesses along South Kihei Road. There're lots of tourist and clothing shops that mostly sell the same stuff quite near here."

Walker thanked her and briskly walked to his second-floor unit, sweating profusely even though it was a short distance. When he got inside, he checked the locks on the doors and windows to make sure they couldn't be opened from the outside, and then, from habit, made certain none of the rooms were bugged. When he finally looked around at the furnishings, he was very pleased that it was clean and modern, the kitchen was fully stocked, and, most importantly, it was air-conditioned and had a panoramic view of the sidewalk, the street, the beach, and the ocean; especially from the lanai just outside the sliding glass door and picture windows that looked out at the pictur-esque vista and down on the entrance to the resort. The perfect "crow's nest," as he thought of it.

FIVE—MAUI, LATER THAT DAY

Figuring that it would take at least a day or two for anyone to find him and then make their way to Hawaii, Walker felt less of an immediate sense of urgency and started to unwind. He stripped down to his creased shirt and slacks, put on his shoes, leaving off his smelly socks, and ventured out to buy new clothes. Passing by the shave ice stand, he was pleased that the three young women were no longer there, so he wouldn't have to engage with them again. After going into stores in the two closest strip shopping centers, he realized that the woman at Surfland was right—theyall carried basically the same merchandise, so at the last one, he bought some lightweight shorts and shirts, a bathing suit, sneakers and flip-flops, and a yellow cap with an embroidered pineapple on the green brim, which he put on to keep the sun out of his eyes. A little farther up the road, he was able to get toiletries, sunglasses, a bag of Maui Kettle Chips, a pair of binoculars, and a prepaid burner phone.

Walker decided to walk back to Surfland on the sand of the beach, on the other side of the road from the shops, so he put his shoes into one of the three shopping bags and donned the flip-flops. He passed a number of condo buildings on his walk along the Pacific under the still-hot sun, and by the time he reached the public beach that was across the road from Surfland, sweat was once again drenching his face and body, so he sat down on one of the semi-unoccupied benches on the end that was shaded by the leaves of a coconut palm tree.

A grizzled older man with a stubbly beard, who Walker estimated to be in his late seventies or eighties, was sitting on the far end of the bench, bathed in sunshine, with his bright-red floral Hawaiian shirt unbuttoned and opened wide, his deeply tanned bare chest soaking in the blistering sun.

"Hey, man," Walker addressed the guy. "Why're you sitting there? Isn't that much sun bad for you? And it's so damn hot, how do you stand it?"

The man pointed at the tree above Walker. "Don't want one of those coconuts falling on my head. That'll kill you faster than the sun." Then he paused and kiddingly said, "Nice cap. Nice pineapple, tourist."

Walker smiled, gave a slight unconscious tug on the brim of the hat, and looked up at the tree above where he was sitting. It was indeed loaded with coconuts. "Never thought of that. Happen often? One of them falling on someone?"

"Nah," the guy replied, "but I don't wanna take a chance. Hell, I'm gonna die anyway, better from the sun than a split-open head."

"We're all gonna die someday, what's it really matter how? When you're dead you don't really care how you died," Walker countered.

The man turned away from Walker and stared at the ocean. "It matters to me. I'm dying now, son. I got terminal cancer."

Walker looked at the man before responding. "You've got cancer and you're sitting there soaking in the rays so you can get more cancer? That makes no sense to me."

The man turned back to face Walker. "Listen, son, I'm from Chi-town. I lost my job—too old they said—and then I ran out of money and became homeless. Couldn't imagine that happening to me, not after all the years I put in working. Came out here ten years ago. Figured it was better to be homeless warm than homeless cold. Been living in an abandoned, rusted-out VW bus and on the beach. That's no life I care about. The only things I *do* care about are my daughter and grandson back in Chicago. I regret not being able to help them out. Financially. Other than that, there's nothing for me to live for anyway. So, what the hell do I care how I die, or when?" He paused. "Except, I don't want no coconut splitting open my skull."

Walker, who was hardened by the deaths of many men, felt a strange sense of sadness for this man. "What's your name? If you don't mind my asking."

"'Course not. It's Fred," was the reply. "Fred Harding. What's yours?"

As he was about to reply, an idea popped into Walker's head, and he said, "Fred, what if I could help your daughter and grandson out?"

"That would be wonderful," Fred replied, "but why would you do that? We just met. You don't know me. You don't owe me anything. You some crazy do-gooder? Or maybe, a total bullshit artist?"

"No, I'm neither," Walker answered. "I've got a little, uh, situation going on. I got some people who're gonna be looking for me, and I don't particularly want to be found by them."

"Bill collectors?" Fred asked.

"Yeah, collectors of a sort," Walker replied, thinking, but not saying, it was more like body collectors. "What if I sent a lot of money to your daughter in return for you giving me your ID. I could become you and you could become me for a while. You got any ID?"

Fred perked up and replied somewhat sarcastically, "Of course I have ID. I may be homeless, but I'm still a person." He paused before continuing. "How much we talking about?"

"How much do you want?" Walker asked.

Fred cocked his head and then scratched it before responding. "Probably more than you'd spend."

"Try me," Walker said.

Fred moved closer to Walker and stared directly at his face. "I can always tell if a man's lying to me by looking into his eyes, and you look like you're not. Tell you what, I'm gonna speak to my daughter tonight, and if you meet me here on this same bench at ten tomorrow morning, I'll tell you what it's gonna take."

Walker smiled. "I'll be here. Make sure you're here too."

"Oh, I will be," Fred replied. "At this point, I'd do anything for my kid. Don't need anything for myself, too late for that. And I don't really care what happens to me, so see you tomorrow. What's your name, by the way?"

"Walker."

"Is that your first name or last?"

Walker nodded. "You'll find out tomorrow."

Fred rose from the bench as he said, "Fair enough, Walker," and started sauntering down the beach in the direction Walker had come from, his open shirt flapping with each step.

Walker watched Fred walking away for a moment and then turned to gaze into the ocean before rising and heading to his condo with his shopping bags to take a short nap.

He fell asleep on one of the chaise chairs on the lanai, and when he awoke, he was hungry, so he walked a few blocks to Maui Fish Tacos, to try what the guidebook advertisement said were their award-winning mango salsa–topped tacos. While he was ravenously downing two unexpectedly tasty, non-Mexican style tacos, Walker thought about how he was going to get a gun. He figured that if he could find a bar that had gambling going on, he'd probably meet some locals he could purchase one from. So, after he finished the tacos, he went back to the cashier and asked the pimply-faced teenager at the register, "What's the best bar around here? Someplace I can get some action tonight? Do you have any idea?"

While the kid was shrugging his shoulders, an older apron-wearing man walked up from behind him and motioned Walker to meet him at the side of the counter. "The kid's an innocent," he reported. "What kind of action are you looking for?"

Walker replied, "Gambling mostly. Where does the lowlife hang out around here?"

The man looked Walker up and down. "You're not a cop, are you?"

Walker smiled and replied, "I am definitely *not* a cop."

The man nodded like he understood Walker's implication. "You got dough?"

"Sure do. Plenty. But I don't want any high-class action, I want down and gritty. That's my scene."

The man took out an order pad and wrote on it, ripped out the sheet he had written on, and handed it to Walker. "That's the place you want to be. Tell them Phil Kahale sent you. The action starts around midnight."

Fortunately, the bar was an easy mile walk from Surfland, and when Walker arrived at twelve fifteen, Phil's name got him into the backroom that had three mostly filled poker tables. Walker looked around and surmised most of the men were locals, from their complexions and clothing. He sat down at one of the empty chairs, pulled out part of his roll, and said, "Mind if I join?"

Walker played for over four hours, and while bantering with the other players he learned who the "baddest ass" in the room was. When the badass guy got up to take a break, Walker followed him into the bathroom and, lying that he was one of Phil's friends, worked out getting a piece when the night's festivities were over.

At six the next morning, Walker was walking back to Surfland, the new owner of a .22 revolver that had no markings, and a box of ammunition. He would have preferred a longer-range magnum, but he took what he could get. He felt much safer having a way to defend himself.

SIX—THAT MORNING

Walker took a short three-hour nap, then showered and dressed, made a pot of coffee, and called John Hank's son, who answered on the second ring.

"Junior, this is Walker."

"Hey, man," Junior replied. "How ya doin'?"

"Forget the pleasantries. Anyone been asking about me?"

Junior said, "Actually, yeah. First off, I got a call from a broad yesterday afternoon. She said she'd been trying to get you on your phone, but there was no answer. She said she knew you and my old man were tight and maybe I'd know where you were."

"She say what she wanted?" Walker asked.

"Yeah. Said her boss wanted to hire you. Want her number?"

"Nah, hold on to it for me. You said that was first, what's second?"

Junior paused a moment before responding. "Not exactly sure how to put this, Walker, but the word on the street is that someone wants you dead. Something about your killing his brother and then disgracing him at the funeral. Some tough guy was shooting off his drunken mouth last night at Sammy's bar and one of my pals happened to be there. He called me right away. The guy said they're trying to find you and they're sending somebody really good to off you. Someone from the coast, named Lou. Be careful."

Walker thought for a moment before replying to Junior, "I will be. Thanks for the info. Listen, forget this call. If anyone asks, tell them you haven't spoken to me, but you've heard I'm on a job upstate. Will do you do that for me?"

"Of course I will, Walker. You've always been good to me, and my old man vouched for you. And he didn't do that for many people."

Before ending the call, Walker said, "Thanks, Junior. I'll call you in a day or two to see if you hear anything else, but if you hear anything before then, call me on this number. It's a burner that I'll keep for another few days."

Junior said, "Sure will. Bye."

When the line went dead, Walker took his coffee cup out to the lanai, sat on one of the lounge chairs, looked across at the ocean and then down at the street, and smiled, thinking no one was going to take him by surprise from his vantage point.

At almost that same moment back in New York, Smokey, hoping Lou was as good as his cousin claimed, picked up his phone on the second ring. "I expected to hear from you sooner than this, Lou. I got that sketch for ya. You got anything yet?"

Lou replied, "I'm good, Smokey, but I ain't the damn Flash. No, I don't have anything yet, but I'm heading your way now to get that picture. I'm right around the corner. See you shortly."

When the phone went dead, Smokey looked at Walker's face in the drawing and muttered, "You're gonna get yours soon, dipshit."

Five minutes later, when Lou walked into his office, Smokey handed over the sketch and the somewhat blurry still from the video and said, "Use the drawing. It looks way more like the bastard than the photo. What's your next step? You got a plan?"

"Of course I do," Lou replied. "I've always got a plan. That's why I never fail, Smokey. I've already got my people working on finding the cab driver that picked Walker up, and when I learn where he went, I'm gonna go there and use this picture to see who recognizes him. Depending on what information I get, I'll track him to wherever he is now."

Smokey growled, "Well, I know where he *isn't*. I sent my guys to his place, and he wasn't there. Wasn't at his gym, wasn't anywhere he usually goes. So, he musta skipped town or he's hanging with a friend we don't know about."

Lou quickly responded, "I think he went someplace else. I asked a few questions and checked around a bit, and no one's heard from him or knows where he is."

Smokey lit up a cigar. "Find him, Lou, no matter where he is. Find him, and kill him."

Lou smiled. "Count on it."

Smokey blew a smoke ring. "I am."

SEVEN—LATER THAT MORNING

When Walker arrived at the bench, Fred Harding was already sitting there, shirt open, with the sun beating down on his chest. Fred looked up as Walker sat down under the shade of the tree. "Don't go telling me not to sit in the sun again, pineapple-hat man."

Walker smiled. "I won't. You come up with a number?"

Fred reached into the pocket of his shirt, took out a small piece of paper, and handed it to Walker. "It's on there, but you ain't gonna like it."

Walker looked at what was written and shrugged. "It's a lot for one temporary ID, but I got more money than I'm gonna spend in this lifetime, so yeah, you got a deal."

Fred's look of surprise told Walker that he hadn't been expecting the deal to go through, so Walker asked, "You got the ID? And where I send the money?"

Fred said, "Just like that?"

"Just like that," Walker responded.

Fred asked, "So how do we do this?"

Walker told him they'd go to a bank where he'd make a wire transfer to Fred's daughter and then he and Fred would trade IDs.

Fred said, "Let's go," and they walked together to the nearest bank, where Walker made the transfer to Fred's daughter.

When they left the bank, they traded their driver's licenses and then Walker peeled ten hundred-dollar bills from his roll and handed them to Fred. "For you. Have some fun as me."

Fred stared at the bills. "You sure?"

"Absolutely," Walker said.

Fred pocketed the bills and Walker's ID. "Thanks, son. You're okay. I'm gonna enjoy being someone else for a while. It's no fun being me, and like you, I'm just gonna go by Walker."

As Fred started to cross the street, Walker called after him, "Be careful, Fred. They'll be coming for me. Or maybe now, you."

Fred stopped for a moment. "Ain't afraid of no collectors. They can't kill me any more than this cancer is already doing," and then he headed to the beach.

Walker watched him go until he was lost from sight. *Actually, I hope you flash that money and let people know you're Walker. Maybe they'll kill the wrong guy.*

A few hours later, Lou called Smokey. "I found the cabbie and talked with him. He took Walker to United at Newark Airport. Fortunately, one of my friends is married to a United flight attendant, and she was able to check their records. Walker went to Maui. That's where I'm heading. See you in a few days."

Smokey considered Lou's intel and responded, "I been there once. Maui's a big place, how're ya gonna find him? You don't know which part of the island he went to."

Lou answered quickly, "I'll show his picture to the taxi drivers and the car rental places, or maybe I'll hear something. Plus, I got another avenue I'm chasing down."

Smokey was intrigued. "What's that?"

"One of my former business associates in LA, a guy who calls himself the Piranha, thought about opening a club on Maui a few years ago. Even though he never did, when he went there to check it out he made some good contacts he's stayed in touch with. He's giving one of the guys a call and asking him to let him know if he hears anything about

Walker. He'll call me if he does. Don't you worry, Smokey, one way or the other, I'll find him."

Before hanging up, Smokey said, "Sounds good."

Lou responded, "See ya soon. I'll text you a photo when it's done."

EIGHT—THE NEXT DAY

When Lou landed at Kahului Airport the next day, there was a voice message from the Piranha saying he had information about Walker. Lou called him back and then phoned Smokey. "We got lucky. One of the Piranha's contacts on Maui told him that Walker was hanging at a bar last night spreading some serious C-notes. Also said he's seen him before but never knew his name. Usually wears a red Hawaiian shirt and spends part of his day on a bench at the last beach in South Kihei, looking at the ocean and soaking up rays. That should narrow it down a lot. Make it easy for me to find him."

Smokey was impressed. "Good goin', Lou. You know I'm countin' on you, and it feels like you're gonna come through for me."

"No doubt about it," Lou replied before ending the call.

Lou got into a taxi and told the driver, "Take me to the last beach in South Kihei."

During the drive, Lou rummaged through the mostly empty backpack and, seeing the dark-blue gun inside of it, was reminded about how easy it was to get the small plastic weapon an associate had made with a 3D printer, and its silencer and bullets, past TSA at the airport—and how good it was going to feel to take out Walker. Lou put on the Los Angeles Dodgers cap that was also in the backpack, so the sun wouldn't be a problem when the taxi reached the beach.

The cabbie pulled into the public parking lot of the shave ice stand. "This is as close as I can drop you to the beach. It's just on the other side of the road next to that condo building. I'd suggest you change into a bathing suit if you're going there, though. Hard to enjoy it in what you're wearing. Can't go swimming in that outfit."

Lou thanked the driver for his advice, paid him, exited the cab, donned the backpack, and looked around at the surroundings. Seeing not many people in the area except three young women sitting at one of the tables at the stand, Lou approached them and said, "I'm looking for a guy."

One of the girls looked up and said sarcastically, "Aren't we all?"

Lou replied, "Not like that, sweetheart. I got a picture of him. Mind looking at it and telling me if you've ever seen him around here?"

The second girl replied, "Sure. Why not."

The third girl asked, "Buy us some shave ice if we look?"

Lou opened the backpack and pulled out the sketch of Walker. "Sure. Seen him?"

The girls looked at the drawing and said, almost in unison, "Yes."

Lou was taken by surprise by their instantaneous recognition of Walker. "You sure?"

Two of the girls nodded while the third girl said, "We won't forget *that* guy. Bluer eyes than I've ever seen before."

"Where'd you see him?" Lou asked.

"Right here," was the answer from girl number one, "and then he walked that way." She pointed down South Kihei Road.

Lou smiled. "Well, thank you, ladies, you've helped me immensely."

Girl number two piped up. "So how about buying us some shave ice since we've been so helpful."

"Gladly," Lou responded.

After purchasing three large shave ice cups with their syrup choices, Lou thanked the girls again and started walking down the road. Remembering what the Piranha had said about Walker hanging out at the beach, Lou decided to check out that area first, crossed the street, and went looking for someone sitting on a bench wearing a red Hawaiian shirt.

At the same time that Lou was walking to the beach, Walker was calling Junior. "Hey, Walker, didn't expect to hear from you so soon."

Walker, sitting on the lanai with the binoculars on the chaise next to him, quickly took a drink of the iced coffee he'd made. "Sorry, Junior, but I had to take a sip of something cold. It's so damn hot here. Anyway, I was just wondering if that guy who was blabbing at the bar gave any kind of description of who was coming for me."

There was silence on the line as Junior attempted to recall everything his friend had said, "I'm thinking . . . Nope. He just mentioned the name Lou. That's all."

"Thanks," Walker replied. "Just checking. Speak to you soon," and then he ended the call.

Lou stopped halfway between the street and the beach, crouched down, reached into the backpack, loaded the plastic gun, and screwed the silencer on. Once that was done, Lou stood up and surveyed all the benches that lined the path along the beach. Some were empty, a few had younger couples sitting on them, and one had three kids noisily jostling and shoving each other for dibs on who'd sit next to the woman who appeared to be their mother. Lou thought, *If I had kids like that, I'd shoot 'em.*

And there on one bench, sitting on the sunny end away from the shade of the coconut tree that covered the other side, was an older man in a red Hawaiian shirt.

Lou slowly and quietly walked toward that bench, holding the backpack in one hand and fingering the gun inside of it with the other.

Lou got right behind the man, took the gun out, and whispered, "Walker?"

At first, there was no response.

Fred was not used to being called Walker, so it took a moment for the name to sink in.

Then, as he started to turn toward the voice, he said, "Yeah."

That word was the last thing Fred Harding ever said.

When the bullet entered the rear of Fred's head, he instantaneously slumped forward, but Lou pulled his body back and leaned him against the bench, which was starting to be covered in blood.

Lou reached into the backpack, pulled out a wad of tissues, took off the Dodgers cap, packed the tissues into the back of the cap like a lining, and then put the cap on Fred's head to stem the blood flow, and so it would look like he was sunning himself or napping. Then Lou put the gun back into the backpack and walked to the front of the bench. It was then that Lou realized that the man was not *the* Walker. Lou reached into the man's shirt pocket and pulled out the driver's license, which had Walker's name and picture on it.

"Shit," Lou cursed, "they musta traded IDs. Sorry, pops."

Lou put the ID back, looked around to see if anyone was gazing in their direction, made sure the pseudo-Walker looked like he was relaxing or dozing, and quickly walked away from the bench, toward the street.

Once across the road, Lou walked a little farther south, and then stopped to call Smokey. "I'm sure I'm pretty close to Walker. Some girls I showed his picture to recognized him and pointed out where they saw him going. I thought I had him, but he switched identities with some guy, unluckily for him. I'm on my way to check out the two resorts near here. I know he must be in one of them. There's nowhere else he could be staying down here. These are the last resorts on this road."

Smokey blew a smoke ring that Lou couldn't see over the phone. "Don't leave a trail of dead bodies, Lou. Just get Walker. I don't have a beef with anyone else. Okay? Be sure next time."

Lou cringed a bit at being chastised. "Sure, Smokey. Just one more dead body. Walker's. I'll call you when it's done."

Smokey disconnected the call without responding.

Lou walked up to the office of the Aloha Lani Resort and took out the counterfeit US Marshal identification card and badge, forged years ago by another associate, which Lou always carried for just this kind of a situation. Lou showed it and the drawing of Walker to the woman at the front desk. "This man is wanted in New York. Do you recognize him? Is he staying here?"

The manager studied the drawing. "I'd be happy to help you if I could, Marshal, but I've never seen this guy. Try next door at Surfland. Maybe he's there."

Lou thanked the woman for her time and then walked down the

path that went from the office to the road, where Lou turned left and walked toward Surfland.

Walker was sitting on his lanai, drinking his third cup of iced coffee and watching the street and the beach through the binoculars. He mostly saw families wearing bathing suits with towels slung over their shoulders or tied around their waists, older couples in walking shorts, a cleaning-service truck that drove up the hill to Surfland, a few teens with surfboards, and some obvious locals. He smiled when he saw Fred in his red shirt lounging on the bench through the field glasses. *Good for him*, Walker thought, *he used some of the money to buy a cap to keep the sun off his head.*

Before he went in to refill the coffee cup, Walker noticed a very attractive woman with blond hair that went halfway down her back, wearing a miniskirt, probably in her late thirties or early forties, stop at the same trash can at the bottom of the Surfland hill in which he had disposed of his shave ice cup. *Darling, another time and place I'd find out who you are. You look like one fine lady, and I'm not seeing a ring on your finger. But now is not the time.*

Walker followed her with the binoculars as she walked up the path toward Surfland's office and said aloud to himself, "Well, well. If you're staying here, maybe when this is over, we *can* connect." However, just before she was lost to sight, he realized that she had no luggage, just one of those minibackpacks that he knew were so popular with girls and women, and so he speculated that she was probably a salesperson trying to get Surfland to take a product or service they really didn't need— trading on her looks to at least "get in the door."

Walker then went back into the apartment to relieve himself, missing out on seeing anyone else entering Surfland over the ensuing five minutes.

Lou walked up the path to Surfland's office, huffing a bit from the somewhat vertical walk. The man behind the desk looked up from his computer. "Aloha, can I help you?"

"I'm looking for someone. I wonder if I showed you his picture if you could tell me if he's staying here."

The man replied, "We value our guests' privacy, so I'm not sure I'd be agreeable to that."

Lou took out the fake identification and showed it to the man. "I understand, but this man is a wanted fugitive who I'm trying to apprehend." Continuing the lie, Lou added, "He might be alone, or he might be part of a couple. No matter which, I've tracked him to Maui from New York, where he's Wanted."

"What'd he do?" the man asked. "Is he dangerous?"

Lou, not wanting to alarm the man so much that he might call the local police, leaned in and said softly, "Drugs. The hard stuff. Heroin. He's a major kingpin in a syndicate. Not dangerous, but a drug lord."

The man thought for a moment. "All right, show me his picture."

Lou took the drawing out of the backpack and handed it to the man, who looked at it and quickly said, "Not anyone I've ever seen."

Lou, expecting this to be where Walker was staying, said, "Are you sure? Totally, certain?"

The man said, "Yeah. I've never laid eyes on this man."

"That's surprising," Lou responded. "I *really* thought he was here."

Suddenly, the man looked like a light bulb had turned on over his head. "Now, wait a minute. He could have checked in with my wife. She's in the back room. I'll show it to her."

Both the husband and the wife came out less than a minute later. The wife held up the drawing and then told Lou, "That's Mr. Cashman. I checked him in a couple of days ago. He was alone and he seemed nice. Is he really a drug dealer?"

Lou confirmed, "He is."

The woman asked, "You told my husband he could be with someone else. Do you really think he is?"

Lou answered, "Very possibly. Do you keep an eye on his unit day and night?"

The man responded, "No, we don't. In fact, except when our cleaning crew comes in once a week, we wouldn't have any idea how many people were actually staying in a unit."

"So," Lou countered, "he could have someone in the condo with him and you wouldn't know. Can you tell me which unit he's in?"

The manager pointed to the building at the front of the property. "The Pikake. 2F. That's the front unit on the second floor. It's that place there." Then he asked, "How're you going to confront him? Just knock on the door?"

The wife wondered, "What if he doesn't let you in?"

Before Lou could answer, the husband suggested, "We could give you a Surfland Staff shirt and you could say you work here. Pretend you're one of our room-cleaning crew. They're on-site today."

Lou smiled, thinking how easy it would be to get into Walker's room using that cover. "Sure. That sounds great."

The wife went to the back room, came out with a shirt, a mop, and a bucket, and handed them and the drawing to Lou. "These'll make you look official. Good luck."

As the husband walked back to the computer, he asked, "Can you let us know what happens?"

Lou responded, "Believe me, you'll know what happens." Then Lou turned and headed to the Pikake building carrying the cleaning implements.

Walker was sitting on the rattan couch in the living room of the condo watching a *Family Feud* rerun when he heard a somewhat faint knock on the front door to the unit. Not expecting anyone, and taking no chances, he turned off the television, went into the bedroom, took the gun out of the dresser drawer, and made sure it was loaded. Then he tucked it in the waistband of his shorts at the small of his back.

He walked to the door, and standing to the side of it in case anyone tried to shoot through the door, asked, "Who is it?"

A woman's voice answered, "Cleaner. Today's the day we clean the units."

Walker softly walked closer to the door to make sure he wasn't heard moving about and looked through the fisheye peephole in the door. He was able to see an attractive blond woman standing a foot in front of the door in a Surfland shirt that said Staff across the front, holding a mop and a bucket.

Walker looked around the apartment and said, "Honey, I just checked in two days ago. This place doesn't need cleaning. I would have put it out if there was one, but there's no Do Not Disturb hanger for the door. Can we hold it off until next week?"

The woman replied, "Sorry, but we have to clean the units every seven days. It's a rule, no matter how long anyone has been here, we have to clean every week. We can't adjust the schedule every time someone moves in or out. We'd be here every day if we did that."

Walker really didn't want to let her in, but what she said rang true, and she did look very alluring even through the peephole. Before letting her enter, he touched the gun to make sure it was there, and then he unlocked the door and held it open a crack.

Seeing her in person, Walker was surprised to see that she was the same woman he had seen, and admired, standing at the trash can a few minutes earlier, but with her hair pulled back he guessed with a scrunchie. He thought, *I wouldn't have taken her to be a cleaner—with her looks she could do a lot better than that—but I guess you never know.*

Walker said, "Okay, come in," and opened the door wider to allow her to enter.

Once she was inside, Walker asked her, "What's your name?"

"Louisa," she replied.

Walker said, "That's a name I haven't heard in a while. Kind of an old-fashioned name for a younger woman."

Louisa smiled. "My mother's favorite book was *Little Women*. She named me after . . ."

Before she could finish the sentence, Walker interrupted, "Louisa May Alcott—its author."

Louisa was impressed. "I didn't know if you'd know that or not. I don't think a lot of men have read that book. Especially not these days."

Then, looking Walker up and down, she said, "And you look more like a Ludlum kind of guy than a *Little Women* one."

Walker laughed. "I'll take that as a compliment. And let me return one to you—I saw you when you were walking up the hill and noticed how attractive you were, Louisa."

Louisa smiled. *I've got him relaxed. That's good. He's probably letting his guard down. Time to get this over with.*

Walker's mind wandered. *I wonder what she's like under that Staff shirt.*

Louisa reached into her bucket and at the same time she leaned over to give Walker a kiss on the cheek. "Thanks, what a nice thing for you to say about my looks." As she did that, Walker's mind stopped wandering and something clicked in his brain.

Louisa . . . Lou . . .

He moved back a step just as her lips brushed his moving face.

Walker reached behind his back and pulled out his gun at the same time that Louisa got hers out of the bucket.

Simultaneously, two shots rang out, one loudly and one muffled.

The bullet from one gun went into brain matter, which splattered onto the wall. The bullet from the other gun harmlessly went into the wall.

One of them fell dead on the floor, while the other bent down, gave the fallen one a kiss on the lips, and said, "I am the best. Make no mistake about it."

HOTEL CALIFORNIA

JENNIFER GRAESER DORNBUSH

On a dark desert highway during an arid day in late September, the Santa Ana winds chase Penelope Elizabetta del Fuego along California's PCH, both of them blazing a fevered passage to Los Angeles.

Windows open, the cool wind in her hair, the smell of Penelope's *colitas* rises up in the air as she takes a long exhale and eases into a hairpin turn. The ocean spreads before her, endless as the future she has lined up at 3462 Fountain Avenue, Apartment 4B. The smoke sucks out the window, along with any guilt she harbored about finally leaving her third-world existence to capitalize on the success she's built as a growing social media influencer.

Penelope ascends the side of the mountain which peaks onto a scenic overlook and cannot resist the lure of the view, if only because it is nearing magic hour. The most flattering time to be on camera.

She pulls over on the cliffside and parks the car. Phone in hand, Penelope bounces from the car and positions herself in the backdrop of the sun's buttery yumminess spreading over the surface of the ocean, the perfect set piece for Penelope's TikTok video.

Penelope checks her teeth in her camera's selfie mode and then applies a coat of MAC's Keepsakes coral lipstick before posing. She puckers and pouts at the lens, then breaks into a smile and blows her fans a kiss over the ocean. She adds a few filters, creates a boomerang effect, and uploads her video with a satisfied sigh.

At just age twenty years, three months, and six days, Penelope Elizabetta del Fuego has the social media world on the edge of their apps with the touch of her Essie gel-manicured fingertips.

Penelope hops back into her car for another toke of colitas. She can't help checking her post. Already over two hundred engagements. She loves the waterfall of adulation. She could live off one sip for days.

Penelope pulls back onto the unfamiliar road, taking it easy and slow. She has never driven this far from home. Never even been outside Santa Clara County.

Within the next two hours, the sky darkens to night and her headlight beams illuminate the narrow road as she concentrates on the white line in the middle. Penelope's excitable mind fogs over with the incoming marine layer to somber thoughts. The parting conversation with Mama had just been an extension of every conversation they had had in the past six months.

Evelia Rodriquez del Fuego had not said much all day as she'd watched her only child pack the last of her toiletries. When it was time to leave, Penelope had latched her arms around her mother's four-foot, eleven-inch frame. She'd taken her mother's hands, hands that had worked the San Jose soil for twenty years. Soil that had taken and taken and taken from Mama. And now one more thing, the most valuable thing, was being taken from these hands.

"Oh, Mija," said Mama, her eyelids swollen and red.

"I can't stay," Penelope told her. Mama nodded. Evelia had come to a reluctant understanding after they had done nothing but fight for the last six months. Mama didn't understand that Penelope's dream was not Mama's dream for her life.

"I had a nightmare you were drowning," said Mama.

"That's crazy, Mama. I'm a strong swimmer. I love to swim."

"Not in the water. Your hair. It was very long and blond and wound around your neck."

"It's a crazy dream." Penelope pulled a box from her purse and put it in her mother's hands. "I have something for you."

Mama stared at the turquoise-blue lid and white satin ribbon.

"Open it, Mama."

"I don't need this," said Mama.

"You deserve the best things. Por favor."

Mama tugged on the ribbon and caught it from falling to the dusty driveway. After opening the lid, Mama frowned at the eighteen-karat gold tennis bracelet. Penelope plucked it from the box and tried to clasp it on her mother's sticklike wrist.

"This isn't who we are," Mama said, pulling away. She shoved the box back into her daughter's bag.

Penelope reached for the box. "I promote it. I keep it. That's how it works, Mama. It's how I get paid."

Mama pursed her lips and looked away.

"I should have never put you in that pageant when you were four," said Mama.

"That one pageant is not to blame for what I want to do with my life."

Mama turned her dark-brown eyes on her daughter's trademark aquamarine ones, a gift from Penelope's Scandinavian absentee-father. Penelope was wrong. She left that pageant high on adoration from the audience and judges. An addiction Mama fed and fed before she understood just how poisoned Penelope had become.

"You had good grades in school. You can go to college. Become a nurse or teacher. A real job, Mija."

Penelope was about to bark back that social influencing was a real job when she stopped short. She was so sick and tired of getting into it. Mama wasn't on social media, and Penelope was careful about what posts she shared with her mother. Over the past year, racier images brought in more sponsorships and engagements. She understood since she was a child that her unique look was her currency, and she was sure it would buy her a spot in Hollywood.

"I'm going to get you a house with all the money I'm going to make," she told Mama, hoping she would see the positive side of her dream.

"I have a house, Mija."

That shackhole! The words regurgitated up her throat, and Mama saw her swallow them down. Penelope knew all would be forgiven the moment she marched Mama out of her rundown apartment and into a three-bedroom, three-bath house with a garage and pool. Mama's hands would never be cracked again. She would have people to clean for her. She could go to lunch with friends like rich people did. She could get her nails done and buy her meats from a butcher, not the Aldi.

"I have to go, Mama," said Penelope with the impatience of an energetic puppy straining on its leash.

"Wait, Mija." Hand passing over her face and chest in a reverent genuflect, Mama blessed Penelope Elizabetta del Fuego with the sign of the cross. "God bless you and keep you and cause his face to shine on you. May he keep you from evil and temptation and restore your soul. *Te amo*, Mija." As she hugged her daughter, Penelope slipped the jewelry box into her mother's apron pocket.

"Te amo, Mama."

Penelope had rushed to her car and hadn't looked back. If she had, she would have been forced to consume a helping of Mama's hurt.

Now, four hours later, Penelope's head grows heavy and her sight dim. She relies on Siri to guide her two more miles as she passes the city sign for a small coastal town where she will stop for the night. Penelope makes a turn off PCH onto a frontage road.

It would be nice to find a hotel. Nothing fancy. Maybe a place with a pool. She likes to unwind with late-night swims. Back in San Jose, on a dare, she and Henley snuck into one of those fancy gated communities in the middle of the night. The pool lights at night were absolutely unbeatable for stylized shots, and Henley had convinced her to slip off her top and pose underwater. A vintage filter, some light editing, and a well-timed post had caused Penelope's social media to explode. She topped 100K followers and a few more sponsorships followed. Flowing into this next phase of social media stardom felt natural. Almost as natural as breaking up with Henley after she found him cheating on her with the blond Rebecca Perkins, who lived in that fancy gated subdivision.

It didn't matter. Penelope was never planning to stick around San Jose anyhow. She had worked out her plan long before Henley broke her heart. Partner with a brand-name fashion designer and live off the residuals while pursuing roles in film and TV. Did she have an agent? No. A reel? No. Headshots? No. She had built her social media platform with adoring followers. Each one of them, star currency she could cash in on.

***

A mile and a half up the winding mountain road past Chateau Cambria lay a two-hundred-year-old mission church tended by a very good-looking fifty-eight-year-old mission priest, Asa, who once held a lucrative career as a runway model in Paris and New York in the early 1980s. At the tender age of twenty-four, four years after his first magazine cover, Asa found himself in a Belgian hospital, overdosed on cocaine and testing positive for HIV.

After receiving the devastating news, he spent six months wandering Europe's cathedrals, begging the Father, Son, and Holy Spirit for a miracle. When none came, he climbed to the top of the Duomo in Milan, ready to throw himself from the heights rather than reveal his scandalous infirmity to the world (and his mother).

Asa claims he was saved by an animated gargoyle that spoke to him from one of the spires, instructing him to give up his riches and go through the eye of the needle.

He ran down the steep, narrow steps of the Duomo di Milano, hailed a cab from the square, and went immediately to the clinic to be retested. The results came back after three painstaking days. HIV negative. And this healing he attributes as the Miracle of Milan. The very next day, he entered the seminary in Rome. But upon completion of his studies years later, knowing full well the stronghold temptation had on his soul to the niceties of the world, Asa beseeched the bishop to allow him to serve the Church in solitary service, penance for his youthful sins. His request was granted, and Asa was sent to the central coast of California to tend after a dying mission parish. The parish had been dead long before he arrived, and there was nothing left to resurrect. So Asa took meticulous care of the grounds and spent his hours praying for the souls of the lost and seeking.

Tonight, the mission bells strike eleven o'clock and Asa exits the rectory building into the arid heat as the Santa Anas pick up. He feels his skin tighten, the moisture sucked from it in the desert wind, as he trawls his way to the mission chapel along a dirt path. He is headed for his nightly adoration at the foot of the cross, which usually lasts well past midnight. Asa gazes up at the hotel, as he does every night, and sees that, again, every room is lit on every floor. The sounds of music and laughter spill across the valley, growing louder with each step to the chapel, rising through the air to make fun of his lonely pilgrimage. Although he has never entered the castle, he can clearly envision the festivities therein. Chateau Cambria is a constant reminder of his former life. And constant fodder for his prayer life.

". . . and lead me not into temptation but deliver me from evil. For thine is the kingdom, the power, and the glory. Amen." Asa clutches his rosary and completes the Lord's Prayer as he arrives at the threshold of the chapel, a place only he and the occasional wayward tourists have stepped through in all his years here. Mass is offered daily and twice on Sundays, but the mission has no registered parishioners.

Asa moves down the center aisle, stopping once he is in front of the altar. He lights the altar candle, and it creates enough light to see his rosary and the crucifix that hangs above him. He moves his fingers to the first bead of the rosary to pray a Hail Mary. The high stained-glass windows at the top of the clay chapel walls let in the faint notes of revelry. Roars of laughter and shouting become a constant menace to his reverent hour of prayer. So Asa speaks the prayers aloud, rolling back his eyes under his lids in concentration.

His torso sways to the rhythm of incantation as he strains to find a place of deep meditation.

A particular explosion of laughter causes Asa to stumble over "Glory be to the Father." He recognizes it as Sharon's. He loves when she comes to visit him because their time together is contagious with laughter. And for days afterward, his obliques ache.

Forgetting where he left off, Asa's eyes open and he decides to redirect his attention to the prayer book laying on the communion table. He rises, still clutching his rosary, and grabs the sides of it, holding it as if it might careen off the table and slam to the floor. With fervor, Asa begins to pray for the repose of the souls listed.

Norma Jeane.

Natalie.

Sharon.

Elizabeth.

Peg.

Tim.

Kate.

And the list goes on.

***

Penelope coasts into a two-stop-sign tourist town whose sidewalks have rolled up hours ago. Penelope tries to tell Siri to find a hotel, but there's absolutely no internet service along California's mountains.

Driving a few more blocks, she debates if she should just get back on the PCH and keep going, when up ahead in the distance she can see a shimmering light coming from a Spanish-style structure. Perhaps a hotel? Penelope begins a slow ascent up the side of the mountain and out of the marine layer.

The light is coming from the interior of an old Spanish mission, long ago forgotten except by school children who recreate the mission trail for their fourth-grade school projects.

Perhaps there is someone inside to show her the way to a hotel, and if nothing else, it'll give her a chance to stretch her legs and shake off the sleepiness.

Stepping into the back of the nave, Penelope hears a man's voice droning on in prayer in front of the cross, but the words are indecipherable. In the soft glow of a single overhead light, she recognizes the black priestly robe and is swept with a strange comfort. Out of respect, Penelope waits for the priest to complete his utterances before she steps forward to speak.

"Hello? Excuse me, Father, I don't mean to interrupt but I'm wondering if you can help me?"

He turns to her with an open look as if he's been expecting her all his life.

"Of course."

"I'm looking for a place to stay for the night?"

"How many in your party?" says Asa.

"Just me. I'm passing through."

He nods. "You're most welcome to stay here at the mission retreat house. Plenty of room. The accommodations are humble but reasonably priced. We ask only for a donation."

"I see," says Penelope. She doesn't remember seeing any other cars parked out front, and she did not relish the thought of being the only guest here. Church or not, there was safety in numbers.

"Where are you headed?" asks Asa.

"Los Angeles."

"To become a star," he confirms in a way that does not make her feel mocked or belittled, like when Mama or Henley says it.

"To become a bigger star," she corrects.

"Of course. I beg your pardon. And you are well on your way, Penelope Elizabetta del Fuego."

"How do you know my name?" *This is taking a creepy turn.*

"I follow you on TikTok," Asa replies.

"You . . . What? Why?" She laughs out loud at the aging priest.

"Priests have social media, too," he says with a grin.

"Do you follow many young women?" Was he some kind of sex-starved sicko?

Asa reads her expression and replies softly. "My charism is to pray for those who seek adoration in the public eye."

She didn't know what a charism was, but it didn't sound healthy. "I just need to find a place to crash for the night. Is there a hotel somewhere nearby?"

"Only one. Up the mountain. Chateau Cambria. Maybe you have heard of it?"

Penelope shakes her head.

"It's one of the most beautiful castles ever built in the United States. Built by shipping magnate Johnathan Beauford Carlisle IV in the 1920s, it is now a luxury hotel and little-known getaway spot for Hollywood's rich and famous."

Penelope perks up.

"Are there celebrities staying there now?"

"Always and forever," Asa says.

Penelope reasons that a place like this will be brimming with TikTok fodder. She's learned enough about being an entrepreneur that she can easily justify her stay as a business expense.

"Have you been?"

"No. But reliable sources fill me in."

"Are you not allowed to leave here or something?"

"Or something," he laughs. "It's better I am kept from temptation."

"What exactly goes on there?" says Penelope, her curiosity growing.

"The best of everything."

"That doesn't sound so bad."

"There is a very dark side to glamour and excess if you let it take you, Penelope. It is very easy to become Tiffany-twisted," says Asa, speaking with a well of experience and as an actual, former model for the Tiffany Company. "And very difficult to unravel from it. A good many never do. There go I, but for the grace of God."

She didn't know what that meant either. She was so over dealing with this crazy priest speaking in riddles.

"I have a room made up if you've decided to stay."

"I'm good. Thanks." And with that Penelope quickly darts back to her car.

***

Penelope weaves up the mountain road to the estate, and before she even arrives she senses the magnificence in it. As Penelope enters the iron gates and winds down the long drive to the castle, she gasps with delight as Chateau Cambria comes into view. She can't believe such a treasure exists in California. Like a set piece lifted from Baz Luhrmann's *Great Gatsby*.

What a lovely place. Such a lovely place.

In preparation for her own Hollywood career, Penelope has been studying up on Hollywood history. She has taken special interest in the dark stories about stars whose destinies had been ill-fated by untimely crashes, suicides, or murders.

She loves all things vintage and era because her followers are trending in that direction. They can't get enough.

Penelope pulls her aging car past dozens of luxury vehicles and the valet station to the guest parking spots. Once she's not getting paid in yoga pants, perfume, and purses, she'll buy a designer car. Something that would tempt a valet to drive away in it.

Grabbing her purse and overnight bag, Penelope takes the sidewalk path down a Spanish-style courtyard to the open-air entrance of Chateau Cambria. She stands aghast, drinking in the most opulent place she has ever experienced when a deep voice calls to her.

"Welcome to Chateau Cambria," says a handsome hotel clerk who looks more like a 1930s Clark Gable than a hotel servant. He's so era in his black tuxedo, patent leather shoes, and suede driving gloves.

"Are you checking in, Miss?"

"I hope so," Penelope says. "Do you have room?"

"Plenty of room any time of year. Your name, Miss?"

"Penelope Elizabetta del Fuego."

"That's a movie star name if I've ever heard one. I'm Denver.

Please call on me for whatever you desire during your stay. May I take your bag?"

Dapper Denver. His TikTok post was writing itself.

Denver draws her past a large seating area, and Penelope notices a spread of magazine covers, past and present, hung along the walls of the lobby. She recognizes every face and fantasizes that someday her famous image will be among them.

Penelope's gaze drifts to the aesthetic of the room. "I'm seeing like a million photo ops here." She stops to dig out her phone. "And Denver, you're just the most . . ."

"Era?"

"Exactly. Except for your skin. You don't look a day over twenty-five. How long have you worked here?"

"Since 1969."

"That can't be right. Your face is so fresh."

"An old family secret, Miss Del Fuego." He winks at her.

She pulls out her phone. "For my followers," says Penelope, who promotes several lines of skin care but doesn't actually use them. She prefers coconut oil because it smells like Mama.

Denver puts up his hand and shakes his head for her to stop recording. "Please respect the privacy of all our guests and staff here," he says. "No cameras."

"Do you have celebrities staying in the hotel tonight?"

"Yes. You can find them here any time of year."

Penelope reluctantly slips her phone into her bag. She'll play by the rules. For the moment.

"And if you must know, my secret skin-care routine is the same as yours." He smiles. "Coconut oil."

How did he know?

"May I show you to your room, Miss Del Fuego?" Denver lights a candelabra and guides her through the lobby and down a long corridor to a sweeping staircase. "A little history, if I may. Chateau Cambria is over one hundred years old. There are forty-two rooms, thirty-eight bathrooms, and thirty fireplaces. And no electricity."

"Oh. Wait. So, no internet service?" Penelope says.

"I'm afraid not," says Denver. "Our guests seek us out specifically for a chance to unplug from the world. I think you'll find it most refreshing."

Penelope finds it annoying, as she treks up the endless marble staircase. By the time she reaches the third floor, Penelope is completely winded. Despite being a sponsor for lululemon, Penelope does not like to work out. And she doesn't have to. Her body is perfectly proportionate, because last year when some of her followers started noting her curves were looking curvier, she quickly swapped Mama's lard-heavy cooking for vegan dishes.

They head down the marble corridor lined with suites. Gold-engraved nameplates adorn some of the suite doors. Norma Jeane. Natalie. Sharon. Elizabeth. Peg. Kate. Tim.

Denver stops and unlocks the door to her suite. Penelope actually squeals when she sees it.

What a lovely place. Such a lovely place.

Denver sets down her bag and leaves the room, closing the door behind him. Almost immediately, a breeze from the open window blows out the candles. Penelope fumbles around in the dark, searching the drawers for matches and thinking maybe era isn't as glamorous as it seems when a twinkle above catches her eye. She lifts her gaze and a second gasp escapes.

Transparent mirrors on the ceiling reflect the night sky in a thousand pinpoints of light. It's the most brilliant starry landscape Penelope has ever seen. As she is drawn into the wonderment, she kicks off her shoes and sinks into the biggest four-post king bed she has ever been in. The day of tears and tension melts away as she enjoys her starry, starry night. *A most fascinating feature.* She picks out a few landmarks in the Milky Way. Orion's Belt. The Big Dipper. The last time she was lying face up, looking at the stars, she and Henley had snuck off to the fields to smoke colitas and have sex. Henley never took her to his house, his bedroom. She had never met his family and only once a couple of his friends. When she asked him why, he told her he was going to name a star after her. A bright-blue one. Because of her aquamarine eyes. No. Henley said blue stars were the hottest and most energetic stars. Just like her. The hottest Mexican girl he knew.

Penelope instinctively reaches for her phone and snaps a photo of the night sky. When she goes to post it, a No Service message glows back at her. *Right.* Hollow frustration swells within, making her feel insignificant and alone. If she can't share it, what's the point?

But Penelope is not one to sit around and feel bad feelings. And she certainly is not going to let a place like this go unexplored. There are things to see, people to meet. But first, she will change into the most stunning thing she owns.

***

Penelope's heels click-clack down the first flight of marble stairs as she balances the brass candelabra in one hand while the other is on the rail to steady herself. Self-conscious about the noise her shoes are causing against the echoey walls, she slips them off and pads barefoot on the cool floor two more flights down. Landing on the garden level, she feels a pulse through the floor on the soles of her feet. Thump, thump, thump, thump. It's a steady beat. Like club music pumping from somewhere inside the hotel.

By light of the candelabra, Penelope can see no one. But her feet still feel the pulsation. Penelope takes a few cautious steps down the corridor and thinks she hears voices calling to her. Winding down another corridor, her ears pick up the faintest sound of music.

Penelope's feet do not question their direction, scurrying toward the throb of the beat until it resounds through the halls, luring her through the castle on a maze to the revelry that ends at a carved oak door, ten feet in height, with a placard reading 'Master's Chambers.'

The beat drives through her chest. Electronic club music. Intoxicating. The beat hollows out your soul, cleansing the negative and making you forget. Tonight, on the precipice of a new life, Penelope desires only to leave behind sleepy, hopeless San Jose and embrace whatever is behind those doors. She was born for this.

Pulling on the brass handle, she unleashes a sound explosion. Bass. Snares. Trumpets. Sax. A frenzied electronica synced to a light show strobing through an open-air ballroom. The Spanish-style courtyard houses a thirty-foot cascading water fountain, towering palms, and monstrous bougainvilleas planted all over the room, dusting the floor with their fuchsia flowers. Oh, how they all dance. Hundreds of them in that courtyard. Late summer's sweet sweat mingled with the tropics. Gardenias. Roses. Plumeria. So overpowering Penelope is certain they are being piped through the air ducts. *And wait! Electricity!* The candelabra was just a quaint gimmick to keep things era. Penelope quickly blows out the candles and steps inside.

The priest has grossly understated the enormity of what was going on here. The guest list alone! She has found them here, all right. Reality show celebrities. Talk-show personalities. Actors. Musicians. Movie stars. Models. Social media influencers. The rich. The famous.

The adored!

Penelope has stumbled on one of those hidden Hollywood parties she read about. Places where celebrities gather without the public or paparazzi. And to think she could have been sleeping in a monk's bunk at the mission.

On the balcony above, Penelope recognizes her favorite EDM DJ, Avicii, dressed like he just stepped out of a carnival parade in Rio, but looking like he just came from a street fight, with fresh jagged gashes on his wrists and under his chin. *But of course, it can't be the real Avicii.* She'd lit a candle for Tim in her bedroom when he'd died.

She turns back to the crowd and gulps in the social media meal. Enough clickbait here to feed her followers for weeks.

Behind the eye of her camera, she begins to pick out guests of note like a sharpshooter trained on each target. Her pointer finger rapid fires the shutter.

Click. Click. Click. Click. Click.

Click. Click. Click. Click. Click.
Click. Click. Click. Click. Click.

There are others here, too. The ones who created the famous. Men with crisp haircuts and manicured nails. The suits. She studies how they move among the crowd, trailing after the blonds. And oh, how the blonds dominate, tossing back long thick manes to tease. Penelope feels a twinge of envy. She knows the best Hollywood roles always go to blonds, but reassures herself that she only has to latch herself onto the right suit. If all goes well, she will avoid months, if not years, of studio apartments and soup. And if things don't go well, she will invite him up to her suite for a blue-star experience. Others have suffered more for much less. Her mother, for one. Penelope would do it for Mama's future as much as her own.

As Penelope's lens moves around the room, she notices a few anomalies that stir her curiosity. On the dance floor, a woman with a short, blond bob leftover from the 1920s, dances the Charleston in a navy chiffon day dress and white gloves. Penelope watches as the woman's entire body goes boneless to the floor, her limbs twisting at unnatural angles. In the next instant, the woman stacks herself up again. Her dance partner doesn't seem a bit fazed. *What a weird party trick.*

Near the bar, Penelope becomes captivated by a starlet with green eyes who stands tall and sleek in her black suede high-heeled shoes and a black '40s skirt, encircled by men grappling for her affection.

Penelope can't stop staring at how gorgeous and era she is. As the woman bends down to pick up a cocktail napkin that has floated to the floor, her skirt separates from her sheer blouse to expose a surgical scar circumventing the width of her waistline. *Strange.*

As Penelope struggles to reconcile these guests, Denver suddenly appears, planting himself in front of her. She lowers her phone to her side.

"Miss Del Fuego. I need you to erase those images, please."

"If you think these people will be upset because their picture is splashed all over the internet, I can assure you. They won't."

"My house. My rules."

Penelope sighs. "Fine, but answer me this. Why are some of these people dressed up like dead celebrities?"

"This is no costume party, Miss Del Fuego. Everyone here is a celebrity."

"Dead or alive?" says Penelope in disbelief.

"All are welcome." Denver points to a green-eyed starlet. "That is the actress Elizabeth Short. You probably know her as the Black Dahlia. She was found severed at the waist and her body left in two in a field in East LA."

"And they put Humpty Dumpty back together again?" Penelope jokes.

Denver smiles. "The young lady dancing the Charleston is less well known. That budding actress is Peg Entwistle—broke almost every bone in her body jumping off the Hollywood sign in 1932 to commit suicide."

"Is telling Hollywood ghost stories part of the whole Chateau Cambria experience?"

"They aren't ghosts. They're spirits."

"Spirits who spin records?" Penelope points to Avicii in the DJ box. "Come on. Tim killed himself with a glass shard from a wine bottle."

"And quite a bloodbath when it happened," says Denver. "Hence those nasty wounds."

"Are there others?" Penelope plays along.

"Yes. You will find them here. Some dance to remember. Some to forget," he says with a serious look. "Please understand, Miss Del Fuego, that I cannot have those images going out to the public."

Denver looms over her, waiting for her to delete the photos. Penelope meets his gaze with her own stubborn look. This is definitely the most bizarre rave she has ever, ever been to. And if she doesn't have the pictures, she can't prove anything. Strong-willed as the day is long, Penelope slides her phone back into her clutch and takes off into the throng, zigzagging through the grand ballroom until she is safely on the other side and through French doors leading onto a patio. Another run-in with Denver seems likely, so Penelope saves the images to a hidden back door location in her phone, knowing she will be able to download them later.

"You have such a lovely name, Penelope Elizabetta del Fuego," says a sultry female voice coming up to her. "But you should change it. How about Elizabeth Donovan? That's a solid stage name."

Penelope turns to see a glamorous woman approaching.

"Welcome. I'm Norma Jeane." She sticks out a hand to shake Penelope's.

"As in Marilyn Monroe?" says Penelope. She decides to play along with Denver's game.

"Yes, but here I prefer to use my birth name. I used to go by Jean Norman when I was modeling. How dull. Dull is the worst thing to be. Word of advice. Do yourself a favor and dye that gorgeous mane blond. Gentlemen prefer blonds."

A waiter passes by with a bottle of pink champagne on ice.

"Sir, excuse me," Norma Jeane calls to him. "Could you bring me my special wine, please?"

"Ma'am, you know Denver hasn't stocked that since 1969," he says, offering them two glasses. "Champagne?"

"Fine." Norma Jeane takes a glass.

"I could use some champagne courage to talk to one of these suits," says Penelope.

"Denver throws the most exclusive soirees in the world. You should have no trouble meeting just the right career handler. Here's to your future." Norma Jeane clinks the rim of Penelope's glass. Penelope tastes the sweet pop-pop over her tongue and down her throat.

Soon, she guzzles it down, not realizing how parched she is.

"Oh, look. The clouds finally lifted," says Norma Jeane, and Penelope raises her gaze to the same starry night she saw from her bedroom suite. "Is it not the most magnificent celestial view you've ever laid eyes on?"

"Stunning."

"He knows the number of stars and calls each one by name," Norma Jeane says.

"Is that from a poem?" says Penelope.

"Oh, just something I heard from the priest up at that mission."

"You know him?" asks Penelope.

"Father Asa? Oh yes. Quite well. I visit often."

"You do? Why?"

"He's a great listener. I always imagined that's what my dad would be like if I had known him."

"You picture your dad like a crusty old priest?"

"Asa's not crusty, doll. He's lived a fuller life than I ever will. He's been everywhere. Used to model in Europe."

"No? Really?"

Norma Jeane reassures her with a nod. "I love talking to Asa. I can unload all my regrets, and then he hugs me and tells me it's going to be okay."

"I'd give anything for the kind of silver-screen life you lived," says Penelope, starting to buy into the ruse.

"Oh, darling. Don't say that. The cost can be severe."

"You left behind a legend."

She wags her warning finger at Penelope. "I don't have a cent to my name, despite the fact that I made millions. I was never able to have children. As for love . . . Just strings of terrible relationships. What I wouldn't give for someone who truly, deeply loves me."

"Are you telling me that the queen of Hollywood was never really happy?" says Penelope.

Norma Jeane's face dims and she pours Penelope a second glass of champagne. "Drink up, buttercup. The night is young."

The second glass goes down faster than the first. Penelope's head starts to feel fuzzy and her inhibitions melt.

Penelope lifts her index finger to Norma Jeane's face to pluck off the fake mole and expose her silly ruse. But the mole is really glued on, forcing Penelope to pick at it from the top to see if she can loosen one edge.

"Stop," says Norma Jeane, swatting her away.

"It's real?"

"Of course it's real. I took a defect and made it a trademark. That's the secret to success right there, darling."

Penelope instinctively reaches for her phone and snaps a picture of the glamour queen.

"What are you doing?" barks Norma Jeane, snatching it from her and marching off.

"Hey!" Penelope takes a step to go after her when a stern grip jerks her back.

"You have more moxie than I first gave you credit for," says Denver.

"She stole my phone," says Penelope.

"I will never understand the strange addiction to that device. Acting as your own paparazzi. Creating your own stardom. I've seen a lot of narcissism in my time, but your generation has certainly elevated it to an awe-inspiring level."

Penelope never looked at it like that, and she takes it as a compliment.

"Miss Del Fuego, someone wants to meet you, and if this guest likes you, you won't need to work so hard at achieving adoration."

"Oh? Who is it?"

"Come with me," he says, and leads her to the upper level of the ballroom to private quarters, where the tone is subdued but sophisticated. He parades her through a room of lounging models and fashion designers when a guttural retching and gasping sound sends an alarm through the room. An African model jumps to the rescue of a woman Penelope recognizes as Kate Spade.

"Happens all the time. She'll be fine," Denver addresses Penelope's concerned look.

Penelope watches Kate sip the water, only to induce another round of choking.

"She never takes that scarf off. It's the one she hung herself with," says Denver, passing her a sad glance over his shoulder as he leads them to the far corner of the room where a velvet curtain partitions a small living room area. He pulls back the velvet to reveal the bleachiest blondest Donatella Versace, smoking on a chaise with her dog, Audrey, at her side. Denver commences the introduction, and the conversation runs its course quickly.

"When you arrive in Los Angeles, contact Marco, my media guy," says Donatella through eyelids drooping with faux lashes. "Then, you'll go to Drake for wardrobe, and finally, Julia on Melrose. She'll do your hair."

"Do what to my hair?"

"Bleach it out." She exhales a curl of smoke with the rest of her instructions. "We'll start you out with small accessories and see how things go."

"Handbags?"

"God, no. Socks. Please tell me you have cute feet. No. It doesn't matter. We can always swap in a foot model."

Penelope stands in awe before the greatest icon and inspiration in the fashion world. Penelope can hardly believe she's talking to *the* Donatella Versace. And she has to ask, "Why me?"

"I like your eyes," says Donatella, lifting her gaze to Penelope for the first time. She waves her cigarette at Penelope. "But that's not going to be enough. It's up to you to suffer for your dreams and show the world your worth."

Penelope is unable to find her voice, which makes Donatella impatient.

"Are you willing?" demands Donatella.

"I am," says Penelope with an unwavering tone.

"Good," says Donatella, satisfied. "That's all, you may go."

Penelope scurries behind Denver in complete shock.

"This is a dream, right?" she says to Denver when they get outside the suite.

"The best kind of dream. The one that comes true," he tells her, leading her down the staircase back to the main ballroom.

Penelope turns to Denver. "What is it about this place? Why do you want to keep it a secret? It's amazing."

"You do understand the gift you've been given here tonight, Miss."

"What do I do? How do I find those people she wants to me see?" asks Penelope.

"I'll contact you with the details," says Denver, skirting left to make room for a sopping wet brunette in white pedal pushers and a navy striped sailor top, puddling the floor everywhere she steps. She's a dead ringer for—

"Denver, can you please have extra towels sent to my room?" says the woman coming up the staircase.

"Right away, Miss Wood," replies Denver.

Penelope stares in recognition. "Natalie Wood?"

"Poor dear, she'll never dry up, no matter how many towels I bring to the room," sighs Denver.

Penelope knows her tragic backstory. Mysterious death at sea. Rumored to have been thrown overboard her yacht by her husband. And suddenly, all comes into stark focus.

Denver turns when he realizes Penelope is planted in alarm on the step behind him.

"Everything okay, Miss Del Fuego?"

"Natalie will always be wet, won't she?" says Penelope. "And Tim will always have open wounds. And Peg will always be broken. And Elizabeth will always be severed. And Kate will always be choking."

"Yes, I'm afraid they will."

"They must be miserable."

"Do they seem miserable? Does this place seem like a miserable place?" asks Denver.

Penelope shakes her head. It seems like heaven. "You give them whatever they desire. The most. The best. The grandest. It's perfect."

"And did you not get what you were seeking, Miss?"

"And more," admits Penelope with a sinking feeling.

"Penelope Elizabetta del Fuego, this is all yours now, too." Denver withdraws with a wry smile.

Penelope, dizzy with alcohol and ambition, steps right into the path of a very pregnant blond, dancing past in a flowered minidress and knee-high white leather boots.

"Woah! Hey, you okay?" says preggo, reaching out to help. "Denver only buys the best champagne but, wow, it goes right to your head. I've been there. You feel better?"

Penelope shakes her head. Dread was setting in.

"Deep breaths, deep breaths. There you go." She rubs Penelope's back. "You'll get used to it."

"Get used to what?"

"Denver. He does everything over the top."

Penelope gets a better look at the woman and decides she is an uncanny doppelgänger for Sharon Tate. If she was, then she really would be pregnant. But if not?

Penelope pats the woman's belly, praying it's just a fluffy fake bulge.

It is taut and solid.

"Oh, you want to feel the baby?" says Sharon excitedly. 'Lemme have your hand." She lifts her dress.

Penelope gags at what she sees. Crisscrossed over her abdomen is an oozing, jagged, X-shaped incision. The skin is held together by only a few sinewy muscle fibers.

Sharon presses Penelope's hand to her belly, and through the gaping, leaky flesh a tiny finger touches Penelope's.

Two glasses of pink champagne and stomach bile rush into her throat, projecting onto the floor and Sharon's white boots.

Penelope retreats before the next wave of vomit can surface. Unloading the rest of her stomach in the hallway. She then gathers herself and wills her body down the maze of corridors to find the passage back the way she came before. With feet on fire, she finds the lobby.

"Miss Del Fuego? Checking out?" Denver plants himself between her and the door.

Penelope halts and with panting breath, says, "Sharon . . . she's never . . . she's never gonna have that baby, Denver."

Denver hangs his head. "I just love the way her contagious laugh fills the castle."

Penelope tries to power past him, but Denver snatches her by the arm and squeezes it until she can feel the pressure of her blood trying to pump its way through.

"You must never, ever, ever speak of this night. What you saw. Who you saw," he hisses in her ear.

"I won't." She will scratch this nightmare from her memory.

Penelope wriggles from his grip and races for the parking lot. Her car is not where she parked it. It's not anywhere in the lot. Even if she could find it, Penelope left her key in the suite. And she'll be damned if she's going back!

In the distance, the mission bell clangs, offering Penelope the saving solution. She charges across the parking lot to where the steep decline meets the mountain path to the church. And with all her effort, Penelope claws her way down the side of the shrubby hillside.

***

Once inside the mission gates, Penelope spots a dim light from a chapel window. Entering the chapel through the back door, she dashes down the center aisle to the front and drops to her knees at the foot of the wood beam cross. Penelope's hands instinctively fold together in prayer. She utters the first words of the only prayer she ever learned: "Our Father, who art in heaven . . ."

The last time she tried to pray, she had been forced to attend mass with Mama. She had spent the entire service glued to her phone. After that, Mama just let her sleep in on Sundays.

"Our Father, who art in heaven . . . Our Father . . ." The rest of the prayer is stunted somewhere deep within.

"Our Father, who art in heaven, hallowed be thy name. Thy kingdom come, thy will be done, on earth as it is in heaven," whispers Asa in a quick cadence from the front pew where he has been praying.

Penelope whips around, her aquamarine irises now black and wide with fear.

"Are you okay?" says Asa.

"What is that place?" Penelope's voice trembles.

"It could be heaven. Or it could be hell." He goes on to explain, "Time is a continuum at Chateau Cambria. A never-ending adoration of excess and extreme."

"Do they ever leave?"

"The living do. But the dead, they have become prisoners there of their own devices."

"They are trapped there, forever?"

"Only if they die to self, will they truly live," says Asa, shaking his head sadly. "Until then, they languish at Chateau Cambria."

Another damned riddle. Why couldn't this guy make any sense?

"Are *you* the dead or the living?" asks Penelope with a steadier voice.

"Very much mortal, as you are."

"Why should I believe you?"

Asa removes a small knife from his pocket and moves slowly toward Penelope. She should be worried about a man coming at her with a knife, but something about his calm manner causes her to stay put.

"Here."

He reaches out to give her the knife. Her fist unfurls to take it. Then, he raises his sleeve and holds out his palms, giving her his flesh. "Make a cut. Go ahead."

"What? No." Penelope, now sobered, is unsure what kind of game he is playing.

"You seek the veneration of those pretty, pretty followers you call friends. But they are nothing but an algorithm. And you, nothing but a click and a commodity. And I'm afraid that's how Donatella sees you, as well."

"What do you know about Donatella Versace?"

"I used to model for her in Milan. Until one day, I didn't show up to set."

"How do you know about the offer?" Penelope scoffs.

"She comes to visit me when she stays at the Chateau."

"Why would she still visit you if you ditched her like that?"

"Because I got out. And some part of her wants out, too." He reads Penelope's mistrust. "I know it's hard to believe. But if you doubt, go back. Ask her about Asa, or Astoria as I was known during my modeling days. She will remember."

"If this is true, then I think your decision was stupid," says Penelope.

"When you bow to the world, you give it permission to use you as it wishes," he explains. "Donatella will use you. And you will let her. And in the end, you will both get what you want."

"That sounds like a fair exchange," says Penelope. "It's just business."

"Not to your soul it's not."

Asa's eyes transfix themselves on her aquamarine ones, and even though she wants to look away, Penelope can't detach herself from the feeling that is snuggling its way into her. She remembers what Norma Jeane said about Asa being like a father. Is this the way Norma Jeane feels being in Asa's presence? Loved. Whole. True. Good. Pure. With increasing waves, this feeling overtakes Penelope until she is sure she must be going under. With every gasp for breath, Penelope digests another swallow of this beauty and goodness. Nothing has ever made her feel this way and she panics, immediately deciding to mistrust this feeling in order to save herself. She fights it, and fear pushes her to the surface of rational thought. Penelope comes up for air, clinging to the life raft that Asa, and *this feeling*, is not real.

Penelope wields the knife, coming down fast and deep into the priest's flesh.

Asa does not flinch, nor do his eyes move from hers as blood streams from his palm onto the floor at the base of the cross. Instantly, she is gutted with guilt.

The pool of blood grows wider on the Sausalito tile.

"What do you want from me?" whispers Penelope.

"Accept it. Believe," says Asa, knowing exactly the conflict within this young star.

He rubs the sleeve of his robe over the bleeding wound. When he removes it, his flesh has been sewn back together. Not a scratch nor scar remains.

Penelope drops the knife. It clinks on the tile and skitters to a stop under the cross where the pool of Asa's blood has miraculously evaporated, leaving no stain.

This unbelievable healing is by far the strangest and most curious and most powerful thing she has witnessed tonight. And yet, her stomach does not churn. Her mind is not horrified here. This place does not feel haunted like the Chateau, but holy. For a brief flicker, this stirs up a wonder in her spirit.

Penelope's gaze travels up the length of the cross to the punctured, bloody sculpture of Christ. It sends a suffocating fright to her soul. Her mother embraced that, and where did it get her? Slaving away in the pesticide fields. Scrapping for crumbs like a dog around the dinner table. If Penelope bows herself to what her mother adores, she is certain He will take away all the things she has attained; especially and most importantly, those things forming in her future. This was a priest going loco in solitude, listening to the voices of crazed spirits.

No, gracias!

The only real thing she knows is real, is Donatella's offer. And with that small stepping-stone, Penelope will build everything she wants into the highest mountain. And from its peak no one can look down on her. Not the father who abandoned her. Not the mother who wants to hold her back. Not the boyfriend who's embarrassed of her. No one.

Penelope turns and runs for the door.

In the middle of the night, Penelope flees south along the shoulder of the PCH toward LA on shaking legs—away from Asa, away from that grisly cross, away from the harrowing spirits. She rides the hot Santa Ana winds and they push her down the coast, growing stronger and stronger. They boil the ocean, and each wave crashing against the shore grates on her already frayed nerves.

In the distance, she can hear the mission bell ringing. And from the castle, their voices are calling her from far away, *"Penelope Elizabetta. Lovely face. Lovely place."*

Penelope focuses on her escape and does not hear the sound of tires squealing around the tight curve as headlights narrow on her and the bumper of a passing SUV narrowly misses hitting her. As the car blows by and blasts its horn, it sends Penelope off-balance, tottering to the edge of the cliff. She drops to her knees, feeling her long hair dancing around her face. She's alive! Very much alive.

Penelope rises and sets out again, sending her thoughts to her adoring followers and her promising future. These give Penelope a warm inner sensation. Soon, her mind and her heart are so, so full of them. And with this fuel she is carried right to the doorstep of 3462 Fountain Avenue, Apartment 4B.

Hollywood.

***

Penelope wakes to the sound of the ocean and the sweet, sweet smell of gardenias, roses, and plumerias, as if they are being piped into her room through the ducts. She sits straight up, filled with disturbing puzzlement, to find herself back in the four-poster bed in the suite at Chateau Cambria. She had tried to convince herself that Chateau Cambria was a convoluted dream her tired subconscious had conjured up, until a few weeks after that hypnotic night ten years ago, when she received a text on her new phone containing an address that mapped her to Julia's salon. Thus began her rapid transformation into bleach-blond Penelope, TikTok fashion star and, eventually, sought-after actress, sculpted by the best surgeons in Beverly Hills.

She no longer worries about Mama or what Mama thinks because Mama succumbed to cancer two years after Penelope moved to Holly-wood. As much as she misses Mama, her death freed Penelope from guilt and regret.

Penelope Elizabetta del Fuego springs out of bed, throwing back the curtains to expose a cashmere yellow sky. Sea breeze opens every pore in her lungs. The marine layer retreats from the side of the mountain like a down comforter being pulled over the sea. She reaches for her phone to capture herself in the moment. But her phone is not on the night-stand where she always leaves it.

Last night. Last night. Where was she last night?

Last night was drifty and shifty in her memory. For several years now, cocaine had replaced colitas. Its awakening influence made the coastal drive feel glorious, until tiny tormenting memories from San Jose prick through. No amount of powder, pill, or syringe kept them at bay anymore.

The voices began calling from far away.

Penelope had gotten into her car, recorded a message to her followers, then pressed down on the gas pedal of her Mercedes Benz. Her car sailed off the road toward a large pine tree and, upon impact, she flew gloriously through the windshield, her long, blond hair flowing out behind her; then, as she slowed in midair, it retreated, wrapping around her neck like a scarf. Penelope's beautiful body landed in the tree, and the remaining locks tangled themselves around limbs, jerking her to an abrupt halt.

And that was the last thing she remembered.

This morning, her head feels light and cool. She sits up and realizes that her long blond locks do not tumble down. She reaches for her head in shock and horror. Her hair has been chopped off at the nape. Utter panic bolts through Penelope. Her beautiful hair! And . . . her phone! Where was her phone? There would be some clues in her phone. And if it isn't in her room, then it must be in her car. She'll run down and ask the valet to retrieve it.

Tying a scarf around her butchered locks, Penelope darts out of her suite and barrels into a woman passing by.

"Oh my God, Penelope!" says Norma Jeane. "What a nice surprise."

Penelope's grit dissolves, replaced with a look of complete bewilderment and despair.

Norma Jeane presents Penelope with one of her famous smiles as she links her arm into Penelope's. "Darling, the breakfast solarium is this way."

"But—my phone—"

"You and that phone," says Norma Jeane, shuffling them down the hall. "Relax. First order of business: coffee. Denver brews the best beans."

As Norma Jeane drags Penelope from her suite, Penelope notices there is a gold nameplate on her door, engraved in sweeping calligraphy with her beautiful movie star name.

***

Up in the mission church, Asa begins morning prayer. Ten years more at the mission church had aged this handsome former model. He moves with plodding steps to the book of names. He lights a fresh candle at the altar, takes up the pen, and wills his hand to scribe a new name at the bottom of the list.

Penelope.

His eyes go blurry, and after a long inhale he begins his rosary with "Our Father." When he reaches, "*lead us not into temptation and deliver us from evil*," despair seizes his throat.

Sometimes, you just can't kill the beast.

ABOUT THE AUTHORS

ANDREW CHILD was born in Birmingham, England, in May 1968. He went to school in St. Albans, Hertfordshire, and later attended the University of Sheffield where he studied English literature and drama. After graduation Andrew set up and ran a small independent theater company which showcased a range of original material to local, regional, and national audiences. Following a critically successful but financially challenging appearance at the Edinburgh Fringe Festival, Andrew moved into the telecommunications industry as a "temporary" solution to a short-term cash crisis. Fifteen years later, after carrying out a variety of roles including several which were covered by the UK's Official Secrets Act, Andrew became the victim/beneficiary of a widespread redundancy program. Freed once again from the straight jacket of corporate life, he took the opportunity to answer the question, what if?

DON BRUNS, *USA Today* bestselling author, has written three mystery series. His first novel, *Jamaica Blue*, was championed by author Sue Grafton and became the cornerstone for his Caribbean series. His second series, the Stuf series, involves two twenty-four-year-old private detectives in Miami. The books have been praised for their humor, their compelling storylines, and the characters. Bruns's newest series, the

Quentin Archer Mysteries, involves a New Orleans homicide detective and a voodoo practitioner who team up to solve crime in the Big Easy. Traveling the country as a guitar-playing comic, Bruns worked the Playboy Circuit, Las Vegas, and a number of night clubs across the country. As a writer, he has traveled the country for book signings, signing twice at the Playboy Mansion.

When **JOHN GILSTRAP'S** first novel, *Nathan's Run*, hit the market in 1996, it set the literary world on fire. Publication rights sold in twenty-three countries, the movie rights were scooped up at auction by Warner Brothers, and John changed professions. A safety engineer by training and education, he specialized in explosives and hazardous materials, and also served fifteen years in the fire-and-rescue service, rising to the rank of lieutenant. That "first" book was really his fourth, and that one call from an agent (after logging twenty-seven rejections) changed the trajectory of his life. Twenty books and seven movie projects later, it's been a good run, and it's still running. Outside of his writing life, John is a renowned safety expert with extensive knowledge of explosives, hazardous materials, and fire behavior. He lives in Fairfax, Virginia.

REED FARREL COLEMAN, called a hard-boiled poet by NPR's Maureen Corrigan, is the *New York Times* bestselling author of thirty-one novels including six in Robert B. Parker's Jesse Stone series. His new novel, *Sleepless City*, will be released by Blackstone Publishing in 2022. He is a four-time recipient of the Shamus Award and a four-time Edgar Award nominee in three different categories. He has also won the Audie, Scribe, Macavity, Barry, and Anthony awards. Reed lives with his wife on Long Island.

HEATHER GRAHAM, *New York Times* and *USA Today* bestselling author, has written over two hundred novels and novellas in numerous genres and has been published in approximately twenty-five languages. She has been honored with awards from booksellers and writers' organizations for excellence in her work, is a proud recipient of the Silver Bullet from Thriller Writers, and was awarded the prestigious Thriller Master in 2016. She is also a recipient of the Lifetime Achievement Award from the Romance Writers of America. Heather's books have been featured in such publications as *The Nation, Redbook, Mystery Book Club, People,* and *USA Today* and appeared on many newscasts including *Today, Entertainment Tonight,* and local television. Married since high school graduation and the mother of five, her greatest love in life remains her family, but she is grateful every day to be doing something that she loves so very much for a living.

AMANDA FLOWER is a *USA Today* bestselling and Agatha Award–winning mystery author. Her debut mystery, *Maid of Murder,* was an Agatha Award nominee for Best First Novel and her children's mysteries, *Andi Unexpected* and *Andi Under Pressure,* were Agatha Award nominees for Best Children's/YA Novel. *Andi Unstoppable* won the Agatha Award for Best Children's/YA Novel 2015. Amanda is a former librarian living in northeast Ohio.

RICK BLEIWEISS started his career in music as a rock performer, produced over fifty records, was a songwriter and record company senior executive, and worked with the Backstreet Boys, Kiss, U2, Whitney Houston, the BeeGees, and other industry legends. Since 2006 as a publishing company executive, he has acquired works by bestselling and award-winning authors including James Clavell, Gabriel García Márquez, Rex Pickett, and Catherine Coulter, among others. In his latest creative endeavor, Rick has crafted the Pignon Scorbion historical mystery series—blending his love of the past with the twisty deliciousness of a whodunit. Follow Rick and Scorbion at www.RickBleiweiss.com.

JENNIFER GRAESER DORNBUSH, as a daughter of a medical examiner whose office was in her home, investigated her first fatality, an airplane crash, when she was ten years old. Since that first case she has had decades of on-site experience in death investigation and 360 hours of forensic training through the Forensic Science Academy. Jennifer now uses these experiences to pen crime fiction for film and TV. Her female-driven crime drama, *The Coroner's Daughter*, is being developed for TV. Her half-hour forensic comedy, *Home Bodies*, received a Humanitas New Voices Award. Wanting to share her love of forensics with other storytellers, she scribed *Forensic Speak: How to Write Realistic Crime Dramas*, published by Michael Wiese Productions, hailed as a north star to creating authentic crime dramas.